BURIED ABOVE GROUND

Also by Mike Ripley

The Albert Campion Mysteries

MR CAMPION'S FAREWELL *
MR CAMPION'S FOX *
MR CAMPION'S FAULT *
MR CAMPION'S ABDICATION *
MR CAMPION'S WAR *
MR CAMPION'S VISIT *
MR CAMPION'S SÉANCE *
MR CAMPION'S COVEN *
MR CAMPION'S WINGS *
MR CAMPION'S MOSAIC *
MR CAMPION'S MEMORY *
MR CAMPION'S CHRISTMAS *

The Fitzroy Maclean Angel Series

THAT ANGEL LOOK
BOOTLEGGED ANGEL
LIGHTS, CAMERA, ANGEL
ANGEL UNDERGROUND
ANGEL ON THE INSIDE
ANGEL IN THE HOUSE
ANGEL'S SHARE
ANGELS UNAWARE
Etc.

Other Novels

DOUBLE TAKE
BOUDICA AND THE LOST ROMAN
THE LEGEND OF HEREWARD

Non-Fiction

SURVIVING A STROKE
KISS KISS, BANG BANG

* *available from Severn House*

BURIED ABOVE GROUND

Mike Ripley

SEVERN
HOUSE

First world edition published in Great Britain and the USA in 2025
by Severn House, an imprint of Canongate Books Ltd,
14 High Street, Edinburgh EH1 1TE.

severnhouse.com

Copyright © Mike Ripley, 2025

Cover and jacket design by Piers Tilbury

All rights reserved including the right of reproduction in whole or in part in any form. The right of Mike Ripley to be identified as the author of this work has been asserted in accordance with the Copyright, Designs & Patents Act 1988.

British Library Cataloguing-in-Publication Data
A CIP catalogue record for this title is available from the British Library.

ISBN-13: 978-1-4483-1561-1 (cased)
ISBN-13: 978-1-4483-1562-8 (e-book)

This is a work of fiction. Names, characters, places and incidents are either the product of the author's imagination or are used fictitiously. Except where actual historical events and characters are being described for the storyline of this novel, all situations in this publication are fictitious and any resemblance to actual persons, living or dead, business establishments, events or locales is purely coincidental.

No part of this book may be used or reproduced in any manner for the purpose of training artificial intelligence technologies or systems. This work is reserved from text and data mining (Article 4(3) Directive (EU) 2019/790).

All Severn House titles are printed on acid-free paper.

Typeset by Palimpsest Book Production Ltd., Falkirk, Stirlingshire, Scotland.
Printed and bound in Great Britain by TJ Books, Padstow, Cornwall.

The manufacturer's authorised representative in the EU for product safety is Authorised Rep Compliance Ltd, 71 Lower Baggot Street, Dublin D02 P593 Ireland (arccompliance.com)

Praise for Mike Ripley

"A refreshingly surprise-packed entry in an always
excellent series"
Publishers Weekly Starred Review of *Mr Campion's Christmas*

"Outstanding . . . A joy to read"
Booklist on *Mr Campion's Christmas*

"[A] lively adventure"
Kirkus Reviews on *Mr Campion's Christmas*

"Clever, witty, and packed with intriguing characters, period
ambiance, and unexpected twists"
Booklist on *Mr Campion's Memory*

"The plot thickens in utterly unexpected ways"
Kirkus Reviews on *Mr Campion's Memory*

"Impressive . . . brilliant inventiveness"
Publishers Weekly Starred Review of *Mr Campion's Mosaic*

About the author

Mike Ripley is the author of more than thirty books, has written for radio and television and has reviewed almost 3,000 crime novels over the last three decades. His 'reader's history' of the heyday of British action and spy thrillers 1953–75, *Kiss Kiss, Bang Bang*, won the H.R.F. Keating Award for non-fiction in 2017.

To librarians everywhere.
Nos qui lecturi sumus te salutamus

Author's Note

This is not a conventional crime novel, rather a novel about writing crime novels, written by someone who has probably read too many. There are numerous references to well-known writers and their books hidden within, which are revealed in an appendix should anyone be remotely interested. No real publishers or editors were hurt in the writing of this book.

Part One

The Librarian

ONE

'How long is it since you were in London?'

'Beer was less than five pounds a pint.'

'So last century then.'

He said it without a trace of humour, simply stating a matter of fact after a moment of mental arithmetic which was, sadly, accurate.

'It has been a while,' I admitted. 'Things will have changed so much.'

A quicker mind and sharper tongue could have taunted me by pointing out that no one used cash to pay for a pint of beer these days, so the price was never noticed, or that CDs were now four for a pound in charity shops and DVDs had gone the way of VHS tapes and what the hell was Betamax, Grandad? But this young tearaway did not have the wit, or more likely the inclination, to score points off an old dog like me. I simply was not worth the effort, though his body language had made it quite clear that simply talking to me *was* an effort.

'How long has it been . . .?'

He spoke without taking his eyes from the bright screen of an iPhone which I suspected would have to be prised from his cold, dead hand.

'Since I was found to be surplus to requirements? More than twenty years.'

He looked up at that, perhaps wondering whether or not to express sympathy. 'The requirements of publishing have changed exponentially in that time frame, even affecting houses such as Boothby and Briggs.'

'Not that B and B is a publishing house anymore, not since the sell-out,' I said as pointedly as I could. 'Now it is no more than a potting shed in the kitchen garden of a European conglomerate.'

'But we still persist with the Boothby and Briggs name as the imprint for our crime fiction, which is what it was famous for.' He said it as though generously conceding something.

'And profitably so,' I pointed out calmly, not wanting to let him see that his very presence irritated me, but he shrugged dismissively, irritating me more.

'B and B kept its head above the surface in its day, but it was treading water in a small pond. Publishing is now an ocean, not a pond, which touches every continent. It has to be international, and it has to encompass modern technology and operate on numerous platforms. There is simply no room in the market these days for the small, traditional publishing house which relies on print formatting.'

That sounded almost convincing. I wondered where he had read it.

'By print formatting, you mean what I used to call *books*?'

'We still call them books, but today they can be downloaded and viewed on screens or listened to; they don't have to involve paper and ink. You left publishing before ebooks, didn't you?'

His eyes widened and his voice softened as he said that, as if trying to imagine a pre-industrial past where dinosaurs, if they did not rule, still wandered the leafy glades of Bloomsbury.

'To be accurate, publishing left me,' I pointed out.

His name, he said, was Jake Philbin. I might have known he would be a Jake, as every young male in publishing these days had to be a Jake or a Jasper or a Nic (without the 'K'), to differentiate them, if they had not preferred a pronoun, from the Catrionas, Abigails, Emilys and Laurens. He had probably started life at the firm as an unpaid 'intern', which in my day would have been 'the work-experiencer' unless they were related to someone senior in the company and been assigned as the assistant to the person they would invariably replace in a matter of months.

When I was the age of a Jake – or an Abigail or a Catriona – the first step on the editorial ladder was as a secretary (experience of booking fashionable London restaurants essential) or in the post room unpacking and repacking boxes of books or, occasionally, as a *reader*, where a respectable degree and/or some specialist, even arcane, knowledge was required. That was, of course, assuming that one did not have family connections to the publishing house, in which case acceptance would be immediate and promotion hot on its heels.

I was lucky in that I had a respectable degree, though from one of the less respected universities, in Russian Language and Literature, and my embarrassingly crude and honest CV – grammar school and chess club before university and morris dancing society, plus a one-term student exchange programme with Volgograd University (which would have been more impressive had it still been called Stalingrad), accompanied by holiday jobs in local bookshops – had somehow found its way across the desk of Edward Jesser.

As the main shareholder in Boothby & Briggs – thanks to a fortuitous marriage to the only remaining member of the founding Boothby clan – Edward Jesser took an active role in the firm and was rather good at it, claiming the titles of Publisher as well as Managing and Editorial Director. The recruitment of very junior, short-contract employees would not normally come within the remit of such a high-powered executive, but the company liked to think itself steeped in tradition and fostered the myth that all incoming mail was, as in Victorian times, opened by the managing director at a standing desk or lectern. Of course, Boothby & Briggs had never actually existed in the Victorian era and did not possess a standing desk, and a personal secretary did the actual opening of the morning post before placing it on her master's desk, but Edward Jesser's eagle eyes were always the first to peruse it.

It was pure chance that Mr Jesser was currently reading – or, to use a technical publishing term, skimming – a recently submitted manuscript from a debut author, a thriller set in Russia (still communist in those days) about a gang of rebellious students raising funds for an escape to the West by smuggling caviar. Our loveable, non-violent group of outlaws are pursued by an ageing, remarkably honest police officer who has a secret weapon: a cat which has been trained to sniff out the rarest and most expensive types of caviar. Hence the book's title, *Caviar Cat*.

Being a lover of caviar but knowing little about its production or, indeed, the Soviet Union other than what he had gleaned from a clutch of 'crash bang' (as he called them) spy stories, Edward Jesser found himself in need of a second, more expert, opinion but also in receipt of an application for employment from a young man who seemed both ideally qualified and cheap.

6   Mike Ripley

Thus my job interview for Boothby & Briggs was to be given the manuscript – fortunately typed – of *Caviar Cat* and told to go away and return in three days' time, preferably after lunch, with a 'reader's report' on it, complete with an estimate of its publishing potential. I had, of course, no idea what a 'reader's report' was, but I had written essays (usually scoring in the B+ range) on Tolstoy's books and Dostoyevsky's, even Lermontov, for goodness' sake, and I had been to Russia. How hard could it be? I set to with a will and gushing enthusiasm, raving about the accurate setting, the intriguing plot and the endearing characters of *Caviar Cat*, and then ripped up my reader's report and started again.

I knew enough, or thought I did, to recognize that the object of a critical review – essentially what a reader's report was – was to be critical but at the same time optimistic, if only to prove that the reader had read it. Consequently, I leavened my endorsements with some minor suggestions for improvement to the Russian idioms used and, crucially but fortuitously, the recommendation that the manuscript could lose 10,000 words without detriment to the plot or pacing of the novel. I had no idea at the time that this recommendation would give the manuscript a word count of around 90,000 which fitted exactly into Boothby & Briggs' ideal economic publishing model, a model I was to discover was ruthlessly adhered to as printing costs continued their inexorable rise.

The manuscript had been handed to me by Edward Jesser's secretary, Miss Robina Robinson, who always wore a businesswoman's pearl-grey suit and tan stockings with seams in the office, giving her a spine of steel. When I delivered my reader's report on *Caviar Cat* – painstakingly and neatly typed – my boyish enthusiasm and naivete blinded me to any warning signs that this was a person I should be frightened – or at least wary – of. That realization came later, but to give Robina her due, she must have passed on my assessment of the manuscript fairly promptly as five days later I received a letter offering me a six-month contract as an editorial assistant, my initial responsibilities to include 'tasting' unsolicited manuscripts (I had no idea there were so many would-be novelists out there) and making recommendations as to which, if any, might graduate from the 'slush pile' and on to the lists of Boothby & Briggs.

Although I had little more to do with it as its future was above my pay grade even before I had a pay grade, *Caviar Cat* was published the following year by B & B, and although it probably earned out its no doubt paltry advance, there would have been little in the way of royalties, with only one print run of hardback copies all of which would be destined for the shelves of public libraries, the main customers of Boothby & Briggs. Which was, in a way, a pity, as I had thought it entertaining enough, but the firm put little effort behind it when it became clear that the author had no plans to write a sequel and develop a series of novels using the same characters and setting.

I was to learn, fairly quickly, how important a *series* was when it came to publishing crime fiction. Publishers love an established market for a new novel, and readers of crime fiction, although they do not want to read the same book again, do appreciate more of the same. Familiarity in crime fiction rarely bred contempt, except among authors who tired of their characters – often longed to kill them off in spectacular ways – when faced with the contractual need to produce a book a year.

Thanks to *Caviar Cat,* fortunate timing and having a rudimentary knowledge of Russia, I gained my objective of a job in publishing and did so by reading a manuscript – or 'scrip' as I was to learn to call them – and writing about it, but without any formal interview. I had been working in the B & B post room as part of my 'induction' for almost a month before I actually met Edward Jesser on one of his infrequent tours of the office 'to keep staff on their toes', although most old hands at the firm regarded these walkabouts as him taking a passeggiata after a good lunch rather than a serious tour of inspection.

To give him his due, he was familiar with everyone's name, even mine, and as he greeted me, he did so with the words, 'You're the young fellow who helped out with that Russian story. Got any more specialist skills up your sleeve?'

'I'm a very fast reader and I read quickly; I don't skim or speed-read,' I said honestly.

'And do you like crime fiction?' Mr Jesser asked, generously ignoring my cringe-worthy attempts to ingratiate myself.

'I love it – can't get enough of it!' I lied.

'You'll get quite a sufficiency if you stay with us,' he said, and he was not wrong.

8   Mike Ripley

It was not difficult to overindulge on crime fiction at Boothby & Briggs as it was the company's bread and butter; almost ninety per cent of their annual lists were crime novels or thrillers of one species or another. And I immediately began to indulge myself, reading voraciously to familiarize myself with the type of books my employer was most famous for.

Which was how I discovered Duncan Torrens.

'So . . . I'm here to pick your brains about Duncan Torrens,' said young Mr Philbin, carefully sweeping a lock of well-trained hair from his eyeline.

Now he had my undivided attention.

TWO

'There's a name from the past,' I said cheerfully.

Young Jake seemed neither relieved nor impressed and casually flicked an imaginary mote of dust from the sleeve of his suit jacket – making the double point that his suit had probably cost more than the furnishings of my squalid little bedsit, which had dust on every surface touched by sunlight.

'You knew him in your time at Boothby and Briggs.' He did not pose it as a question.

'When I achieved the exulted position of Editor, Duncan Torrens became one of my regular authors. I liked his books; they were often very clever and usually well written, if not great literature. The copy was always very clean and didn't really take much work on my part. I may have some of his titles from those days.'

I waved an imperial hand vaguely in the direction of an unstable bookcase overloaded with books, mostly hardbacks, their dust jackets faded and frayed, crammed on their sides into the central shelves and then piled haphazardly and precariously on a top shelf, as if in an experiment to defy both gravity and physics. I had already made a mental note that young Jake had barely given it passing glance since his arrival, which was a black mark against him. I have always been the sort of person who scouts visually for books upon entering a room.

'So . . . you got on with him . . . professionally?'

'Professionally, yes. He was never any trouble; certainly not compared to some of our other authors. He was always willing to accept editorial notes without running off in a hissy fit, screaming that we were stifling his creativity.'

'He wrote a lot, didn't he.'

Again, it was not a question, and he seemed to be reading from a script. Perhaps he did have a script on the screen of the smartphone he rarely took his eyes off.

'A book a year, regular as clockwork in his Inspector Seeley series. Never missed a delivery deadline in all the years I was with B and B.'

'So . . . a backlist of something like twenty books.'

Again, not a question, Jake following the modern trend of using 'So' as a filler word to give themselves thinking time while speaking. There is probably an official linguistic term for it, but I was no longer being paid to look such things up.

'More than that,' I said, cheerful to be able to show this old dog was still of some use. 'He'd written a few before I joined the firm.'

Young Jake looked up from his telephone, clearly in need of further information but not capable of asking for it.

'Inspector Seeley was Duncan's most popular creation and his main series, but he tried other things: a few historical thrillers and a short series featuring a country parson as a detective, but they were just potboilers; his bread and butter came from the Inspector Seeley books. Edward Jesser cut him a fair bit of slack over the ones he did under his pen names because the Seeley books were steady sellers.'

'To libraries,' said Jake, and I was sure I detected a slight sneer.

'They were very popular in libraries, and libraries were our main customers.'

'So . . . Torrens had pseudonyms?' he said, dismissing me with a raised eyebrow, and this time it did seem like a question.

'At least two with Boothby and Briggs in his early days, before he invented Inspector Seeley, and, of course, Duncan Torrens was itself a pen name.'

Now *I* had *his* undivided attention.

'It was? What was his real name?'

'I have no idea,' I snapped, furious with the young oik for not doing any basic research.

'But you helped edit his books.'

'But I never met him.'

'You never met him?'

'I did not. Nobody did.'

Well, I suppose Edward Jesser must have, when he commissioned that first Inspector Seeley way back when, but in my time at the firm, Duncan Torrens was a mystery man. Not that anyone

Buried Above Ground

ever thought of it as a mystery. In those days before 'social media' existed (something I was sure young Jake could not possibly imagine), authors did not enjoy the high public profiles many now aspire to. Few of his fans would have recognized Duncan Torrens in the street as it was B & B policy not to include an author photograph on the back flap of their dust jackets.

Edward Jesser would say this was to keep them grounded and in their place. He would justify this using examples (from other publishers) where authors both male and female were using black-and-white head-and-shoulders shots clearly fifty years beyond their sell-by date. Vanity, Jesser used to say, was the monkey always on the back of a writer, clinging on next to the twin succubae of alcoholism and praise.

It seemed perfectly normal for authors never to visit the offices of their publishers. There were exceptions, of course, particularly in the big houses which boasted superstar writers who had either had a genuine bestselling book, or a face well known from television, but at Boothby & Briggs they were not encouraged. There were telephones, for goodness' sake, and if there was an unavoidable need to deal with an author, or their agent, face to face, then there were plenty of nearby pubs or, if a delicate subject was likely to be raised, several reasonably priced restaurants.

What had marked Duncan Torrens out as slightly unusual was his penchant for conducting all his literary affairs solely by fax. (I was not willing to say this out loud and give young Jake the chance to say, 'What's a fax, Grandad?') Editorial notes, copy changes, corrections, contracts, even replies to the odd fan letter (rare but invariably odd) were communicated through humming fax machines all long since consigned to the municipal scrapheap with as little ceremony as I had been.

This particular quirk never affected the way B & B thought about Duncan Torrens; if anything, it was a point in his favour. Where other authors would complain to their agents about arrogant editors, nugatory advances and lack of promotional marketing ('Why aren't my books advertised on television?') or, quite often, complain to their editors about their agents, Duncan Torrens kept any concerns he had to himself. He never complained about his advances or the occasional royalty payment; nor did he ever suggest a more aggressive publicity and marketing campaign for his books. He reacted to editorial notes (by fax) with polite logic, accepting some, arguing against others and always reaching a consensus. He never once complained about the artwork on his dust jackets or attempted to design his own. For this in particular, he was much appreciated by his publisher as something of a prince among writers.

When Edward Jesser died suddenly – not following a three-bottle lunch at the Groucho as had often been predicted but quietly in his sleep – the remaining shareholders in Boothby & Briggs took the decision, with indecent haste, to put the company up for sale, take the money and run for the Channel Islands. The fact that with Edward's passing, there was not a single person in the firm who had ever met Duncan Torrens, or would recognize him if he delivered his next manuscript to the office in person, went totally unnoticed.

The new owners retained the B & B imprint and naturally honoured all extant contracts – it was only later that the great cull of lower midlist authors began – and more Inspector Seeley novels followed, the script, neatly typed, arriving by post whilst any other business continued to be conducted via the fax machine. As the books were as good as ever, required only minimal copy-editing, continued to be popular among librarians and readers, and the author made no demands for an increased advance, all seemed right with the literary world of Duncan Torrens – or at least not worth upsetting. Torrens was a boat simply not worth rocking.

Young Jake leaned forwards in his chair, having thought of a question important enough for him to set aside his phone.

'Did Torrens have an agent?'

'Not that I was ever aware of.'

'Wasn't that unusual?'

'Not at all. Edward Jesser always preferred authors without agents. He always quoted Raymond Chandler's maxim that authors could always apologize to publishers and publishers could always apologize to authors, but with agents it was enough that you let them live.'

Jake Philbin's face remained impassive and I genuinely thought he was going to ask me who Raymond Chandler was.

'So Torrens did not have an agent and you never met him?'

'That's right.'

Buried Above Ground 13

'But you were his editor.' He was either accusing or complaining – I could not tell which.

'For some of his books. Edward Jesser handled his early ones, and the series was well established when I took over, initially as his copy editor. I suppose someone else took him on after I was pushed out.'

'There were no more Seeley books after you left,' he admitted, 'as it was decided they didn't fit the profile of the new owners.'

'So Robina Robinson dropped them?'

'She had to rationalize the list,' he said as if reciting a mantra, which he probably was. 'B and B were churning out forty-eight or more detective stories a year; that was just insane.'

'Detective stories were always popular, still are, and we also did thrillers and some romantic fiction. Most of them broke even and the company didn't lose money; in fact, it was a profitable concern when it was sold.'

'It was on borrowed time, stuck in a rut: no paperback operation, no ebooks, no marketing strategy, no interest in selling translation rights, little presence in high street bookshops, none at all in supermarkets.'

'Public libraries were our main market.' It sounded weak, even to me.

'And look what's happened to libraries. They've gone.'

'Not all of them; I work in one.'

Young Master Philbin looked up from his phone in surprise, either at the news that some libraries still existed out in the wild or at the fact that I had managed to find a job and a life after Boothby & Briggs. His eyes flicked around the room, as if assessing the rental value of my flat if it could somehow be transported lock, stock but without the book collection to somewhere fashionable in London – or at least on the Northern Line.

'Do your customers still take out Duncan Torrens' books?'

'I prefer to call them readers,' I said, not wanting to admit that he was absolutely right and that following a local government edict, libraries had customers and staff could not discriminate against those unfortunates who actually liked books. 'As a matter of fact, the Inspector Seeley books still issue quite well, though many are old and falling to pieces. Most are out of print, of course.'

'They all are, which is why we need to secure the rights to Torrens' works.' He tapped the screen of his phone with a fingernail as if ticking a box.

'I was wondering why I was honoured by this visit. There had to be a reason for head office to send somebody out into bandit country.'

'That's what you get for being the junior dogsbody.' He slipped his phone into his pocket and gave himself – not me – a wry smile.

'You're an intern?'

I was pleased that I had placed him from the start and disappointed in equal measure that I did not rate a visit from anyone at a higher level in the firm.

'I see it more as a gap year spent in London,' he said casually, as if it was a subject hardly worth mentioning, apart from the fact that it was about him. 'My mother was dead against me going backpacking in Thailand, got really hysterical about it, so my father calmed her down by renting me a flat in town. I got a car out of it as well.'

I had noticed the small but spanking new Audi parked on the street and had wondered about the salary scales at B & B these days, but now it was clear.

'Publishing is just a stopgap for you, then?'

'So . . . stopgap, gap year; same difference. Gives me a chance to hone my networking skills' – I wondered where he had read that – 'before I go off to uni.'

'And you get a nice trip to the Hertfordshire countryside out of it.' I was resigned to being no more than an expense chit for petrol money to him and certainly not part of his networking agenda.

'So I was heading for Cambridge anyway, to check out a couple of restaurants before I take my place.'

'You're going to Cambridge?'

Of course he was.

'I offered to swing by here and see you and combine pleasure with a bit of business. Nobody else volunteered.'

I knew I was unlikely to be invited up to London for what passed for a publisher's lunch these days, but it seemed that I did not merit a visit unless I happened to be a convenient stop on the way to somewhere else.

Buried Above Ground

'You haven't said exactly what you volunteered for.'

'To look you up and pick your brains.'

He said it as if it should have been perfectly obvious, his face as blank as someone who had been approached by a charity collector in the street and was gauging how rude he could be without causing a scene.

'About Duncan Torrens,' I nudged him.

'That's right,' he drawled, as if he had won some big admission from me. 'So we need to resolve the situation.'

'The "we" in question being Boothby and Briggs or the dreaded Pabulator?'

Pabulator International, to give it its ridiculous proper title, was the giant publishing concern which had taken over Boothby & Briggs. A force to be reckoned with in the book trade, Pabulator and its subsidiaries had extended their dominance of the Scandinavian market across all of Europe and finally Britain. The rest of the world would surely follow. I had often wondered how many of its employees – especially young Jake Philbin – knew that the name of the company came from the Latin for 'forager' or would appreciate the irony of a concern whose mission statement seemed to be engulf and devour rather than carefully selecting choice morsels.

The double irony was that Pabulator's founding success, which gave them deep pockets, came from a series of lavishly illustrated cookery books promoting the Norwegian (or was it Danish?) fad for chefs foraging in forests, hedgerows or on the seashore every morning before presenting those who could afford it with an extravagantly priced twenty-seven-course tasting menu for lunch. The way to a Michelin star these days seemed to lie among the bracken and dead wood or under the seaweed, yet in publishing, Pabulator's philosophy was exactly the opposite.

Instead of foraging for and selecting tasty morsels for their fiction lists, or nurturing, like the first seedling shoots, the writings of newly discovered talent, Pabulator preferred to buy titles job lot 'off the shelf' and off as many shelves as possible. Any publisher with a substantial backlist of novels was a prime target, and it did not matter how old or forgotten were those titles and their authors, as Pabulator would repackage and reissue them as cheap paperbacks with garish covers and as ebooks and in audio editions. A 'new' book, went the mantra, is simply one you haven't read yet, which I suppose is fair enough, but quantity rather than quality rapidly became the company's prime directive.

'So it's a Boothby and Briggs matter,' Jake was saying, 'but the incentive comes from Head Office.'

'An interesting use of the word "incentive".'

I had been on the receiving end of one of Pabulator's incentives and knew they were predominantly stick rather than carrot.

'So it's part of a general overhaul and consolidation of rights, particularly electronic rights across all the imprints.'

I suspected I knew what was coming, but as I had no intention of easing Mr Philbin's path, I remained silent.

'You never did any of the Duncan Torrens books as ebooks, did you?'

'Most of his books were written before there was such a thing as an ebook. It was something Boothby and Briggs just didn't do, at least not in my time there. When I was let go, ebooks were a fad, a ridiculously small part of the market, and it was not a market we were interested in getting in to.'

'Which is why B and B is no longer independent.'

'I think the size of the Pabulator cheque book had more to do with it as far as the main shareholders were concerned.'

Master Philbin had no wish to go down that particular rabbit hole. 'Very few of B and B's crime list were ever done as ebooks. Why was that?'

'I know it must be difficult for you to get your head round, but in my days at B and B, ebooks were only just getting going,' I repeated, slowly this time, 'and no one thought they could ever compete, let alone replace real books. Edward Jesser was quite passionate about reading fiction being a physical thing, where you could hold and feel and smell the pages and not be glued to a screen. Most of our authors would have agreed with him if they'd been asked. In fact, one of them – I won't say which – wanted a written assurance from us that we would *never* put his books into ebook formats, he hated the idea of them replacing printed books so much. Which, of course, they never quite did. Rumours of the death of the book have been much exaggerated.'

He gave me a look which, for him, passed as pity. 'So you never asked Torrens if his Inspector Seeley series could be ebooked?'

'The situation never arose in my time. I take it that they have not been digitized since, otherwise you wouldn't be here asking about them.'

'No, they haven't.'

'Is there a demand for them nowadays?'

'Head Office policy is to exploit all known assets across all platforms in accordance with the theory of marginal gains.'

'Squeezing the lemon until the pips squeak.'

I had confused the poor chap again, though I doubted 'poor' was an appropriate adjective, for young Jake had clearly been brought up having someone squeeze his lemons for him.

'The instruction has come down from Head Office that everything should be ebooked, even old stuff which is popular with the ageing demographic of ebook readers these days.'

'That would be me, then,' I said, straight-faced. 'The ageing demographic that is, not the ebook reader. I've never read anything on a Kindle.'

'You can read on your phone these days.'

'I don't have one, and before you ask, the only tablets I use are for blood pressure, but that's just me. I've been out of publishing for two decades now, so what do I know? Maybe the Inspector Seeley books are due for a revival as ebooks. Goodness knows there are enough of them to choose from.'

'The plan is to do them all and parcel them up in box sets so that readers can binge five or six books on the trot. Keep the initial price low, give 'em five or six ebooks for the price of one; an introductory offer they can't refuse.'

'Can you make money that way?'

'Sure, if titles go global. That's the beauty of ebooks – worldwide sales without shipping or warehousing costs.'

'And does the author make any money?'

'More than they would without an ebook version, especially if the book is out of print.'

'Fair point,' I said, 'though I still don't see what this all has to do with me.'

'So it's a question of the rights to the Inspector Seeley books.

If Torrens did not have an agent, all rights would have been with the publisher, but not for ebooks.'

'Because back then, we never asked for them.'

Jake nodded, glad that I was keeping up.

'But surely after this length of time, with the books out of print, the rights would have reverted to the author. Except' – I paused and looked at him to see if it was a test – 'the standard B and B contract, as drawn up by Edward Jesser, did not include an automatic reversal clause. After a certain amount of time – ten years, I think – authors could request, in writing, their rights back if a book was out of print and Edward had no plans to do a reprint. I suspect Torrens never asked for reversion.'

'Correct.' He raised an eyebrow a millimetre or two in appreciation. 'We still have the rights to the books, but not the ebook rights, which would normally just be an addendum to the normal contract.'

'So?' Saying that felt like I was getting my own back.

'So we have to get an agreement to the addendum. If we can't find Duncan Torrens, we have to find the executor of his literary estate.'

'Well, good luck with that.'

I knew he couldn't find an executor – because there wasn't one – and would not find Duncan Torrens.

Well, not above ground.

THREE

I did not say that aloud, of course; I merely thought it. The reference would surely have been lost on young Jake, as I doubted he was aware that the title of one of Duncan Torrens' Inspector Seeley books was *Buried Above Ground*, a fairly predictable mystery based around a group of potholers and caving enthusiasts in the wilds of Derbyshire. A first edition (the only edition) of that very book was on a shelf only an arm's length from Jake's chair and clearly within his eyeline if he ever chose to focus on something other than a screen.

'We were wondering if you knew how you used to contact him.'

His phone had materialized in his hand and he was poised as if to make notes on it. I was not sorry to disappoint him.

'My usual means of communication with him was by fax, but that was years ago. I presume he continued that way after I was let go.' I don't know why I said 'let go' when I meant 'thrown out' as it was an expression I disliked almost as much as when people said someone had 'passed' rather than died. Passing implied the chance that a person was temporarily moving away but might return. Dead was more definite. 'Robina Robinson took over as his editor, didn't she?'

I knew she had.

'Yes, technically, but then he was . . . let go.'

'Dropped.'

'If you like.' He wasn't being deliberately dismissive – it just came naturally. 'It happened at the time the company got rid of its fax machines and everyone was computerized.'

'But not Duncan Torrens. Let me guess, he was simply forgotten about.'

'All copies of his fax messages were thrown out when the fax machines were. No one thought they were worth keeping. Unfortunately, all his other paperwork went too in the general rationalization, everything which might have had his name and address on it.'

'Everything?'

His original manuscripts, which had been neatly typed and cross-tied with red ribbon like state documents, had always arrived by first-class post, the title page bearing his address in the bottom left-hand corner. But, as was the tradition at B & B, once the typesetters had done their job, original manuscripts were returned to authors so they could stack them in dusty lofts until they became famous and an obscure American college offered to buy them.

'Even our copies of his contracts?' I persisted.

Jake nodded and shrugged in a what-can-you-do? gesture. 'That may have been a mistake, but the assumption was that all contracts had been computerized.'

'But Torrens started writing in the days before computers, either at home or in the office.'

'And nobody noticed because he had been dropped from the list . . . until now and the company realized it didn't know how to get in touch with him.'

'That's disgraceful!' I tried to put surprise in with the indignation. 'One of Boothby and Briggs' most popular, not to say prolific, authors lost to posterity because nobody computerized his details? Doesn't anyone keep a Rolodex anymore?'

'A what?'

'Oh, never mind,' I said before he had another opportunity to add the epithet 'Grandad'. 'You must be desperate to have to come begging me for help.'

'I wouldn't call it begging.'

No, he wouldn't, but suddenly I really wanted him to beg.

'It can't be that important,' I said airily. 'I mean for a company the size of Pabulator, the ebook rights to a few detective stories written by a forgotten author years ago surely can't be worth the petrol money you'll be claiming on expenses.'

'You'd be surprised. Have you seen the amount of reviews some ebooks get on Amazon and Goodreads and sites like that? Get your laptop out and I'll show you.'

I resisted the urge to smile like a Bond villain as I dropped the bombshell.

'I don't own a computer.'

It took him a while to digest that clearly unpalatable fact, his face going through more contortions than it would during an early morning shave with a hangover.

'So you'll just have to trust me on this. Nobody's saying the old Torrens books will set the world on fire done as ebooks, but it is a revenue stream Pabulator wants to exploit. It's all a question of marginal gains. That's the name of the publishing game these days.'

I could not resist unsettling him further. 'And Pabulator has just suddenly discovered that the forgotten works of Duncan Torrens are an untapped revenue stream, years after dropping him?'

He squirmed slightly but not nearly enough.

'Pabulator did an internal audit of rights that they took over from B and B and found . . . '

'A big hole where all those Torrens titles should be,' I finished for him. He looked surprised, but before he could ask how I knew, I said, 'You've told me all his faxes and contracts were destroyed and because he had the temerity to start writing before the age of office computers, he might as well not have existed. I'm just surprised it's taken them so long to realize what an asset they had.'

'So yes, red faces all round because no one remembered him, but there's no record of the rights ever being reverted, so it's a question of finding Torrens and getting him to sign off the ebook rights. Your name was suggested . . .'

'By Robina Robinson I'll bet, and I'll double the bet that she was one of those red faces when the audit found she'd lost an author.'

'It was actually. Can you help us find Torrens?'

'You have really got no idea?'

'Not a clue. We don't even know if Duncan Torrens is his real name.'

'Yes, you do,' I said smugly, 'but no, it isn't.'

'I don't follow.'

Of course he didn't.

'Follow the money. The finance department will have paid him royalties even after the sell-out to Pabulator. It used to be run by a woman called Mandy, and we always did what she told us to do, though I don't know if she's still there.'

22   Mike Ripley

'There's nobody in Accounts called Mandy,' Jake said defiantly.

'Another casualty of the takeover, but there will be *a* Mandy who will have a name and bank details, maybe even an address where B and B used to send cheques to, though I don't suppose you know what a cheque is.'

Jake shook his head so that a well-rehearsed forelock of hair fell over his right eye, only to be flicked back into place before it could hide a manicured eyebrow.

'Not really,' he said with his upper lip curled, 'but surely the company would have stopped paying Torrens when the books stopped.'

'Now *you* might be surprised. If the rights were never reverted and the company still owned them, then as long as there was one copy in a warehouse somewhere, the bean counters would know about it, and if it was sold or remaindered, they would make sure the author got their cut – or at least a note on their annual royalty statement saying the amount was too small to pay but would be carried forward. I know of one author who had £1.87 carried forward for ten years. That wouldn't even pay the postage on his statement these days.'

'So you think the people in Accounts would have an address for Torrens?' He was almost licking his lips.

'They might still have, and at least they would know his real name.' Poor Jake was confused again, so I put him out of his misery. 'Hadn't we agreed that Duncan Torrens was a pseudonym? I'm pretty sure the name he wrote under would not have been the name on his bank account.'

Oddly, that never occurred to many both inside and out of publishing. There had been the well-publicized case of the winner of a £5,000 literary prize for a book written under a pen name. The sponsors of the award had proudly presented her with a cheque – a real one, not one of those giant fake cardboard jobs – made out to her pseudonym. On the podium, to the horror of the organizers and the selected, Prosecco-sipping audience, she declaimed that she 'couldn't cash that thing' and tore the cheque to pieces in front of the predatory cameras.

'Good thinking,' said young Jake, then came up with a thought of his own. 'But a bank would not give out somebody's address details, would they?'

He asked as a child would, almost pleading, which made me think he was worried about his own financial security.

'Probably not,' I reassured him, 'but it would be a start. I'm sorry I could not be of more help.'

'You're sure you can't remember anything about Torrens? A phone number? Some idea of where he lived? Did he never give any clues?'

'I'm sorry, I never knew Duncan Torrens.'

That was almost true.

But I had known Alan George Hibbert.

FOUR

I don't count exchanges of lengthy fax messages with 'Duncan Torrens' as a conversation, but those faded sheets, some hand-written though mostly typed on his antique Underwood type-writer, covered more topics and ideas with more generosity of feeling and wit than would be found over many a married couple's breakfast table.

The thing I liked most about Duncan Torrens was that when it came to being a published author, he had absolutely no side to him. I know that is an old-fashioned thing to say, the sort of thing people said about my father even after the award of his George Medal, but Torrens had the same realistic sense of self-worth. He knew his place in the universe of crime writing – a rare commodity indeed – as a journeyman author of reliable potboiler mysteries, the sort of books Dorothy L. Sayers, from lofty heights, would classify as 'for train journeys only'.

He knew he would never produce a true bestseller and often joked that he was aiming for 'the bottom rungs on the midlist ladder'. He had once beautifully explained his classification of crime writers in terms of football clubs. The real bestselling authors were in the Premier League (the Liverpools, Arsenals and Manchester Citys), then there were those who had early success but had slipped into the Championship, though still harboured hopes of promotion (Norwich, West Bromwich Albion), while the rest, the majority, struggled along in Divisions One and Two. Torrens described his books as 'midtable Division One – a bit like Peterborough'. They had dedicated fans among library users, who kept supporting them, and many readers thought they should do better, but they never did.

He was equally phlegmatic when it came to his earnings as a writer and once again turned to a football metaphor. The problem he said (faxed) was that the average reader, and the vast majority of the population who had never visited a library or ever darkened the door of a bookshop, assumed that anyone who had published

Buried Above Ground

a book must, automatically, be very rich and actively seeking relocation to a tax haven. The truth was that whilst the real international bestsellers did earn the fabled 'six-figure advances', they were the Premiership players, who earned far more (and similarly commanded higher transfer fees if poached by a rival publisher) than the journeyman footballer down in Division Two. He even joked (by fax) that he had once been offered a six-figure advance by Edward Jesser: 'Ten pounds, nineteen shillings and eleven pence.'

I had always treasured that joke, though I was glad I had not tried it on Jake Philbin, who would not have understood it at all.

I had been deliberately vague with young Jake about the number of Duncan Torrens titles B & B had published, as I saw no need to help him out – or rather, help out dear Robina Robinson, whose messenger boy he surely was. If Pabulator were rooting around finding untapped income streams and looking for a long-running series to be ebooked, then the Inspector Seeley books would, on paper, be a prime target. The trouble seemed to be that Robina had, in her desire to suck up to the new owners, destroyed the paper trail – quite literally – which led to Duncan Torrens and now, when she needed it, couldn't find it.

My unexpected visit from Jake Philbin had been my first physical contact with anyone from B & B or Pabulator since I was made redundant or, as the office wags had it, been awarded the DCM (the 'Don't Come Monday'). Even the corporate Christmas cards stopped coming after the first year, and I suspected Jake had been acting, if in all innocence, in order to save Robina's blushes.

Well, good luck with that. Jake wasn't going to get any help from me.

It wasn't that I had anything personal against Robina; I couldn't really blame her for looking after number one during the takeover and sucking up to the new regime. It was what I should have done, but Robina had far more gumption than I had ever had, and I could understand why. For years she had suffered – I had seen it with my own eyes – from the curse of being a lowly 'secretary', a position which seemed to be particularly looked down upon in publishing, and not just by senior male executives. I remember one occasion at the London Book Fair when the

Boothby & Briggs stand was visited by the (female) commissioning editor for a national fiction publisher. Robina proudly introduced herself as an associate editor, which she most certainly was by then, to which the visitor responded with a haughty, 'And whose secretary were you?'

By the time of the takeover, Robina was more or less in sole charge of B & B's output of romantic fiction, small but regular sellers which would never set the book world alight but were popular enough on the library circuit. She ran a tight ship and kept a beady eye on production costs so that her little part of the firm always made a profit, yet she also had ideas on how the market for romantic fiction was evolving, had an eye for spotting emerging trends and was willing to talk in staff meetings and use terms such as 'demographics' and even – whisper it softly in the hallowed halls of Boothby & Briggs – 'promotional opportunities'.

Under the old regime, such suggestions would have been greeted with patronizing smiles – after all, she was only a secretary – but the new owners, determined to flaunt their progressive Scandinavian work ethic, positively encouraged their employees to contribute to the 'philosophy and well-being' of the company. Robina was not slow in coming forward, which is why she is still employed by Pabulator in a senior editorial position and I am an invisible librarian working in our small town's satellite branch of a cash-strapped county library.

Within a week of the takeover, the staff of B & B were examined, some might say interrogated, by a crack team from Pabulator's human resources department. From the looks on their shiny young faces, they seemed surprised on arrival to find we were not actually still using quill pens and ink, though to many of us it was they who looked like visitors from another planet. The employees of B & B had never enjoyed the benefits of human resources, and most of us, not even in coffee breaks or over the (very) occasional pub lunch, had never been asked to list our personal goals and ambitions or predict where we thought we might be in five or ten years' time. (In my case, the answer to that question was measured in weeks, not years.) Nor were we used to filling in so many questionnaires or having to declare what we thought were our 'competencies'.

Buried Above Ground

We did receive feedback from those exhaustive, and exhausting, exercises in the form of a one-line verdict delivered personally by the Head of Human Resources, a sharp-suited Viking who spoke irritatingly perfect English, on his one visit to the office in the week the redundancy notices went out with the payslips. The conclusion they had made in my case was that I was a 'determined underachiever'. It sounded like an epitaph, and in my case it was.

I have no idea how Robina scored on her corporate evaluation but clearly higher than me. It would have been churlish to suggest she might be the 'determined overachiever' in the workforce, as I was sure there were several of those, but Robina must have impressed our new lords and masters into seeing beyond her shorthand and typing skills, skills which were soon to be as redundant as I was. Perhaps she had mugged up on computers and marketing and was able to speak to the new owners in their own language, whilst us of the old guard simply stared, slack-jawed and nervous. Whatever she did, she was flagged up as promotion material, and good luck to her.

It seemed she proved herself to be a competent editor, which is to say she made no notable mistakes, such as the editor who rejected the first crime novel written under a pseudonym by J.K. Rowling, throwing petrol on the fires of self-immolation by returning the manuscript with the helpful suggestion that the author enrol in a creative writing class. And she innovated, slowly and gently, by accepting first novels from new writers, something which Boothby & Briggs had always been reluctant to do, and cleverly stayed clear of any unpublished novel featured in a 'heated bidding war' according to *The Bookseller*. She also spent more money – not a lot – on dust jackets, using Pabulator's in-house designers so that B & B's crime list got a new, more modern look, which did not necessarily please the bulk of the stable of writers.

When Pabulator's human resources hit team conducted their star chamber interviews to decide which of the old guard would be culled and denied the brave new world on offer, Robina had clearly endorsed herself far more than I ever could, or indeed did, making sure Pabulator spotted her talent. Her progress to senior fiction editor had been as inevitable as my being put out

28   Mike Ripley

on my ear. With Edward Jesser gone there was no one to stand in my corner and sing my praises; Robina was more than capable of singing her own, and it seemed that the new owners were keen to join her choir.

Not that I blame her or bear her any animosity. She did, after all, sign the 'Sorry You're Leaving' card I was presented with on my last day, although she did not come to the pub for farewell drinks that evening.

But then nobody did.

FIVE

'I'm putting you on discards this morning, Roly,' said Mrs White in lieu of a greeting.

'That's fine, Val,' I answered, glancing around to make sure we had no early-bird customers, as in front of the library-going, tax-paying public it was always 'Mrs White' out of respect for the chain of command.

Not that it was a long chain of command, more a short leash. Valerie White was the senior librarian in our town's little local satellite branch of the county library, in command of a staff of one assistant librarian (myself) and two part-time library assistants (note the distinction) – a pair of jolly grandmothers who bravely supervised the unruly toddlers and their often unruly young mothers in the daily Early Readers clubs. I knew they were paid a pittance and always said they loved the job because it got them out of the house, but I often thought that Mrs Sharpe (Janice) and Mrs Cook (Sally) deserved danger money for keeping control of a dozen or so four-year-olds dumped unceremoniously by their mothers in search of a couple of hours of 'me time' each morning.

Being assigned to discard duty suited me down to the ground. It not only put me in the stock room out of sight and earshot of Janice and Sally as they press-ganged reluctant Early Readers into circular groups on rubber floor mats and fought for their attention, but it was a job I relished.

Someone probably said – or should have – that there can be nothing sadder than a library book which has been discarded and had the word WITHDRAWN rubber-stamped on the inside of its cover, only partially obscuring the borrowing record sheet which exposed the humiliating fact that the book had not been borrowed from the library for an embarrassing number of years. They often nestled uncomfortably next to books which were being discarded for exactly the opposite reason: they had been read to death, their spines broken and their leaves loosened by a voracious readership, as witnessed by a Date Due sheet so

30 Mike Ripley

covered in overlapping date stamps it looked at first glance as if it was a page from a Japanese novel.

Whether they had been too popular for their own specially strengthened library jackets, or simply unpopular enough not to have justified the additional expense, many of the books headed for the discard pile came with fond reminders of the library's borrowers in the form of ad hoc bookmarks signifying, in most cases, the extent of their reading of a title, or perhaps marking the point where their interest, and patience, ran out. Most were harmless, some quite endearing. I had personally removed several (opened) letters, usually from insurance companies, or offers of double glazing addressed to 'The Occupier', the odd postcard (including one from an 'Auntie Jan' sent from South Africa in 1931), a receipt from an apparently excellent lunch in Cherbourg in 1970 (I took a note of the restaurant's name), numerous bus and train tickets, and once a pristine high-denomination banknote in a currency no longer used in Bulgaria.

On the downside, of course, there were items which had been pressed into service which should not have been. Teabags, mercifully unused, were more popular than one would have thought, and among the more curious – and thankfully rare – enclosures had been a Rich Tea biscuit; a double sheet, carefully folded, of Izal toilet paper; and an extended, but luckily (for the library) unused, male condom.

One could not say that life in the discards department was ever dull, and at times it was positively exciting, as it was that day when my rubber WITHDRAWN stamp hovered, like a Damocles blade, above a book jacket I knew only too well. It was almost fate, following the visit of young Jake Philbin, that one of the books unceremoniously dumped in the large plastic box which served as my in tray would be a Duncan Torrens title, and one I knew well.

It was a mid-period Inspector Seeley novel and the last one of a mini trilogy within the series, by which I mean three books with a theme that did not interrupt or add to the narrative, but was there merely at the whim of the author. In this case, *One Who Is Afraid of Death,* which followed on from *Small Is the Span*, which followed *Most Wretched of Deaths*. Each novel was a complete, standalone case for Inspector Seeley, and the titles

Buried Above Ground 31

had no direct connection to the mayhem and detection described, other than for dramatic effect.

Few readers would have known, and even less cared, that those three titles all came from random dips into the *Meditations* of Marcus Aurelius, the Roman philosopher emperor and one of the very few emperors regarded by historians as A Good Thing. I was not aware that anyone had wondered why Torrens had trawled Marcus Aurelius for suitable titles, other than perhaps to show he was well read, although the purist might argue that *Most Wretched of Deaths* was in fact Aurelius quoting Socrates. But then, titles can be difficult things and some sources have been done to death, which itself is not as common a title as you might think, and virtually every other line in *Macbeth* and *Hamlet* is the title of a crime novel. I know of one bestselling – genuinely bestselling, not just marketed as such – author to whom their titles were of little interest and would submit untitled manuscripts, leaving it to their editor to come up with one.

That soon-to-be discarded copy of *One Who Is Afraid of Death* was in near pristine condition or 'fine' as the collectors would say; though they would always add the stigma of the label 'ex-library' which in their obsessive minds always trumped all favourable descriptions of condition. A book may be spotless, its edges un-yellowed, its pages crisp and clear of creases, grease spots and – heaven forfend – free of any turned-down corners by members of the lower classes who had not come to terms with the concept of bookmarks, but to a true collector, the designation ex-library meant instant rejection, and the Mylar plastic covers used to protect library books were equally hated, especially on older books where they were often secured with cracked brown strips of Sellotape.

But I am not a collector; I am a *reader*, and to me a new book is simply one I have not read before, whatever its condition and however sad its history of rough mistreatment. *One Who Is Afraid of Death*, of course, was not a new book in any sense, for I knew it well, although I did not own a copy, so to find one scheduled for discarding was an offer I had no intention of refusing.

I put the book to my nose and inhaled deeply. Apart from must and age, it was free of suspicious odours as, thankfully, most library books are these days.

32   Mike Ripley

I did once, at the request of one of our regular customers, agree to value their grandfather's collection of first editions of James Bond novels now he was too old to enjoy them. The books were all intact, their spines undamaged and their dust jackets present and correct, most with their famous illustrations by Richard Chopping. They had been kept out of direct sunlight, and potentially the collection could have been rather valuable. There was one problem, though, in that Grandad had been a heavy pipe smoker for more than fifty years and even the gentlest of page-turnings assaulted the olfactory senses to the extent that *The Spy Who Loved Me* reeked like a burned-out cattle shed. I knew there was an odour-neutralizing chemical which worked on paper and was used by antiquarian book dealers, but I felt, sadly, that this collection of Ian Fleming's finest work was beyond reclamation and so directed our hopeful customer to the nearest Oxfam shop.

The only sad thing about the copy of *One Who Is Afraid of Death* was the reason it was now being discarded: the almost virginal Date Due sheet which recorded only two withdrawals, the most recent being eight years ago. I gently blew away the thin patina of dust which had settled on its Mylar covering and slipped the book into the canvas tote bag bearing the logo of a national paperback publisher in which I carried my sandwiches and Thermos flask of coffee.

I had no qualms of conscience about taking the book and certainly never thought of it as stealing. After all, no one had bothered to read it for free in eight years, so why would anyone pay for one when the library held one of its periodic sales (hardbacks £1, paperbacks 50p)? And if withdrawn volumes did not sell, they were unceremoniously crated and shipped off to one of the big online dealers who paid the local council by dead weight, offered the half-decent copies for resale on the internet and sent the rest to the recycling centre – the Elysian Fields of many a good book and almost certainly the resting place of a fair number of Duncan Torrens titles, though this one was coming home with me.

I am not superstitious as a rule and therefore thought nothing about my acquisition of a Torrens title I did not possess coming so soon after the visit of young Jake Philbin. I regarded Duncan

Buried Above Ground 33

Torrens as a closed book in every sense, and when Val White poked her head round the stock-room door and announced that I had a visitor at the front desk, my suspicions went only so far as to wonder who it could possibly be. I never had visitors here at the library and I had never advertised the fact that I worked here.

'Are you sure they asked for me, Val?'

'Quite sure, Mr Wilkes, and you know the rules,' she said firmly, using my surname instead of just Roly, to indicate her disapproval of personal visits to the workplace and her delight in reminding me that although she was two decades younger, she was in charge. 'He asked for you by name and if you were available to answer a question about an author. He's rather young, looks like a student and is very forward. He said his name was Jacon Archer and stressed that was Jacon with a "C" and not an "S", which is the sensible way of spelling Jason if you ask me.'

Nobody had, but I did not point this out.

'I don't know anyone called Jacon Archer, however he spells it.'

'Well, it sounds as if he knows you. Please come and deal with him because I'm alone on the desk.'

'Of course, Mrs White,' I said politely. Then: 'Did he say which author he had a question about?'

'Yes, it was one in your special area of interest: crime writing.'

She said 'crime writing' in a tone which reminded me of the famous crime writer who, tongue firmly in cheek, had a character who also found the expression loathsome.

'Who specifically?'

'One of the old ones – Duncan Torrens.'

I know I automatically looked at the canvas tote bag where my recently acquired copy of *One Who Is Afraid of Death* nestled against my clingfilm-wrapped corned beef-and-piccalilli sandwiches, but I do not think Mrs White noticed.

'Happy to help,' I said.

'My name is Jacon Archer. That's Jacon with a "C".'

'So I've been told.'

'It doesn't mean anything to you?'

'I'm afraid not. Should it?'

Val had been right – he did look like a student. Actually, he looked like someone trying rather too hard to look like a student: a knee-length parka over torn jeans and a black T-shirt promoting a heavy metal band, spotless white trainers and the obligatory backpack over one shoulder. He had long ginger hair and a straggly beard to match and wore large round two-tone spectacles with garish blue rims and yellow arms, which gave his face a look of permanent surprise.

'Gadabout,' he said.

'I'm sorry?'

'It's my website.'

'Once again, you have me at a disadvantage.' I knew I must be coming across as a crusty old buffer, but I saw no particular reason to be anything other than polite. He could well be a rate payer and hold a library card, and the rule was to be perfectly polite to customers whatever their appearance or however bizarre their requests. (Val White had often said she was glad the library did not have a dress code for the general public but a pity it didn't have one for their idiotic questions.)

'GADabout.com – capital G-A-D. It's a website about golden-age detective fiction. Basically crime novels and detective stories written in the twenties and thirties, mostly written by British—'

'I know what you mean by golden-age detective stories,' I said patiently, 'but we don't actually differentiate them from our general crime and thriller section, which is over there.'

I pointed towards our largest free-standing unit of shelves, certainly our most popular area with regular borrowers despite the uninspiring sign provided by the county council saying *whodunits*, even if the majority these days featured serial killers and the only questions posed were *who-gets-done* and how many body parts are missing.

'I'm not here to borrow books,' said Jacon-with-a-'C'. 'I wanted to talk to you, if you are Roland Wilkes.'

'I am.'

'The Roland Wilkes who used to be an editor at Boothby and Briggs?'

'In a previous life, yes.'

Jacon blinked behind his stupid multicoloured glasses and swallowed hard. 'Then you are just the person to tell me about the man who was Duncan Torrens.'

Buried Above Ground

35

To say I was surprised at the way he put that would be an understatement, but I think I recovered well.

'Goodness, there's a name from the past! I think we still have some of his books on our shelves.'

Jacon played with his thin, would-be hipster beard with the fingertips of his right hand. I suspected that was one of his least annoying habits.

'I'm not after his books, at least not today. It's him, the man himself, I want to talk about.'

'And what makes you think I can help you?' I looked down at my fingernails in what must have seemed an affected gesture, but I simply couldn't stand looking at him tugging and stroking his beard.

'Because you were the editor on *The Missing Fabergé*, his last novel.' He paused for what he clearly thought was dramatic effect. 'Which was never published.'

'How the devil do you know that?'

'Because I have a copy of – perhaps the only copy – of the original manuscript, and your name's on it.'

I let him have his moment of triumph and looked suitably shocked. 'That's impossible.'

He began to unsling his backpack. 'I can prove it.'

'Not here. And you really should have left your backpack inside the front doors; they're not allowed in the library. If you want to talk to me rather than borrow a book, that will have to be on my time, not the library's. I take my lunch at one and can meet you in the pub across the road, The Foresters.'

'I'm not much of a drinker,' he said limply.

I checked my watch – just after eleven – and said, 'It'll be open now, so you can get in a couple of hours' practice.'

It was, I thought, a good pay-off line, and one to which he had no answer.

Presumably the pub was named after the foresters who had done such a good job at some point in the past that there wasn't a tree for miles except at Christmas. It was the sort of cold, soulless pub you could find on any post-war housing estate in small-town England; the sort that by geography would never attract a passing trade and given its unimaginative interpretation of the mantra 'pub food' (or, more accurately, 'pub grub') was unlikely to attract the discerning diner. Its continued existence rested on the fact that it served a captive audience of residents and local government workers who had nowhere else to socialize and neither the spare cash nor transport to explore greener pastures.

It was not the sort of pub where men went to meet women, or women went to escape men; the atmosphere, or lack of it, encouraged neither pursuit. I suspect I was one of the few customers ever to have arranged to meet a woman there, though it was far from a romantic date of any kind as the female in question was my ex-partner and the occasion was our final parting after a brief, and frankly tortuous, relationship.

I had not patronized The Foresters since that last evening with Alice, but I remembered all too clearly how she had approached the table I had commandeered, sniffed so loudly she could be heard over the sound of the television in the public bar next door and said, 'Is this shithole the best you could do?' It was a typical Alice response to a question she had not been asked, or perhaps just a general comment on me and my lifestyle, which had been a disappointment to Alice from the minute she stepped off the aeroplane.

Jacon-with-a-'C' Archer was waiting for me, sitting alone at a small round wrought-iron table with a glass of what looked like lemonade resting on a beer mat in front of him. He was staring at it as if daring it to move and clearly quite happy to be doing so as it avoided him having to look around the pub and feign interest in the dismal decor or, even worse, make eye contact with the other customers. I knew that look; I saw it every morning while shaving.

He did glance up to acknowledge my arrival but made no attempt to shake hands or offer to buy me a drink. It was not until I had bought myself a half of lager at the bar and pulled out a chair to join him that he spoke.

'I need to find Duncan Torrens,' he said as if I was a stupid pupil who had not been paying attention.

'What on earth for?' I asked, determined not to let my hand shake as I sipped my beer.

'For my website, Gadabout. Do you read it?'

'I know of it,' I said cautiously. 'Customers occasionally ask to consult it on the library computers.'

He seemed mildly proud of that when he should have been grateful. I knew the site, of course, and thought it so dull and nerdily obsessive that I was surprised it had any viewers at all. It was mainly concerned in covering British, more specifically English, detective stories from the so-called 'Golden Age' but concentrating not on the truly notable authors of the period – the Christies, Sayers, Allinghams and so forth – rather on the hundreds of obscure writers who churned out potboiler plots peopled by cardboard characters.

Gadabout seemed to find these authors fascinating, often more fascinating than their books, and went into great detail about how many of them were the sons or daughters of clergymen, saw service in the Great War, married childhood sweethearts, perhaps flirted with a proper job such as teaching and then settled down to a bucolic life of writing in a country cottage in a picturesque part of southern England – always the southern counties, never the industrial north. There they would produce, in incredible numbers and with depressing regularity, the continuing adventures of Inspector This or Superintendent That, their personal foot soldiers in the Grande Armée of Golden Age sleuths.

However fantastic their plots and however indistinguishable their protagonists were from those of the considerable competition, these 'forgotten authors' as Gadabout labelled them, were incredibly prolific, some of them clocking up scores of titles. As one famous crime writer of the Golden Age said (I paraphrase): anyone who wrote that much either had an overactive thyroid or a problem with the Inland Revenue.

The basic ethos of Gadabout was that there were dozens if not hundreds of writers who had been unjustly forgotten, a starting point which allowed no room for the counterargument or even the passing thought that there might be a good reason why the majority of these books, which only ever went through one edition, had remained out of print and perhaps blissfully forgotten for sixty or seventy years.

Invariably they relied upon complex plots depending on railway timetables, the crucial delivery of a letter by the second or third (!) post, increasingly bizarre methods of murder – there was always a murder, though blood and gore were rarely evident – and the closed circle of suspects all had cast-iron alibis (to the minute) for the crime. Clues to the murderer were laid like those in a cryptic crossword and were often obvious to those with a working knowledge of Latin, familiarity with the correct way to address all members of aristocracy and the ability to spot a coded message in a line of knitting or the suspicious foreigner who gave himself away by not knowing in which county Tunbridge Wells was. Characterization was always subservient to plot, and many a character was derided, even at the time of publication, as being of no more substance than cardboard cut-outs. One waggish critic had once opined that such novels should have been made redundant by the invention of the board game *Cluedo* in 1949, when cardboard pieces replaced cardboard writing.

'I'm guessing you're not a fan of Golden Age mysteries.' Even as he said that there was a glimmer of hope in his eyes – or it may have been a reflection from his ridiculous glasses.

'Not greatly,' I said maliciously. 'I once met a man who announced proudly that he never read anything later than 1945 and I made the observation that a quarter to eight was a very early bedtime.'

He had not thought that funny either and had reported me to the head librarian. Fortunately, in those far more liberal days, it took more than one case of 'customer dissatisfaction' to earn a reprimand.

'You can't deny a lot of people are rediscovering the Golden Age and reading a lot of books.'

'Well, as a librarian, I would have to dispute that. There may have been a revival of interest in so-called Golden Age authors recently, but the number of readers hasn't grown; the dedicated fans are just reading more. In terms of library issues, crime fiction is still the most popular category, though it's the contemporary mysteries that are in demand, not the old stuff. Crime novels with something to say about life and society, with characters and situations readers can recognize.'

'At the expense of the puzzle element.'

'Is that a bad thing? Surely there are more things to ask than simply whodunit?'

Buried Above Ground 39

'But the puzzle was the thing; beating the detective in the book to the correct solution.'

'However improbable, not to say far-fetched. However, I'm not here to argue about the Golden Age; I only have half an hour for lunch.' I had sandwiches waiting for me back at the library and I had no intention of wasting money only to be disappointed by the menu at The Foresters – and it would have been my money as Jacon was clearly not offering. 'You claimed to have a Duncan Torrens manuscript.'

'Indeed I have,' he said with what I suspected passed for excitement as he scrabbled into his backpack, which he had slung over the back of his chair. 'Here it is!'

With a flourish, he wafted a sheaf of paper over the table, a bundle of pages held together with a thick rubber band. It was clearly a typescript, the cover page so badly stained with what I hoped was oil that it was almost impossible to read the title and the name of the author.

I did not have to. He had already told me it was the manuscript of *The Missing Fabergé*, and I knew only one author who had submitted manuscripts typed on foolscap-size paper instead of the more conventional A4.

'Where in God's name did you get that?' I knew my eyes were fixed on that filthy pile of yellowing sheets, but I resisted the urge to rip them from his hand.

'I went what the Americans call dumpster diving' – he seemed rather proud that he knew such an expression – 'and found it on a recycling website . . . rescued from a skip.'

SIX

I did not touch it, but I knew I had to have it as soon as I read the handwritten message on the cover page: *Roly – Do what you can with this one, Alan.*

Jacon was speaking. 'You remember this one?'

'I haven't seen it in over twenty years,' I admitted, 'but I remember it. *The Missing Fabergé* was the last Duncan Torrens title I edited for Boothby and Briggs – or would have been except I was made— I left the company before it could be contracted and put into production.'

'That would have been when Pabulator took them over?'

I realized that his stupid multicoloured glasses were fixed on my face as I stared at the grubby manuscript. 'Do you make a habit of rooting around in skips?'

He blinked furiously behind those glasses, and I suspected that was not the first time he had been asked that.

'Not personally; there's a website, as I said.' There would be. 'A recycling website, mostly for furniture but also books, sheet music and scripts which have been rescued from rubbish skips outside publishers and television studios. They were offering technical shooting scripts from episodes of *Callan* from the sixties, episodes where the broadcast tapes were lost, so the camera scripts were the only record.' He realized that I was unlikely to find his enthusiasm infectious. 'Well, the site also had some publishers' manuscripts, including this one by Duncan Torrens. They had no idea who he was, but I did, so I bought it.'

'You bought stolen goods?'

'Not stolen, discarded.'

'And you were going to recycle it and make money out of it?'

'My interest is purely academic.' He refused to give me the moral high ground. 'I consider it too old-fashioned to be worth republishing.'

'Says the big fan of the Golden Age.'

'There's a difference between classic vintage and simply being out of date.' He paused and moistened his strangely bloodless lips. 'That's not to say that others wouldn't be interested in re-issuing the Torrens backlist, even just as ebooks. There's a market for long-running series of detective stories out there.'

'Even what you call old-fashioned ones?'

'A new book is only one you haven't read before,' said Jacon, eerily echoing my own thoughts when I was confronted by Jake Philbin, that other recent irritant.

That was not, of course, the only spooky thought hovering over me. Two approaches from novices in the book business – both a third of my age – attempting to pick my brains about an author who had not been published in over twenty years. Whatever was going on, there would be money involved somewhere. I may not be actually in publishing anymore, but I knew its dark heart.

'Did somebody from Boothby and Briggs, or Pabulator, put you up to this?'

'Up to what?'

I had pulled up a chair and sat down opposite him, but he had leaned forwards over the tabletop and turned his face up so I had the perfect view should I want to appreciate his glasses. It was a strangely subservient but also threatening pose.

'Put you up to playing detective. You have the name for it.'

'Oh, you mean Lew Archer, as created by John Ross Macdonald,' he said blithely, passing my little test, but then he had to show off. 'Did you know that when he was first published in this country, the detective's name was changed to Lew Arliss because there already was a British detective character called Maxwell Archer?'

'As a matter of fact, I did, and I knew that Ross Macdonald's real name was Kenneth Millar, but you haven't answered my question. Who put you on my trail? Was it Boothby and Briggs?'

He looked up at me like a spaniel with a guilty conscience. 'They wouldn't give out your address and they couldn't forward my emails because you don't do email, but she did let slip that you lived out here.'

'*She?* Would that be Robina Robinson?'

'Yes, it would. I went along to a launch party for one of B and B's star authors. It wasn't really my thing, but there were

42 Mike Ripley

free wine and nibbles, and I was invited as I'm on their accredited bloggers list.' He waited in vain for me to show I was impressed. 'When I realized who she was, I asked about you and she said she remembered you.'

'Didn't she want to know why you were asking?'

'I gave her some guff about historical research into crime fiction and said you might be worth interviewing or even doing a podcast on Boothby and Briggs crime writers no longer with us. She agreed you would be the ideal candidate.'

I guessed that Robina's reaction to 'doing a podcast' would have been the same as mine, and she would have got away from Jacon as quickly as possible, using me as a decoy.

I pointed a finger at the soiled manuscript lying on the table between us. 'What did she say about *The Missing Fabergé*?'

Jacon was so shocked his glasses slipped down his nose and he had to throw back his head to make them behave. 'Strewth! I wasn't going down that alley. No fear was I showing her the script; she might have wanted it back.'

'Unlikely, as she was probably the one who threw it away,' I said, curbing the urge to snigger at the way excitement pushed his vocabulary back into the Golden Age he read so much about, which surely could not be healthy for a man of his age.

'But she offered me up as a contact?'

'It was always you I wanted to talk to because you were Duncan Torrens' editor for his last ten Inspector Seeley novels.'

'How did you know that?'

Fiction editors are rarely credited publicly, and few outside the business know who edits which author. Most editors behave like spies and some do not even tell their wives or partners who they are working on (or with, as they like to say). It is a way, not always successful, of keeping out of the firing line of the thousands of unsolicited manuscripts sent to publishers every week.

'*Buried Above Ground.*'

'Excuse me?'

'The book *Buried Above Ground* by Duncan Torrens. I have a first edition.'

It would have been churlish to point out that all books have a first – and often only – edition.

Buried Above Ground

'The dedication!' He was excited and his glasses began to jump about again, though I could not tell if it was his nose or his ears driving the movement. 'It was dedicated to you: *To my new and enthusiastic editor Roland Wilkes with a prospect of much mischief ahead.*'

Bugger. I'd forgotten that. I had been ridiculously proud of that dedication at the time, all those years ago. It had been my first title as a proper editor rather than a lowly copy editor and I felt I had guided it from the opening paragraph, which had Inspector Seeley complaining about the weather (something he did in every book), through the reporting of a murder and the surveying of the corpse, pointing out the obvious to his sergeant Gerry Grimes, suspect, alibis, the traditional second murder and then the apprehension of the murderer in time to prevent the third murder.

In truth, it had been little more than a painless copy-editing exercise as by then Inspector Seeley was a well-established character among readers, and therefore virtually untouchable by editors, and Torrens had produced more than a dozen novels in the same competent, if uninspiring, style approved by Edward Jesser. Any corrections or suggestions, all minor, were done by the exchange of faxes, which made that dedication, from an author to an editor he had never met, rather poignant.

'That was the one where Seeley finds a body in a replica Roman sarcophagus in an ornamental garden,' Jacon offered.

'I know – I remember it. I'd just forgotten the dedication. It was the first Torrens book I was in charge of,' I said truthfully.

He prodded the manuscript. 'And this one would have been the last.' It was not a question.

'Would have – should have – could have. The company got taken over and I was out on my ear before I even got the chance to read the last Inspector Seeley story. It is an Inspector Seeley, I presume. They all were.'

'You mean you never read it?'

'At Boothby and Briggs, no.' I shook my head sorrowfully as I spoke the technical truth.

'So you've no idea what *The Missing Fabergé* is about?'

'Not a clue' – which was certainly not true – 'but I could hazard a guess that it has something to do with a jewelled Fabergé egg of great value which was made for the Tsar of Russia but went missing after the 1917 revolution.'

'That's a pretty good guess.'

'It wasn't that difficult; the title gave it away. Have *you* read it?'

'I have and it's pretty good; I really enjoyed it.'

'Well, thank you for reuniting me with it. It will bring back some pleasant memories.'

I put down my now empty glass of beer and picked up the manuscript, knocking the bundle of pages on the table to straighten them, just as a television newsreader compacts the loose pages of their crib sheets at the end of a bulletin.

Jacon looked horrified and sat bolt upright. He was clearly fighting the urge to rip it from my hands.

'No! Wait! I can't let you have it; I need to copy it.'

'I can photocopy it at the library,' I said, pushing my chair back as if making ready to leave.

'Then I'll come with you.'

I riffled the edge of the block of paper like a card sharp.

'I can't do it *now*; I have to get back to work. I'll have to do it after hours.'

That was certainly true. I would have to wait until Val White had left for the day, otherwise she would insist I paid the 10p per sheet fee we charged the public, and there were, I knew, more than 250 pages.

'I suppose I could hang around and catch a later train back to London. I've got a timetable somewhere.' He began to fumble in his backpack.

'They're very regular; well, I suppose that should be frequently scheduled rather than actually regular. This is commuter country, don't forget.'

'You've always lived here, never in London?'

'I was always a small-town kinda guy – never fancied the big city,' I answered as it seemed only polite to do so, even though it seemed an odd thing to ask. 'I might not have been so easy to find if I lived in London. You never did say how you found me.'

'Yes, I did – Robina Robinson said you still lived out this way, even after your marriage.'

Robina had always thought of my marriage as a joke – with

Buried Above Ground 45

good reason as it turned out – and Jacon clearly realized that the subject rankled me, but he pursued it nonetheless.

'Was she a local girl?' he asked with an innocence I suspected was frighteningly genuine.

'Most definitely not, and she had nothing to do with you tracking me down to the library or anything else for that matter.'

I was suddenly on my feet, looking down into that stupid bespectacled face, and I was doing my best to put some threat into my voice, though I have never been able to put much *heft* into my personality, being naturally averse to confrontation. Even so, a normal person, not a Jacon-with-a-'C', ought to have picked up on the signals I was trying to send.

'I never said she did,' he said calmly. 'I took a chance and caught the first off-peak train out here this morning after I got your address from the phone book. Now that's old school detective fiction.' He was pleased with himself. 'Who knew people were still listed in phone books? Who knew people still had landlines?'

'I do.'

But I had forgotten to opt out of the phone directory, thinking that no one bothered to use them anymore.

'I rang from the station, but there was no answer, and you don't have an answering machine.'

'I am aware of that.' I had no need for one. In fact, I had very little need of a telephone these days.

'So I took a chance and went round to your place. Couldn't find it at first, then I realized it was the flat above the Greek restaurant. They told me you worked in the library here.'

'That was good detective work.' I pretended to be impressed as I hefted the pages of the manuscript. 'And all to bring me this. Let me read it to refresh my memory of Torrens, and if you leave me your address, I'll post it back to you.'

'I'd rather wait while you copied it,' he pleaded. 'I can look around the town this afternoon and meet you after work.'

'Oh, I couldn't put you through that. There's so little to do here. It really is a very dull place, and as you've seen the station and the library already, you've done the main tourist sights.'

'I don't mind. I'll think of something to do. Are there any second-hand bookshops here?'

46 Mike Ripley

'Only charity shops. I might be late, you know. I can't get at the photocopier until six at the earliest.'

Young Mr Archer's face bloomed as a new thought suddenly arrived. 'How far away is Dunkley from here?'

'Dunkley? It's about ten miles, but it takes two buses and they're few and far between after the school run around four o'clock, though you could take a taxi if you have the cash.' From his face, I knew I had made the right call there. 'What on earth do you want to go to Dunkley for anyway?' I asked, though I suspected I knew.

'To see where Duncan Torrens is buried,' he said earnestly.

Damn.

SEVEN

Working on the assumption that Jacon Archer was little more than an irritating fanboy when it came to crime fiction – they do exist and are usually less annoying than science-fiction addicts – my plan had been to take *The Missing Fabergé* manuscript on the pretext of photocopying it, return to the library, eat my sandwiches and keep my head down for the rest of the day. At closing time, if he was still hanging around, I would give it back to him and point him towards the London train. After all, I didn't need a copy as I knew its contents very well, but I did need to know what he planned to do with the original, so keeping him hanging around was a sort of test for him, and hopefully he would get bored and go home, where his mother probably had his dinner waiting for him.

But now he had mentioned Dunkley, I needed to keep an eye on him.

He was waiting outside the main doors of the library as I locked up – after making sure Val White had gone first so that we wouldn't be seen together. Quite why he had not come inside for 'a warm and a dry' and read, or pretended to read, a book as several of our homeless regulars do, I didn't know, but it confirmed my view that he was more than a little odd.

It had rained quite heavily that afternoon, so he had put the hood of his anorak up, which should have made him look, under the streetlights, vaguely menacing, a dispossessed youth perfectly blending in to the now empty shopping centre which blighted our small town. The popular press image of a skulking 'hoodie', though, was spoiled in his case by the fact that he had pulled on his anorak over the backpack he had slung over his shoulders, presumably to keep some precious content safe from the elements. The result was that in silhouette he looked like a bedraggled hunchback. When I asked if he had eaten and then avoided the raindrops flicking off his shaking head, it might have appeared that I was taking pity on a vagrant, but no one was around to observe us. I know because I checked before I approached him.

I had his manuscript in a large Jiffy bag, and he followed that rather than me to the early evening delights of Dimi's Taverna, which was transforming itself from daytime café into Greek-themed restaurant like a shop-worn butterfly. I knew he knew I lived in the flat above, but as we passed the side door entrance which led upstairs and took the taverna door instead, I could not tell if he was relieved or disappointed.

Dimitrios, the owner and head waiter, greeted us himself saying, 'So your young friend found you OK?' accompanied by a theatrically salacious and totally inappropriate wink. I responded with a glare and a request for a table for two away from the window on to the street, although I was not too worried about being seen in Dimi's. It was, after all, quite literally my nearest restaurant, and it was cheap if not particularly cheerful.

Jacon seemed overwhelmed by the kitsch decor of the place, or perhaps he had more good taste than I gave him credit for. I dismissed that thought immediately when I saw his reaction to the grease-spotted menu presented to him by the hovering Dimitrios.

Jacon's eyes flicked nervously down the two loose sheets in Dimi's fake leather binder, and then those multicoloured glasses came to rest and his facial muscles relaxed as he reached the 'English Dishes' section at the bottom of page two. I reassured him that dinner was on me, but he still opted for omelette and chips and a Coke to wash it down. I chose my usual kleftiko with a Greek salad and a bottle of Othello, knowing that if I didn't drink it all, Dimi would let me take the remainder upstairs to my flat.

Whilst we waited for our meals, he opened his backpack and carefully packed away the Jiffy bag containing *The Missing Fabergé*.

'Did it bring back memories for you?'

'Yes, but not good ones. I liked the author's initial synopsis of the plot. It was different and it could have been one of the best of the Inspector Seeleys, but it came too late for me. I was made redundant before I had a chance to properly get my hands on it, and clearly the new management discarded it.'

Buried Above Ground

'I enjoyed it, as I've said.' He sipped his Coke as if it was fine wine and looking disapprovingly as I poured myself a full glass of Cypriot red as if it were Coke. 'Much to my surprise because it's more of thriller than a detective story.'

'And what would be wrong with that?'

'There was no puzzle a reader could solve without prior knowledge of the Russian revolution and what happened to the tsars, so it wasn't really fair.'

'Fair? Where does it say thrillers have to be fair? Life's not fair.'

'But it wasn't a whodunit – that was pretty obvious from the start, even to Gideon Seeley, once he remembered his Russian history. Was there a clue in him being called Gideon?'

'I can't think what it could have been; the topic of Seeley's name never came up. There was never, as far as I recall, any reference to the Gideon who was one of the Old Testament judges in the Bible.'

'That's a pity,' Jacon said enigmatically as our food arrived.

His eyes lit up as his plate landed in front of him, and he grabbed his knife and fork as if they were trowels and set about it. I remembered the maxim – one of many when it came to publishers' lunches – of my old boss Edward Jesser when entertaining an author: if they eat their peas with a knife, reduce their next advance by a third. (He also had a long list of rules when entertaining a literary agent, the prime directive being never let them see the wine list – it's enough that you allow them food.)

I picked at my slow-cooked lamb and sipped my wine with what I considered polite restraint compared to his wolfish gobbling, oblivious to my silent disapproval, though his table manners were really the least of my worries.

'I have to admit that I don't understand the current fad for Golden Age detective stories, especially not among people of your age.'

I might have added 'and your background', but I did not have enough information to be quite so snobbish.

'It's a matter of format and language,' he said between explosive mouthfuls. 'You can rely on the traditional detective story. You have a murder, a closed circle of suspects, clues and a satisfactory resolution. Modern crime novels rely on shock value

50   Mike Ripley

both in terms of casual violence and bad language.' His shoulders
produced a theatrical shudder. 'Writers like Elmore Leonard.'

'What have you got against Elmore Leonard? The man was a
genius.'

Jacon pulled a sour face which had nothing to do with his
meal.

'They're not proper detective stories; there's too much cursing
and too many guns and quite often the villains get away
scot-free.'

'I think you've rather missed the point. Leonard was an
American, and America has a lot of guns. When the criminals
use them, usually on each other, they do so without conscience
or fear of retribution. They simply don't see that they're doing
anything wrong. The books say an awful lot about the state of
society there, plus they're very funny in places and he could
create fantastic characters in just a few lines of dialogue.'

Jacon wrinkled his nose to contain a snort of disgust.

'Give me plot over character any time.' He reached for his
glass of Coke and took a swig like an outlaw in a Western saloon
would down a whisky then slammed the glass back down on the
table with a thump.

'That's fairly obvious from what's up on the Gadabout website,'
I said casually.

'But . . . So you follow it?'

'Not regularly; in fact, only rarely,' I admitted, extinguishing
the sudden hopeful twinkle behind those glasses. I was certainly
not going to tell him that was how I had spent most of the afternoon. 'I was impressed at the lengths you go to in order not to
give away plot spoilers.'

'You don't approve?'

I sipped more wine and tried to look imperious. 'If by already
knowing whodunit spoils one's enjoyment of reading a book
again, then I tend to think the writer has short-changed the reader.
Is it really still a state secret who killed Roger Ackroyd, or how
many passengers on the Orient Express were homicidal maniacs?
The books have been around for ninety-odd years – people have
had time.'

'There are some traditions worth preserving,' he said, matching
my pomposity as he finished a last forkful of rubbery omelette.

Buried Above Ground 51

If he expected a dessert, he had better watch his tone. 'Like the play *The Mousetrap*, which has been running forever, but thousands still go and see it without knowing who the villain is.'

'Are you sure about that? I've never seen it, but I know.'

'You're an editor specializing in crime fiction.'

'Was,' I reminded him. 'I haven't been in that business for a while.'

'But I bet you're in charge of crime fiction in your library.'

'As it happens I am, and it's the busiest section when it comes to borrowings, but apart from Agatha Christie, none of the authors would be worthy of inclusion on the Gadabout site even if they were still in print, which most of them aren't. Come to think of it, would Duncan Torrens qualify? He barely gets a mention on Gadabout as it is. So what's your interest in him?'

'I told you, purely academic since I acquired the manuscript of *The Missing Fabergé*. Duncan Torrens became a pet project of mine.'

'Have you run out of Golden Age authors to write about?'

His cheeks coloured slightly, which made me think I had hit a sensitive bullseye.

'The lack of information about him intrigued me.' He said it in a voice which tried to suggest something sinister, but fell well short. 'There's nothing on the internet, and the author biographies on his dust jackets are annoyingly vague – and there's no photograph of him anywhere.'

'You have to remember, or try and imagine,' I said with a sigh, 'there was a world before social media. Even when the internet arrived, most established midlist authors never bothered to set up their own websites, partly because they didn't use computers and having one never sold an extra copy of one of their books. Plus, with writers of the old school like Torrens, there was an element of privacy. Their books were out in the public arena for people to enjoy and, yes, judge. But their non-writing lives were their own business.'

Jacon reached for his backpack, and I thought he was planning to make a run for it before the approaching Dimitrios handed him the bill, but Dimi was bringing a single laminated sheet to thrust at him with a lecherous grin and the query, 'Something sweet for the young sir?'

52   Mike Ripley

I scowled at Dimi to no avail as he loomed over Jacon, holding the dessert menu only a few inches from his face, so that he could wink lewdly at me with impunity. I said nothing and remembered Edward Jesser's acidic view that one could never trust a restaurant which had pictures of food on its menus, knowing that Jacon would go not for one of the authentic Greek honey-and-nut pastries but would be tempted by the garish coloured photographs of ice-cream sundaes and banana splits.

I was right. He opted for the specialty of the house, 'Dimi's Triple-Decker', which was nothing more than three balls of ice cream – strawberry on top of vanilla on top of chocolate – served in a tall glass and eaten with a long spoon. He beamed in antici-pation as he handed back the menu and returned to rummaging in his backpack, eventually producing a small black notebook.

It was the sort of flip-open notebook which police officers traditionally used in amateur dramatic productions to intimidate a suspect or from which they would read things like, 'I was proceeding in a northerly direction when . . .' Perhaps they still use them, despite the proliferation of mobile phones and body cameras, and they can be bought cheaply enough.

'I've checked the author biographies in fourteen Torrens hard-backs,' he said, flipping the notebook open, 'and they are not only unhelpful but downright misleading.'

'I don't know what you mean,' I said, though I did.

'In the earliest titles I found, from the late seventies and early eighties—'

'That would be before my time. Edward Jesser was his editor back then.'

He nodded in my direction; just once to indicate that he had heard me but did not think a reply was necessary or worth his time.

'—on the jacket of *Dead Before Breakfast* it says that "Duncan Torrens is a retired army officer who keeps chickens in the northern Home Counties" and that's it. Hardly illuminating, is it?'

'Perhaps he did keep chickens back then.'

'Then, a few books later, in *The Bloody Heath*, his biography reads: "Duncan Torrens has tried numerous occupations since leaving the armed forces, including teaching, farming and forestry, but finds writing about murder the most relaxing." Still rather vague, wouldn't you say?'

'And slightly tongue-in-cheek. To me it sounds like an author protecting his privacy.'

He looked up at me from his notebook, just as a barrister would confront a hostile witness.

'When you became his editor, you seemed to encourage him on both those fronts. Do you remember *The Herb Border*?'

Of course I did. Torrens had wanted to call the book *Inspector Seeley's Poison Parsnip* after some arcane name for hemlock until I got hold of it.

'Yes, it was the second Inspector Seeley I worked on.'

'Do you remember the author blurb on that one?'

'Not offhand. Remind me.'

'"Duncan Torrens is of Scots ancestry which explains his love of walking and climbing across moors and up mountains as well as his taste for single malt whisky. He lives in splendid isolation miles from the nearest neighbour."'

'Who's to say some of that isn't true?'

'It's not exactly helpful.'

'Author biographies are not meant to be helpful to people like you, but if they intrigue or amuse the reader, they might sell more books.'

I wondered if I had raised his hackles – if he had hackles – by saying 'people like you', but he was distracted by the arrival of his ice cream, and I had a large black coffee to hide behind.

'You have to appreciate,' I said as he dug into his ice cream, 'that the author biog on the back flap was not taken very seriously by publishers back then. There was a famous series of paperbacks by a big bestseller which carried a description of the author as *dark complexion, fourteen stone, six feet tall . . . cruel, sardonic sense of humour* in one novel and, the following year, in his next novel as *fair complexion, nine stone, five feet six tall . . . warm, generous sense of humour*. It was just a bit of fun, not there to contribute to some future history of the genre.'

'An author photograph might have helped sales.' Jacon stabbed his long sticky spoon for emphasis.

'That was company policy. Edward Jesser had a thing about

writers who insisted on using mugshots that were taken in passport photo booths whilst they were students and believed they still looked like that.'

'You never even said that Duncan Torrens was a pen name.'

'Why should we? The author wanted to protect his privacy, or maybe write something different under his real name. If the circumstances were right, it could always be revealed and get some publicity that way. These days you'll see so-and-so "writing as . . ." plastered across a cover, but it wasn't common when Torrens was in his heyday. I think Ruth Rendell coming out as the alter ego of Barbara Vine started the trend.'

Jacon gobbled the remains of his sundae and licked the spoon before starting on a different tack, replacing the spoon with the small pencil usually holstered at the side of his notebook.

'How did you find working with Torrens?'

'I think we had a good professional relationship. His copy was always very clean, and usually I had to make very few corrections or suggestions, other than his titles.'

'Titles?' He scribbled a note, genuinely interested.

'He was terrible at titles; most writers are, unless they have a long-running theme like nursery rhymes or the seven deadly sins, things like that. You'd be surprised how many writers don't have a clue about a title until they've typed those magic words "The End", and some don't even bother thinking of one – they just leave it to their editors.'

'So you suggested his titles?'

'Well, I like to think I improved some of them. It was me who suggested *Buried Above Ground.* When I got the manuscript, it was called *A Catafalque for Cynthia*, which I thought was pretty naff.'

'There isn't a character called Cynthia in that book,' Jacon snapped.

'I thought it a bit of an old-fashioned name and changed it to Kirstie. Torrens agreed completely; he thought it was a good idea.'

In truth, Torrens could not have cared less.

'Did you change any other names?'

'One or two,' I said, not really knowing where this was going. 'Only the minor characters, of course. Gideon Seeley and Sergeant

Gerry Grimes were the stars of the series and couldn't be messed with. There was also the grumpy chief inspector, George Sixsmith, and the local newspaper reporter—'

'Anne Devine, often referred to as The Devine Anne,' supplied Jacon, proving that he had read the books.

'But only by the lower classes and the rude constabulary. Inspector Seeley would never have been so familiar – he was a respectable married man. Those were the key characters in the series; the rest just came and went, some of them in coffins, so their names were not significant.'

'I thought writers anguished over the names of their characters.'

'Not when churning out detective stories. They just pick them out of phone books or take them from local war memorials or – and this is usually a sign of tired desperation – they consult a road atlas and you'll find place names as surnames, so you get Mr Wakefield, Sergeant Bromley, Colonel Merton, Simon Salisbury, Fred Flockton and so on. I understand Mr Rochester was spoken for some time ago.'

'Did you ever give him notes or guidance on the development of his characters?'

'What do you mean?' I poured myself another glass of Othello, noting that there would not be much worth taking back up to my flat.

'Well, in one of the books, Seeley's marriage suddenly turns tempestuous and divorce is even mentioned. It's the first sign of domestic discord in all the Seeley stories.'

'But the Seeleys get over it, don't they? They kiss and make up in time for the next book. Nobody really knows what goes on in a marriage, not even the people who are married.'

I was pretty sure Jacon was not going to engage in a debate about marriage as I was certain I held the high ground on that subject, it being an experience he could only have read about, though he was consulting his notes again.

'Then there was the revelation about Sergeant Grimes in . . . what was the book?'

'Are you thinking of *Most Wretched of Deaths*?'

'That's the one. Nobody saw that coming in the previous thirty-odd Seeley books.'

56 Mike Ripley

'You've read them all?' I gave him my best flinty stare over the rim of my glass.

'No, I haven't, but after I mentioned Duncan Torrens on the Gadabout website, we got a surprising number of comments from readers.'

I suspected that a 'surprising' number for Gadabout would still be in single figures, but I said nothing.

'That was quite a bombshell about Gerry Grimes – caused quite a stir that did,' he pressed, tapping his open notebook with the point of his pencil.

'If you mean by "quite a stir" that it got the book reviewed in the crime fiction round-up in the *Daily Telegraph* – they had a dedicated crime reviewer in those days – then it did. I think it was the only Torrens book to get a review in a national newspaper, probably because someone recognized that the title came from the *Meditations* of Marcus Aurelius. We were proud of that at Boothby and Briggs as only a small percentage of crime novels get review space, but I can't say it increased sales dramatically.'

'According to the Gadabout comments sections, it's probably the most popular Seeley book. Readers are always giving it five stars.'

'Even though it's been out of print for twenty-five years? Your reviewers must have long memories.'

'Readers are still finding copies thanks to the internet. A first edition turned up in America recently for ten quid.'

'There was only one edition, but that's still a bargain for a dedicated fan. Did you buy it?'

He shook his head with genuine sadness. 'No. They wanted thirty quid to cover postage.'

'What a pity,' I said. And then because I could not resist: 'I think I have a copy somewhere.'

The hangdog expression changed to that of a bouncy puppy. 'Do you have his first book, from 1970, *The Body at Starling Junction*? That's really rare and probably worth hundreds.'

'I'm afraid not. In fact, I'm not aware of that one at all. Was it an Inspector Seeley?'

'It was the first Inspector Seeley, and it's a disgrace that it has never been reprinted!'

'Sad but understandable from a publishing perspective – commercially I mean. And remember, I wasn't involved with the Seeley books until 1990, by which time he was in his stride and always concentrating on the next book. In many ways, as an editor, I had to look on *Buried Above Ground* as the first in the series. Authors should never assume a reader has read any of their previous books or indeed that there are other books in the series, as there's a certain type of reader who is compelled to read them *in order* and only in order.'

He looked at me as if I was denigrating perfectly normal behaviour. 'So it was your first Seeley, even though it was number thirty-four in the series.'

'Was it really? He was always professional, aiming for a book a year regular as clockwork.' I did a quick calculation. 'But if your numbers are correct, then he must have produced two novels in some years. I wasn't aware he had written so many.'

'Even though you worked with Torrens for ten years?'

'Something like that. But he was always very relaxed about his reputation as a writer, and I'm sure he stopped counting how many books he'd written. He used to say that if twenty doesn't make you a writer, what number does?'

'So that first book you worked on was in 1990 and the last would have been *The Missing Fabergé* in 2000, but it ended up rejected and thrown in the skip.'

'That's right. The new millennium saw the takeover of Boothby and Briggs, me being made redundant and the last Inspector Seeley book dumped.'

'Because Duncan Torrens was dead.'

'Yes,' I said drily, 'that didn't help.'

EIGHT

I t had been careless of me to let it slip that I did not know exactly how many books Duncan Torrens had written, as it felt as though I was somehow conceding an advantage to Jacon, though to nerds of his calibre, their favourite crime writers could not write enough. The truth was they could and did. The output of new crime novels – books published for the first time – in Britain alone has been around the 500–600 a year mark, virtually every year since Jacon's beloved 'Golden Age', and publishers published as many as they could because the market seemed infinite. No wonder the distinguished critic (and crime writer) Julian Symons pronounced that 'all crime writers write too much', and though he had the good grace to add 'myself included', it did not save him from the opprobrium of his contemporaries.

He had a point though. It was not uncommon for an author to churn out 100 titles; 150 was not unknown, 200 was worth a raised eyebrow, over 400 was, frankly, ridiculous, but sadly true. In my early days in publishing, when I was young and keen to research the crime-fiction genre, I read everything I could get my second-hand hands on, including a battered paperback (these days we'd say 'much loved') with a garish guns-and-girls cover announcing something like *Ferguson .38*. At first sight, I thought this to be a firearms reference; a Ferguson .38 simply being a Magnum .44 I'd never heard of, but on a first rapid (and only) read, I realized that the book was about a private eye called Ferguson and this was the thirty-eighth instalment of his adventures. The publisher, and perhaps his author, had not bothered to give the latest Ferguson a specific title, merely a number. It probably did not affect sales one jot.

An author with a long backlist of forgotten titles long out of print sounded, in theory, the ideal candidate for the Gadabout database, apart from the fact that his books could in no way be classed as 'Golden Age'. Traditional, yes, but more accurately – if

Buried Above Ground 59

one was splitting hairs – they were contemporary 'police procedurals' or, as they were not wedded to the gruesome detail of real criminal investigation, they tended to attract the rather pejorative descriptor 'cosy crime'.

I could not think how the works of Duncan Torrens would sit among the books featured, and at times drooled over, on Jacon's Gadabout website. True, they were murder stories with the murderer(s) always identified and brought to justice in a satisfying, if not happy, ending. They also, more or less, endorsed and supported the social order and avoided gratuitous violence, bad language and sex scenes. They did not, however, tend to involve weekend house parties at country houses, bucolic chief constables, secret passages, long-lost illegitimate relatives making a surprise return from places called Dismal Swamp or suchlike, odd quirks of (unrepealed) medieval English law, aristocratic lords and ladies leaping, or the reliance for an alibi on a railway timetable. In an Inspector Seeley novel, the only darts encountered would be in the public bar of the local pub, not shot from an Amazonian blowpipe having been tipped with a poison extracted from frogs unknown to anyone except Sir David Attenborough.

The only solid common denominator was that Duncan Torrens' books were out of print and the author was dead. On those criteria, Torrens certainly justified a page of his own on the Gadabout website, and certainly Jacon Archer seemed well qualified to write it.

He had read plenty of Inspector Seeley stories, though he had never expressed an opinion on the quality of them, despite making it clear that they were not 'his thing'. So what had got him interested in the first place? I did not buy his claim that it was purely academic interest following his acquisition of *The Missing Fabergé* manuscript (it would have to be that one); surely there was still plenty of Golden Age material still to be mined, as the seam of forgotten authors and out-of-print detective stories seemed inexhaustible.

Only one thing could have sparked Jacon's interest and that was money, something he clearly needed and which could not, as far as I could see, be provided by the Gadabout website, which did not carry any advertising. Perhaps he had a thriving second-hand book business on the side, but he somehow did not strike

60 Mike Ripley

me as a hard-headed businessman, and if a book was published before 1949, he was more likely to keep it than sell it on. Anything published after 1960 he wouldn't be interested in. Unless it had been written by Duncan Torrens, that is.

I had experienced two approaches in quick succession about the work of an author who had been out of sight, out of mind and out of print for more than twenty years. There had to be big money involved somewhere, but I couldn't see where. Jake Philbin had asked about ebook rights, but surely there wasn't that much money in the ebooks of a forgotten author, at least not a reliable but unspectacular one like Torrens.

Jacon gave nothing away and thanked me politely as I paid the bill, and we prepared to leave the restaurant with me having promised to point out the quickest way to the station.

'I suppose I could always get the train to visit Dunkley,' he said once we were on the pavement outside Dimitrios's un-curtained front window, behind which Dimi was sliding cubes of blackened meat off a skewer for two unsuspecting diners.

'I thought I told you: the train doesn't go there anymore. You'd have to get two buses from here.'

'Do you ever go there?' he asked, giving me puppy-dog eyes, clearly a plea for a lift.

'No.' I took guilty pleasure in crushing his hopes. 'And I don't own a car anymore.'

'I could bring my bike on the train.' He brightened immediately and nodded vigorously, as if convincing himself of the wisdom of his plan.

'You have a motorbike?' I said before I could stop myself.

'A road bike,' he said scornfully.

'Of course. It's a fair trek, but probably a safer ride than in Central London. Are you sure you want to go to Dunkley?'

'It was where Alan Hibbert lived, wasn't it?' It was the first time he had used Torrens' real name. 'I think he set some of his books there.'

'It may have inspired him, but I don't think he ever mentioned the place by name. He valued his privacy above all else.'

'He must have had friends, neighbours . . . hobbies, interests . . . Was he a churchgoer?'

'I have no idea. I didn't really know him personally, and most

Buried Above Ground 61

of our business was done by fax, so he did not ever have to come into the office. He hated London – I know that about him.'

'I'm right that he's buried in Dunkley?'

'How would I know? I never went to a funeral there.' Well, that much was true.

'Did he have any family?'

'Not that I ever discovered.'

'But he had a house there.'

'Yes, he did, and I happen to know he left it to the county council.'

'Really? Not to a relative?'

'I don't think there were any, and nobody contested the bequest of the house, though it was quite controversial when the story made the local paper. Yes, we had a local paper back then.'

'I know – the *Chronicle*. I looked at back copies online but must have missed that. What was controversial about it?'

'It was Hibbert's will. It specified that the council could have the house free and clear, but it must be used for the temporary housing of cross-Channel refugees.'

'Illegal immigrants?'

'Maybe Alan Hibbert didn't see it that way, or perhaps he just wanted to annoy the local Conservative Association, which I think he managed to do quite successfully.'

'I'd like to see the house, maybe take a photo for the website.'

'My, my, that's taking your academic research a bit far, isn't it?'

'We see Gadabout as a journal of record, and a record has to be thorough.'

Thoroughly boring, I thought but said, 'Well, if I can help any further, do give me a ring at the library. The number is—'

'I made a note of it while I was there,' he said smugly.

'Well, goodbye then, and have a safe journey.'

Neither of us offered to shake hands. He turned one way towards the station, and I turned the other to the front door to my flat, only a few feet away.

Through the big window fronting Dimi's, I was treated to a close-up of the odious Dimitrios shaking his head and shrugging, making what he presumed was his sad face, rubbery lips pursed as if blowing me a kiss to console me.

62   Mike Ripley

I scowled at him and fumbled for my keys.

When I glanced down the street, Jacon Archer and his backpack had disappeared.

NINE

I did not think I had given too much away, but then there were several things I had failed to get out of young Jacon. He had not told me the real reason for his interest in the Inspector Seeley books – I did not believe his 'Golden Age' website motive – nor had he indicated how he had discovered that the Duncan Torrens pen name hid the identity of Alan George Hibbert.

Even more worryingly, how did he know that Hibbert had lived in Dunkley? Although the local newspaper had carried the story of Hibbert's unusual bequest in his will, there had been no report of his death – why should there have been? – or any obituary or notice headed 'Death of a Local Writer' or suchlike. He had valued his privacy and always said proudly that no one in the village had any idea he was also Duncan Torrens. In those frantic months between his death and my redundancy, I kept a close eye on the local press and was sure that all his literary secrets had gone to the grave with him.

Still, the approach from Jake Philbin – acting, I was sure, as a stooge for Robina Robinson and Pabulator – followed by the investigation of Jacon Archer and the resurrection of the manuscript of *The Missing Fabergé* was all slightly disconcerting.

So too was the attitude of Val White the next day at the library.

'Who was that nice boy who called for you yesterday, Mr Wilkes?'

Good God, she sounded as if she'd stepped out of a seventies sitcom.

'Just a student doing research,' I said through gritted teeth, trying to re-shelve some of the books left scattered like bomb debris by the morning's Early Readers session supervised by Janice Sharpe, everyone's favourite granny, except mine.

'Friend of yours, was he?' Mrs White spoke with a sing-song lilt which made Mrs Sharpe's ears prick up, as it was intended to. 'We never get to see any of your friends.'

'Never seen him before, but I think I answered his questions, which were about crime fiction if you must know.'

My tone was polite but stern enough to hopefully end the matter, as Val White thought less than nothing of crime fiction and was quite happy to leave that section of the library to me.

I hoped in vain.

'When he first came in and before he asked for you, he asked me for directions to Dunkley, and I said if I needed to go there, I'd get a taxi, not that I could think of one earthly reason why anyone would want to go there. But that was odd, wasn't it?'

'Was it?'

'Well, you used to live in Dunkley, didn't you, Mr Wilkes?'

I tried to think when I might have mentioned Dunkley in range of those flapping ears. 'No, but I used to go there on business a long time ago.'

'Was that when you were married?'

Now Janice Sharpe's ears were positively twitching, but I refused to make eye contact with either of that pair of Hecate's handmaidens and concentrated on filing a series of Mr Men books.

'Yes, it was, but, and I stress again, it was a long time ago.'

'Your first wife was foreign, wasn't she? Olga or something Russian?'

How did the woman know these things? I had never spoken of a wife or of living anywhere other than in this dreary town. Perhaps there was a personnel file on me at the county council, which she had access to. If there was, there was no advantage in me lying about things.

'Her name was Alisa, though she went by Alice, and yes, she was Russian.' I resisted the urge to add *if it's any of your bloody business*. 'The marriage was a mistake, but fortunately we discovered that early on and quickly got divorced.'

'There were no children?'

'Certainly not.'

I had a nasty feeling that I knew what was coming.

'I thought I detected a family resemblance.'

Detected? The woman could not detect that I was close to ramming a copy of *Mr Uppity* (wrong sex but otherwise totally appropriate) into her lipstick-stained teeth, but I controlled myself.

'Well, you couldn't be more wrong on that score, Mrs White.'

'But you took the young man for a nice dinner last night, didn't you?'

I could not look at her but did not have to. I could *feel* her nasty, vulpine smile, and I would have bet anything that she was exchanging knowing looks with Mrs Sharpe, who would be hanging on every innuendo.

'You have spies everywhere, Mrs White,' I said with remarkable self-control.

'My husband noticed you on his way home from the City.' She could not resist reminding us yet again that her husband worked in an office in London; I suspected as a janitor or security guard. 'He was walking past that Greek greasy spoon near where you live.'

Over which I live, but she knew that.

'Mr White spotted you through the front window.'

Do women still call their husbands 'Mr' like that? I know I am out of touch with females in general, but that sounded deferential enough to have come from a Golden Age detective story.

'He saw you with that young man and made a mental note of it because though he's seen you in there several times before, you're always sitting on your own, eating by yourself while reading a book. It never struck us as a nice place to go for a meal.'

'I agree entirely, it's not,' I said cheerfully to disconcert her, 'but then you've never tried my home cooking.'

That stumped her for a moment, as did the supportive giggle from Mrs Sharpe.

'I took the student there because he wanted to pick my brains about certain books.' I hoped she registered the emphasis I put on 'my'. 'He turns out to be very well read, but because he's a student, he's penniless and in need of a square meal – that's all there was to it. Now I really have to get on.'

'I never suggested anything otherwise,' Val White said serenely.

You didn't have to.

Duncan Torrens, Robina Robinson and now my ex-wife Alisa. I had been visited by three ghosts and it wasn't even Christmas.

Part Two

The Reader

TEN

What an odd fellow that Roland Wilkes is.

That sounds like something a dizzy vicar would say in a country house murder mystery, whereas the visiting colonel (retired) would have called him 'a rum cove' or similar, and the host of the weekend party, for there would be one going on, would defend him by saying he was a harmless old boy who wouldn't hurt a fly. But then Roland Wilkes would never have been invited to a thirties' country house party, let alone feature in a murder mystery, not even as the most disposable of obvious suspects. He might make an anonymous corpse in a diversionary murder to throw the detective off the scent of the real intended victim, though even that would be pushing it. He simply was not interesting enough to be a character in a crime novel.

Which was disappointing as I had expected him to be more enthusiastic about discussing an author he had edited for ten years and must have thought totally forgotten. Yet he showed little sign of being excited or flattered. If anything, he seemed wary of discussing Alan Hibbert, a.k.a. Duncan Torrens, which was odd considering they lived only ten miles apart. I could well understand a reclusive author not wishing to struggle up – he must, after all, have been getting on a bit when Wilkes edited him – to London to visit his publisher, but when his editor lived more or less on his doorstep, they might have become friends. It was rare but not unknown for publishers and writers to be friends.

On the train back to St Pancras, I went through my notebook, not so much to remind myself of what was in it but rather what was missing.

I did not think I had pushed Roland Wilkes too hard on anything, partly because he could eventually be of use when it came to Duncan Torrens and partly because I had been brought up not to be aggressive with my elders – especially if you hoped to get something out of them.

70   Mike Ripley

Wilkes must be in his mid-sixties, or perhaps not quite sixty-five as he was still working at the library and it was a proper, council-run library, albeit a small satellite one and not one of those culled because of cuts in local government spending which had been 'rescued' by volunteers whose idea of a 'community library' was a coffee bar selling cupcakes with a few books decorating the walls.

In the current climate, it was quite surprising Wilkes had survived to near retirement age. Perhaps it was cheaper to keep him on than to make him redundant, as he could not be earning that much, living where he did above a Greek café in a small town not even important enough to warrant the description 'over-spill', it seemed, and had no family, partner, pets or even a car.

Yet when he was editing the Inspector Seeley books, he would have been in his thirties and must surely have been enthusiastic about his position with a London publisher of crime fiction, reading crime novels for a living being the ideal job, though not necessarily the sort Wilkes had to edit.

I got no feeling from him that he had enjoyed working with Duncan Torrens, and he'd seemed genuinely surprised when I told him that the first book he edited, *Buried Above Ground*, was in fact Alan Hibbert's thirty-fourth published novel. Of course I have no idea if it was – that was just a guess on my part. I had seen a copy of *Death Before Dinner* (a dreadful title) in an Oxfam shop, bearing a publication date of 1982, and the blurb on the back of the jacket announced that it was the twentieth case for 'that perfect policeman, Gideon Seeley'. Assuming that he kept up a high level of output, having started in 1970, then it was perfectly possible that his 1990 book would have been his thirty-fourth.

Usually, publishers are keen to promote an author's backlist, or at least those titles they have published. Books with another publisher would be tactfully ignored. Boothby & Briggs, however, clearly preferred to keep their authors' feet firmly on the ground and on the usual pre-title page headed 'by the same author', they would list only their two most recent titles, perhaps adding a conciliatory 'etc.' to indicate there were more – sometime many more – though not necessarily in print. Given that the Seeley books went out of print fairly quickly, it would have been somewhat

Buried Above Ground

embarrassing to admit that there were ten, twenty or even thirty previous books in the series but all were unavailable. That would be a disappointment to any reader just discovering Gideon Seeley, not to mention depressing for the author.

It might have been a different matter had the Gideon Seeley stories made it into paperback editions, but they never did.

Wilkes did let slip something interesting about the titles of the books he handled, though it was common-enough knowledge that authors often had their preferred titles changed, cases in point being *The Dolly Dolly Spy* and *Ice Station Zebra*. There was even an apocryphal story doing the rounds that one bestselling thriller writer was so fed up with this that he sent in a manuscript entitled *Curse God and Die!*

I wondered just how much influence Wilkes had had on the titles of the Inspector Seeley books – or indeed on Duncan Torrens' work as a whole. I made a mental note to go through those he had edited specifically, as that was, after all, the period I was interested in – or rather being paid to be interested in.

ELEVEN

My mother never believed that I could or would make a living out of the Gadabout website, and she was quite right. My initial hopes of advertising revenue from grateful publishers were soon dashed as the site specialized in books which were long out of print and those smaller independent publishers trying to revive 'neglected classics' from the golden era simply did not have the advertising budgets. Some money came in from subscribers to the Gadabout chat room and some in straight donations from readers grateful to find that their love of classic crime fiction was no longer being ignored.

My main source of income from the site was the service I offered in finding lost books for readers. I had to do this carefully as I could not afford to upset Amazon or AbeBooks or the book dealers on eBay, so I only undertook private commissions without advertising the fact, though the word soon got round the Golden Age community. Most of the requests I received were of the sort where somebody remembers – vaguely, sometimes very vaguely – a plot or a particular character but cannot remember either title or author. Sometimes it's a characteristic or an oddity – 'the detective had a wooden leg in some books but not in others' – for others it might be a unique murder method – 'the victim is shot with an air rifle fired from a hot air balloon' – and, though I say it myself, I have a pretty good record in solving such mysteries. My first port of call in my research is my card index system, which I have maintained since I was twelve and still do, even though it is nowadays backed up on my laptop. I find there is something satisfying about writing the cards (with a fountain pen) and then flicking through them; something positively Golden Age.

What I record on the cards are details of every detective story I have read or read about, their publishers, dates and authors, and I think it a unique source of information which I was confident would come in useful one day. I long ago lost count of how many books I had covered, but it must be well over 3,000. I concentrated on the obscure and the forgotten. Agatha Christie, Dorothy Sayers, Margery Allingham and the like were well-enough known to require only a few cursory notes, and even previously forgotten males such as Anthony Berkeley and Philip Macdonald were getting their due these days. Leslie Charteris, the creator of The Saint, and that master of the locked-room mystery, John Dickson Carr, maintained personal armies, albeit small and ageing, of supporters.

Yet of all the hundreds of cards I had neatly compiled before entering the details into my database, none of them had featured Alan Hibbert or his literary alter ego Duncan Torrens until now.

It began four months ago when, as I told Roly Wilkes, I had bought that manuscript of *The Missing Fabergé* in an auction on the web, after making the winning bid of ten pounds. It was not my usual cup of tea – not that I drank tea or any other hot beverage – but the chance to own an author's original typescript did not come along very often since the advent of word processors. I had heard of Duncan Torrens, even read one of his early Seeley books – *Death Before Breakfast* or *Death After Dinner* or suchlike – to confirm that I didn't like it. His books clearly did not fall into the Golden Age orbit of Gadabout, but I thought the manuscript, as the latest addition to my collection of crime-fiction memorabilia, was worth a mention in the comment column I wrote monthly as the site's webmaster and followed that up with a short podcast.

(I did not ask Roly Wilkes if he had heard the podcast as I doubted he knew what one was.)

To my surprise, that brought a number of messages from regular readers saying how much they had liked the adventures of Inspector Gideon Seeley and Sergeant Gerry Grimes, although the majority had given up on the series following the revelations about Gerry Grimes' backstory. One of them even boasted they had the very first in the series, *The Body at Starling Junction,* signed by the debutant author in a very interesting way. On the title page, the first-time author had written *with best wishes, Alan Hibbert* and then, rather endearingly added in brackets *(and naturally Duncan Torrens!)* as if he had just remembered he had adopted a pseudonym. It could, of course, have been a private joke with someone he knew, as most first novels tend to be bought by friends or relatives of the writer.

So I knew that Duncan Torrens' real name was Alan Hibbert, but I was still not that interested in the biography or bibliography of him as an author, except the more information I could gather might add to the value of the unpublished manuscript I now owned, and so I wrote another comment piece for the website asking for help establishing the order of the Inspector Seeley books. If I could say for certainty that *The Missing Fabergé* was the last, unpublished, case for Inspector Seeley, that too would be added value.

I got more replies than I had anticipated, including one from a fanatical book collector in Canada who bemoaned the fact that the Seeley books had never been published in America, as he always collected American as well as British editions of titles he liked. Thanks to him and other readers chipping in, I compiled a chronological list which I was sure was pretty accurate and even managed to find copies of a couple of later ones (which I now think of as 'the Wilkes era') reasonably cheaply via second-hand book dealers I had used many times before.

I was not prepared to spend much money on what was still very much an academic exercise to satisfy my curiosity until, that is, the chatter on the website produced the last thing I expected: the offer of a job.

As a book detective.

TWELVE

It was a one-off freelance job to research the Inspector Seeley books with a view to writing the introductions to new ebook and print-on-demand editions. There were three stipulations: I was to concentrate on the last decade of Seeley titles (nothing before 1990), I was to establish who held the rights to the backlist and I was not to reveal the name of my employer.

I had to do all this for a flat fee of £300, which I did not quibble about as at last I could show my mother that I could monetize the Gadabout website and that 'all those old books attracting dust' had come in useful after all. To reassure her, though, I had to make it clear that I had no plans to give up the day job just yet, and I would continue my slow ascent up the career ladder of sales assistants in our local Co-op supermarket, employment which, though poorly paid, was wonderfully undemanding.

The initial part of my investigation I called 'desk research', even though much was done on my laptop, which I had smuggled in to the bakery section of the Co-op where we 'baked' fresh bread every morning from a pre-prepared dough delivered in bulk from an industrial estate somewhere just before dawn. That early-morning bakery duty was the most unpopular shift among employees, so I volunteered to make it my own. The early starts were a pain, but the job was far from arduous until it came to stacking the supermarket's shelves from trays of fresh loaves, which required a surprising amount of upper body strength.

I managed to track that last decade of Inspector Seeley books relatively easily with the help of Gadabout readers who had a mutual affection for putting things in orderly lists and had realized that the internet was the perfect vehicle to aid both compilation and sharing.

I was certain that the running order for the nineties, at one book a year, was:

Buried Above Ground

76 Mike Ripley

The Herb Border
Most Wretched of Deaths
Small Is the Span
One Who Is Afraid of Death
Unlawful and Premeditated
Seamless Death
The House Guest Who Never Left
The Attainder
The Missing Fabergé (unpublished)

Whilst Roland Wilkes had not confirmed that list, he had mentioned several titles and admitted that he had been Torrens' editor from 1990 to 1999.

I determined to get hold of a couple of titles to go with my manuscript of *The Missing Fabergé*, which would have been the last case for Seeley and Grimes had it been published – and it would surely have been published posthumously. (I made a note to self to check on the exact date of Alan Hibbert's death.) That was slightly odd as publishers have often made great play of a posthumous work 'discovered' after an author's death.

There seemed no particular rhyme or reason behind those last ten titles, although three or four had the flavour of quotes from the classics, which I was not aware of being a regular source of inspiration for Duncan Torrens. Perhaps, as Wilkes said, some authors simply don't care about titles. There was also one I didn't understand – the last Duncan Torrens book to be published, in 1998, *The Attainder.* I had to look that up, and it turned out to be an old legal term for the forfeiting of land and property as a consequence of a sentence of death for treason, a medieval ancestor of the modern practice of confiscating Range Rovers and houses with swimming pools in Essex from convicted drug dealers. The practice had been known at one time as 'the corruption of blood' which in my humble opinion was a far better title.

Perhaps *The Attainder* had bombed, but I found no reviews of it anywhere, and really bad books are always worthy of review. If it had been a stinker – and all crime writers are allowed one, though some get away with more – it might explain why there was no enthusiasm for *The Missing Fabergé*, even as a tribute to a veteran author. And it could easily have been a poor specimen as Hibbert/Torrens was not getting any younger and crime writers, with a few notable exceptions, rarely get better as they get older, and very few know when it's time to retire.

I realized that my familiarity with Duncan Torrens' books, though patchy, was far greater than my knowledge of the life of Alan Hibbert, the man behind the pen name. From my work on the Gadabout site, I knew that nothing went down better with subscribers than those personal details about Golden Age authors which made them human, more than simply magicians capable of constructing devilishly complex plots.

Somehow it adds to the enjoyment of a book – for the dedicated Golden Ager – to know that the author was born in a fisherman's cottage near Deal in 1882, or was the fifth daughter of a vicar, or served in the Camel Corps in Egypt during World War I, or went to Oxford or Cambridge but being female was not allowed a degree. Frankly, knowing such biographies did little for me. Only their stories mattered, though when depressed I often cheered myself up by imagining an 'author biog' on the back flap of a book jacket which claimed that the author was the fifteenth daughter of a sex-mad clergyman (who had been born in a fisherman's cottage in Kent), had tended camels for Lawrence of Arabia before reading classics at Oxbridge and then becoming a torch singer in Berlin in the twenties. Now that might be an author who would interest me.

Wilkes had admitted that the author details on the Boothby & Briggs books he had edited were so much fluff, designed to protect the anonymity of Alan Hibbert. Those jacket blurbs contained absolutely no personal information about the author: not his age, his education, his professional career, his star sign or the fact that he lived in the small English village of Dunkley.

Interestingly, Wilkes had never disputed that fact, nor asked how I knew it.

THIRTEEN

I cannot claim any credit for dedicated detective work on my part as I was told that Hibbert lived in Dunkley the day I accepted the job to investigate Duncan Torrens by the man who was employing me.

I had never imagined meeting Spencer Crow, though I knew who he was from reading the publishing trade press – or at least as much as I could before the paywalls kicked in. I had been surprised and not a little flattered to find that he actually followed the Gadabout website, which is how he contacted me soon after I had posted a piece on my acquisition of *The Missing Fabergé* typescript.

Spencer Crow was either the future of popular publishing or a pushy public school rich kid determined to drag the book trade down to and along the gutter, depending on whether you were speaking to someone who had just downloaded a fistful of holiday reading by their favourite author for 99p or a collector of Folio Society editions to impress the neighbours.

His biography was easily sourced on the internet, although it was rather light on personal information, concentrating only on his meteoric rise as a financial *wunderkind* and entrepreneur. After university (Cambridge, of course) he was apprenticed – if that's the right word – to some sort of offshore investment company based in the Channel Islands but then graduated to the role of currency trader in the City. As that seemed to offer insufficient challenge for him, he set himself up as the founding publisher of Hooded Crow Books, taking advantage of the most modern technology and applying it to the insatiable appetite for crime fiction, after claiming publicly that he could have got a better degree had he not discovered Agatha Christie.

His business model involved acquiring the reprint rights to forgotten crime novels and producing ebook and print-on-demand versions rapidly and in great volume. Hooded Crow did not pay authors or their agents (especially not their agents) an advance, merely offered a sliding scale of royalties based on copies sold. It was an offer snapped up by the executors of dusty literary estates and gratefully accepted by living writers whose books had gone out of print or who had been dropped by conventional publishers and saw Hooded Crow as the last chance saloon for their crime writing. Spencer Crow was not offended by the 'last chance saloon' epithet; in fact, he used it proudly in many of his public utterings, giving the impression that he was doing struggling writers a big favour.

I doubt that Spencer Crow had ever been accused of being diplomatic and, at least in the trade press and on his company's website, he seemed to revel in being regarded as a bit of a feather-ruffler in the staid, rather snobbish world of publishing. More than once he had referred to himself in print as 'a member of the awkward squad', and when one serious literary figure had commented on social media that Crow was 'the bovver boy of popular pulp' he had encouraged, if not ordered, every one of his employees to 'like' that post.

I had listened to several podcasts he had appeared on. He tended to dominate whatever the topic under discussion, never missing a chance to proudly boast that his philosophy when choosing to publish an author was 'never mind the quality of the writing – look at the length of the backlist'. Should anyone dare to question that philosophy, he would quote both the number of Hooded Crow titles published and the royalties earned for their authors *since the podcast started.*

As no one on the spot could argue with that, the bombastic Spencer always came out on top in podcasts, even those supposed to be on specific topics relating to crime fiction. I was not the only member of the Gadabout community to notice that Spencer Crow much preferred to talk about himself and his marketing skills than about the plot, characters or writers of classic Golden Age mysteries. He cunningly changed the subject to himself whenever the discussion became too detailed, as it often did among dedicated fans. It was suggested, more than once, in the private Gadabout chat rooms that although he had published a hell of lot of detective stories, Spencer Crow had not actually read many.

He was not someone I would have liked to go into a podcast

80 Mike Ripley

with – or be trapped in a lift with, for that matter – so I was surprised and not a little nervous when he contacted me via the website and offered to take me out to lunch without giving any clue as to why.

Publishers' lunches always had something of a mythical quality about them, at least to an outsider who had never been to one. From the days of Arthur Conan Doyle being tempted to bring back Sherlock Holmes onwards, legends abounded about how much had been settled over the tabletop battlefields of trendy Italian restaurants or The Gay Hussar in Soho to fine dining venues such as The Ivy or one of Marcus Wareing's establishments.

For all my reservations about Spencer Crow and what he might be after, I admit that I was blinded by the prospect of a chance to mix with the high rollers of publishing in a venue I could never realistically expect to experience in a normal lifetime. Invitations to book launch parties, often to make up the numbers, or signing sessions where one got to exchange a few words with an author were one thing, but being invited to lunch by a publisher was a big step up for Gadabout. Perhaps now the establishment was taking us seriously as an electronic journal of record rather than dismissing us as a fanzine dedicated to a bygone age.

Not that Spencer Crow would appreciate being called a member of any establishment and so I expected his choice of restaurant would be interesting – probably a radical, off-the-wall eatery of the kind featured in the Sunday colour supplements. The cost would not be a problem; everyone knew Spencer Crow was loaded.

FOURTEEN

'Charles Dickens used to eat here,' said Spencer Crow. 'It always reminds me of the refectory at my old school, though Dickens never went there and we never got claret with our school dinners.'

I had taken the Central Line to Bank and walked up Threadneedle Street as instructed until I found the alley running down the side of a church which led to Spencer's favourite chop house. Not that I was sure what a chop house was, and if I hadn't been looking for it, I could have walked on by it, the alleyway and the church without noticing them.

The place was laid out like what I imagined a Victorian school room might have looked like: dark wood tables, the bigger ones having benches rather than chairs, with large plant pots placed on each. Where these might once have contained pencils or slates and sticks of chalk, they now sported large cones of stiff white paper menus.

A woman in a black dress and white apron, elderly enough to be a grandmother, greeted me as I entered, and my eyes adjusted to the gloomy interior.

'Spencer Crow!' I said, rather louder than I had planned.

'Corner table,' she said, pointing. 'Young Mr Spencer always sits there unless it's a big party. You're not a big party, are you?'

'Not that I—'

'No, he would have said. Go sit down. I expect he'll be here presently. He makes a point of never arriving first. Drink while you wait?'

I wasn't sure of the protocol here, but I was conscious of my mother's advice as I left the house – *try not to be awkward, Jacon* – so I asked for a Coke, only to be served a glass of lemonade and told that their extensive wine list did not include Coca-Cola.

It was clear that Spencer Crow did not need the wine list.

'Bottle of my usual, please, Muriel,' he announced as he swept in, his long leather coat flapping and coming dangerously close to clearing the glasses from the tables of the other diners. If the coat wasn't flamboyant enough, he also wore a black leather fedora, which he took off like a cavalier greeting his king and skimmed it, frisbee-style, to land with a plop on the table next to my glass of lemonade.

As he settled into the chair across from me, he gave me his Dickens speech before introducing himself.

'Spencer Crow. You must be Jacon.'

That didn't seem to require a response, so I said nothing.

'I see you've started drinking without me. Good man. We'll move on to wine though with the grub.'

'I don't drink,' I said.

'So this is as good as you're going to feel today?' He smiled a vulpine smile, an expression I had read many times but never truly experienced. 'Sorry, old joke. Hope you don't mind if I indulge myself, and to be honest, I don't much care if you do as it's my party.'

'Of course it is, and thank you for inviting me.' That was another box ticked when it came to my mother's advice, as ever since I was a child going to birthday parties, it had been drilled into me to thank my hosts on arrival in case I forgot when it came to going-home time.

'So have you scoped out the menu? It's fairly basic, which is why I like it.'

He plucked one of the giant menus out of the plant pot and passed it over. It had been the moment I had been dreading, far more than actually coming face to face with Spencer Crow. I had been terrified of being confronted with a range of dishes in languages I did not understand, even though they might have been written in English, but thanks to Spencer Crow's public school upbringing, I was saved any embarrassment as the menu consisted basically of pork chops, lamb chops, something called a Barnsley Chop, liver and bacon, mashed potatoes and chips.

Granny Muriel appeared at our table with a bottle and proceeded to uncork it, having deposited two glasses. Crow signalled for just one glass to be filled, at which Muriel gave a quiet snort, slammed the bottle down, produced a notebook from somewhere under her apron and asked if we were ready to order.

Buried Above Ground   83

I opted for pork chops and chips, and Spencer asked for his 'usual' liver and bacon.

'Do you want a sausage with that?' Muriel asked.

'Of course,' said Spencer, who then looked at me pityingly before adding, 'It's the speciality of the house: a free sausage with every main course. Do you want one?'

I nodded and must have looked bemused. Muriel made a note and disappeared towards the kitchen. When I glanced back at Spencer, he was refilling his glass from the wine bottle.

'Remind me never to play poker with you, Jacon.'

'What?'

'Your face doesn't give anything away, does it? Christ on a donkey, she was offering you a sausage, not a blow job.'

He shrugged his way out of his coat so that it pooled around his hips. Under it he was wearing an open-necked multicoloured rugby shirt, and I suddenly realized I was the only person in the restaurant wearing a tie. Mother had insisted.

'Now I've embarrassed you.' Spencer was smiling, and I felt my face was now giving me away as it reddened. 'Don't worry about it. Let's move it along. You'll be wondering why I need your help.'

I took a breath, suddenly excited that here was Hooded Crow Books actually asking for my help.

'I presume it has something to do with the books of Duncan Torrens.'

'Dead right, Sherlock.' He reached for his glass again but paused dramatically as if the thought had just struck him. 'That's not a bad title, is it? *Dead Right, Sherlock.* I can see the cover – a bloodstained deerstalker pinned to the ground by an ice axe. What d'you think?'

'Sherlock Holmes is out of copyright, so you could do it and it would probably sell well in America. It's not really my area of interest.'

'No, of course. You're a Golden Age guy, aren't you? Isn't that a bit weird for someone your age?'

'Weird?'

'Don't take offence. I think *I'm* pretty weird, and quite often it's useful if people think you're weird – gives you an edge.'

'I see,' I said, though I didn't, 'but there's nothing wrong with

84 Mike Ripley

appreciating the finest detective stories ever written. The Golden Age is still golden to many of us all over the world.'

'How many hits does your website get?'

'We don't keep track.' I was not going to reveal just how small the Gadabout following was; certainly not when compared to Hooded Crow's massive social media presence. 'But we have a loyal and well-informed readership, particularly in America and Japan. Lots of readers still prefer a good puzzle.'

He drank more wine then smiled that wolfish smile again. 'People who prefer puzzles – the PPP. Sounds like a Middle Eastern political movement, though probably not quite so militant. I was never a member of the spot-the-murderer club, the stereotyped characters, the flimsy motives and the amazing knack of suspects who could remember where they were *to the second* when the murder was committed, even though only the poshest people would have had wristwatches back then. I've got two Rolex and a Patek Philippe' – he pulled up a sleeve to show me one of them – 'and I still need a secretary – sorry, a personal assistant – to tell me I'm running late for a meeting.'

'Spotting the false alibi or the mistakes made by the police, or figuring out how the murder could have been committed in a locked room, those are the puzzles we love,' I said, hoping it did not sound too pathetic.

'Most of which could be solved quickly by modern forensics. Even one of the famous stories, where a chap is stabbed to death in a Turkish bath, no weapon is found and all the usual suspects are stark naked, in the end the solution came down to forensics. Wouldn't even have made half an episode of one of the CSI franchises.'

'But the more fantastical the puzzle, the greater satisfaction in solving it by pure logic.' That came out as more pretentious than I had expected.

'Fantastical, eh?' Spencer sipped more wine as if savouring the word. 'That's a good description of you Golden Age fanboys – The Fantasticals. I'm guessing you are all boys, aren't you? Boys who like things nicely ordered.'

Perhaps he had noticed me making sure my knife and fork were correctly spaced on the table in front of me, but I was saved by the arrival of our waitress – the only one in the place – slamming down a plate containing my pork chop and chips with what looked like a small log lying across them.

'Speciality of the house,' said Spencer. 'You get a sausage with everything, and they are remarkably tasty.'

I couldn't think of anything to say and probably just stared at it like an idiot. It was at least a foot long and bigger than any sausage I'd ever seen.

Muriel the waitress said something I did not catch, but I knew she was hovering as I could smell her flowery perfume.

'Condiments?' she repeated. 'Ketchup? Mustard? Brown sauce?'

'English mustard, my darling, if you please,' said Spencer. 'Jacon?'

'Ketchup for me.'

Muriel disappeared into the kitchen again. On her return journey, she playfully slapped the back of the head of one of a party of four as she passed, telling him to behave himself, causing his fellow diners to roar their approval. Then she deposited two small wooden bowls on our table, one containing a bright yellow paste, the other a similar large blob of red.

'They used to put those plastic squeezy bottles which looked like tomatoes on the table, but the clientele weaponized them and started food fights. Got very messy. Told you this place reminded me of my schooldays.'

I was going to say it was nothing like my time at school, which only allowed plastic cutlery, but I could tell he was not listening. He had fished a smartphone out of his leather coat and laid it on the table next to his plate, checking the screen as he began to carve his sausage and the flappy slice of something bloody which I assumed was liver.

I began to cut up my giant sausage into chunks three centimetres long as near as I could estimate and thought I had the pieces fairly uniform when Spencer began talking again in between slurps of wine. I noted that the bottle he had ordered was already half empty.

'You don't give anything away, do you?' he said suddenly, looking down at his phone whilst managing to refill his glass purely by instinct.

'Excuse me?'

86   Mike Ripley

'You guys on Gadabout – you're very strict about not giving
away whodunit in the books you like. Spoiler alert this, spoiler
alert that. Do you have penalties for anyone who blurts out that
the butler did it? Did the butler ever do it, by the way? I'm sure
I've come across a title which says he did.'

'You're probably thinking of *Why Shoot the Butler?* but it was
a playful cliché that the sour-faced butler should be one of the
usual suspects. Traditionally, though, that was usually a red
herring.'

'And you guys just love a red herring.'

'Yes, we do, and why not? And we do have a strict rule about
not giving away the name of the murderer.'

'Is that like the first rule of Fight Club?'

'I don't understand.'

Spencer gave a delicate snort and grinned into his wine glass.
'Never mind. My serious point was how, once you know
whodunit, can you ever read that book again?'

I suddenly felt on safer ground and actually started to eat my
sausage, which was surprisingly tasty.

'Of course you can. Half the fun is spotting where the author
has fooled or misdirected the reader. The best practitioners of
the Golden Age were meticulous in placing clues in their stories
to give the reader the chance to solve the case before the fictional
detective.'

'And they always played fair, did they?'

'Mostly. One or two got a bit esoteric and relied on specialist
knowledge of medicine, or the law, or train timetables, or poisons
only found in a South American jungle . . .'

'Or bell-ringing, I seem to remember.'

'So you have read some of the classics.'

'Of course I have; they were the raciest things in the common
room at school. Anything written after 1945 was considered
subversive, but teaching young boys hundreds of different means
of murder seemed to be acceptable. I think there must have been
two hundred old green Penguin paperbacks there, all donated by
the school chaplain when the old God-botherer was finally put
out to pasture.'

I smiled to myself as I cut my pork chop into manageable
cubes at Spencer's mention of his school chaplain. It was a

common theme in discussions on Gadabout that the best source of classic 'green' Penguin detective stories in England was a church fete, especially when held at a vicarage just after the incumbent had moved on to 'head office'.

'The English clergy seemed to have a homicidal streak, at least in their choice of reading material,' I said, which produced a wry smile from Spencer.

'If they had ever tried to use them as instruction manuals, to dispose of troublesome members of their congregations for instance, they would not have had much success though.' Spencer paused to drain the last of the wine bottle into his glass. 'I mean half the methods of murder were unbelievably far-fetched or simply didn't work at all. Injecting an air bubble into a vein, building up an immunity to arsenic so the murderer has an alibi, or rigging up a heavy weight on a pulley to smash somebody's head in as they stand in a particular position to wind up the mantlepiece clock at exactly five to midnight. Wasn't it Raymond Chandler who said that any murderer who had to rely on such a combination of circumstances really ought to consider a new profession?'

I knew it was but didn't want to spoil Spencer's moment, although he wasn't interested in my reaction as he was studying the wine list again. Unlike me, he seemed to recognize all the French and Italian words there, whereas I had not really got further than 'White' and 'Red' and had almost choked when I saw the prices. My mother would die rather than pay seventy pounds for a bottle of wine if, that is, she ever thought about drinking wine, which was never at all.

'It was also the motives that annoyed me,' said Spencer, waving the empty bottle at our waitress, signalling for a replacement. 'Characters were forced to murder people, usually their relatives, because they think they've been cheated out of an inheritance or simply don't have enough money to sustain a lifestyle they think is their God-given right. None of them ever think about getting a job; most are just professional spongers.'

'I think that's a bit unfair,' I said quietly, but Spencer did not want to debate the matter.

'That's why I prefer the more modern stuff, written since the seventies, by which time the "play fair" detective story' – he

88 Mike Ripley

made those annoying angry rabbit air quotes with the fingers of both hands – 'had given way to the crime novel and stories which contained credible motives and methods of murder, dealt with the aftermath of a murder and began to explain police procedures and forensics. Not the ones that go over the top with violence and gore, but ones which leave the reader comforted that justice had been done. Some people call them cosy crime, usually with a sneer in their voice.'

The arrival of another bottle of wine prevented any argument on that score, and Spencer quickly made it clear that that second bottle was the signal to get down to business.

'The sort of book that Duncan Torrens wrote – that's what I'm interested in. That's what we're interested in republishing at Hooded Crow, not the Golden Age stuff your website promotes, so there should be no conflict of interest.'

'Why should there be a conflict of interest?'

'Because I want you to do a job for me which has nothing to do with your interest in so-called Golden Age stories, and you must promise not to blab about it on your website until I give you the green light. I can offer you a fixed fee of three hundred pounds, which I know isn't much, but it could lead to other things.'

It may not be much to Spencer Crow – it wouldn't cover four bottles of wine in this place – but as proof that Gadabout could actually generate revenue, it would be invaluable in combatting my mother's nagging.

'To do what?' I asked, arranging my cutlery parallel on my empty plate.

'To do some research into Duncan Torrens. When I read that you'd found that old manuscript of his and then discovered his real name, I knew you were the right guy for a bit of detective work. Real detective work, not fictional.'

I felt a brain swirl coming on, not sure how best to respond without jeopardizing the offered fee.

'I was told it was the pen name of Alan Hibbert by a Gadabout subscriber who had his first novel, *The Body at Starling Junction*, so there wasn't really much detection involved. I know very little else about him.'

'But you've read his books.'

Buried Above Ground 89

'Some of them and the manuscript of his last one. Not really my thing.'

'That doesn't matter. I'm not asking you to be his editor, and I don't really care what you think of his books. I want you to establish where the rights to them reside so I can offer to republish the Inspector Seeley books.'

'All of them?'

He saluted me with a half-empty glass as if I'd made a good point. 'Only the ones since 1990, starting with *Buried Above Ground*. They are the ones which best fit our demographic.'

'How's that?' I asked, knowing immediately that it made me sound stupid.

Spencer sighed loudly into his wine. 'At Hooded Crow, we spend a lot of time and money getting our readers – we don't call them customers, though they are – involved through social media. We ask them to review every book they buy, which makes them feel important and allows us to track their likes and dislikes. We also give them free books and special offers to make them feel valued. In return, they give us a lot of information about themselves, and one of the things we've discovered is that we have a core constituency of readers of retirement age who have taken to reading ebooks like there's no tomorrow, often downloading five or six at a time. Now these are not people who've just discovered reading; they've always read, but now they have more time on their hands and the names of authors from thirty or more years ago will ring bells with them. They read to relax, not to be educated, and a name from when they had a library ticket means a nice, safe, undemanding author they can trust. Duncan Torrens fits that bill perfectly.'

'Were his Seeley books really popular?'

'Popular enough. The important thing is that they are a decent series, a nice run of nine or ten titles with the same characters, all set in the nineties, a period our customers remember without being old-fashioned or . . .'

'Golden Age,' I said boldly.

'Exactly. We leave those to the dedicated specialists like you guys.'

He smiled the sort of smile which said he hoped I appreciated the compliment.

90 Mike Ripley

'But there's only one Torrens title anyone remembers – *Most Wretched of Deaths* – because of the revelation about Sergeant Grimes, and even that one never made it into paperback.'

'You've done your homework,' said Spencer, with a touch of steel in his voice, 'but don't you worry about things like that. Our promotions and publicity people can build up a series so that our readers will be gagging for it, especially if the first couple of titles come free to get them hooked.'

'Like drugs, you mean.'

'Says the guy addicted to country house murders, aristocratic amateur sleuths and out-of-date social attitudes.'

I was relieved that I had not offended him and that he was actually grinning.

'I've never been accused of pushing drugs before, though I suppose I am feeding readers' habits, but in a good way. I mean, nobody ever died due to reading a crime novel, did they? Hooded Crow publish over two hundred a year and we've not killed anyone yet, that I know of.'

'And you intend to feed your readers' habit with the Inspector Seeley canon?' I was quite proud of that.

'Not all of it,' said Spencer, 'just the last ten titles, at least to begin with – and you can help.'

'How? The Seeley books are not the sort we tend to promote on Gadabout.'

'I am well aware of that, and we are very capable of doing our own promotion, though if you fancy writing an introduction to the books, that could be possible. It's Torrens, or rather Hibbert, I'm interested in. To republish the books, Hooded Crow has to get the rights or some form of licensing agreement from the author, which is slightly difficult in this case.'

He smiled around the lip of his wine glass, waiting for me to ask the all too obvious.

'Because?' I jumped into his trap.

'He's been dead for more than twenty years.'

I had suspected as much; no one ever consulted Gadabout about living writers.

'As far as we know, he was unmarried and childless, but we have to be sure he didn't leave the rights to his books to a literary executor. It's called doing due diligence, and our lavishly paid lawyers insist we do it. You know that copyright continues for seventy years after an author dies?'

'Yes,' I said. Of course I did. There were scores of Golden Age titles now reproduced as print-on-demand paperbacks bearing the legend 'Back in print for the first time in XX years' when it should more honestly say 'It's now seventy years and one day since the writer snuffed it'.

'Your website does detailed biographies of dead authors – should be a doddle for you, and whilst you are doing it, find out if anyone has a claim on the rights to his backlist.'

'Surely you could ask his publisher, Boothby and Briggs? Don't they have the rights?'

Spencer was suddenly serious, almost sober. 'Doubtful. If they have, they've done nothing with them for twenty years, and thanks to you, we know they rejected his last book, the Fabergé thing, even threw the manuscript in a skip.'

'It was a bit different to his normal stuff,' I admitted. 'Interesting, though, with all that Russian history.'

'Well, B and B's new owners were not interested in it, or his previous titles, and normally after ten years or going out of print, the rights would have reverted if the author had asked for them. But the point is that B and B or Pabulator *would* suddenly become interested if they discover that someone else was sniffing around Inspector Seeley, especially if they discover it's me sniffing around. Pabulator will think there's an income stream they're not tapping, and of course they'd be right, and the plodders at B and B don't want their corporate bosses finding out they've missed a trick.'

I had no idea how that much wine had affected him, but I risked airing a dangerous thought.

'But Hooded Crow does mainly ebooks . . . How much of an income stream could be generated by bringing back the Inspector Seeley books? Surely not enough to worry a global publisher like Pabulator.'

To my relief, Spencer grinned. 'We might have a policy of piling them high and selling them cheap, but, hey, don't knock it. Our books can be downloaded worldwide, and those dollars, pounds, euros, whatever, they all mount up. We sell a lot of titles in Pabulator's back yard in Sweden, which must piss them off

92   Mike Ripley

no end, and they would certainly enjoy spoiling any deal we might make. So we don't let them get wind of what we're up to. OK?'

'But I don't know where to start,' I said, hoping it didn't come out too weak and lose the finder's fee he had offered. 'I don't even know where Hibbert lived.'

'Oh, I can tell you that.' His grin got bigger. 'He hid himself away in a village out in the sticks in Hertfordshire called Dunkley. You might want to go and snoop around there, see if anyone remembers him.'

'If you know that, why don't you go?'

'Jacon, Jacon, I'm a busy man. At Hooded Crow, we publish and sell books twenty-four/seven and I simply don't have the spare bandwidth in my diary to check out individual titles and authors, especially when it requires some dedicated detective work. Therefore, I hire a detective, and that's you. I thought it might be a job that would appeal.'

It did, and he knew that and knew I was going to accept, but I still had a niggle at the back of my mind. 'Why Duncan Torrens particularly? There must be thousands of out-of-print cosy crime novels crying out for a Hooded Crow revamp.'

'Oh, there are,' he said smugly, 'and their authors and agents would be very grateful at getting a second chance to see their work back in print.'

'Electronically.'

'Hey, don't knock ebooks. Reading is reading, and we don't publish rubbish. Every book we revive has been through the editorial process before and published by a professional publisher. In the case of the Inspector Seeley books, there was a long-running series, so there must have been some sort of readership or fanbase. Boothby and Briggs kept faith with the series characters right up to the takeover by Pabulator . . . who's to say they don't deserve a second chance?'

He put down his glass and placed his elbows on the table – as I had been taught never to do – and clasped his hands together as if in prayer.

'I have a personal reason, which I don't want broadcast. My mother was a fan of the Seeley books. She even left me one in her will hoping I could do something with it.'

I muttered, 'Sorry for your loss,' as one is supposed to do these days, but I don't think he noticed.

'She read them because Torrens, or rather Hibbert, was a local celebrity. Well, hardly a celebrity, as he seems to have been something of a recluse, but he lived in the same village as my mother in her final years. That's how I know he had a house in Dunkley. Not that Mum ever met him as far as I know, but having an author in the village, even a relatively obscure one, seemed to impress her.'

He unclasped his hands and opened his palms in a gesture of resignation. 'Mothers, eh? Who'd have 'em?'

I could relate to that.

FIFTEEN

I had mentioned Dunkley to Roly Wilkes when I tracked him down, partly in the hope that he would offer me a lift out there, perhaps a tour of Alan Hibbert's village if not his actual house, which he'd said was now some sort of hostel for illegal immigrants, but he had given me the brush-off and didn't seem remotely interested. Still, he might be useful depending on what I found at Dunkley, so I rang the library where he worked and told him when I would be passing through the town. I cannot say he sounded enthusiastic at the prospect of meeting up but reluctantly said that he might be free for a drink before my evening train back to London. He didn't offer a single clue to Alan Hibbert's actual address, but how hard could it be to find in a place like Dunkley?

I had Google-mapped the village to find it was the very essence of a one-horse town: a smattering of houses, one of which had clearly once been a pub, and a church now classed as 'redundant'. There was no village pond, though a river looked to run alongside the main (only) road in and out of the place, and no imposing manor house, which meant that it would make a poor map in a Golden Age detective story. Perhaps it had once been connected to the railway and perhaps that had given Hibbert/Torrens the inspiration for his first novel, *The Body at Starling Junction*, though I could find no mention of any such place nearby.

Which begged the question: where did Hibbert get his inspiration from? Roly Wilkes had not said anything about that, and Spencer Crow did not seem at all interested, but I was. It was a point of honour on the Gadabout website that when we feature an author, it is in as much detail as possible to maintain our reputation as a journal of record, although our detractors claim we are obsessed with personal trivia. Normally, of course, we deal with Golden Age authors, but I saw no reason why we – or at least I – should not apply the same approach to Alan Hibbert,

Buried Above Ground   95

about whom there was so little public information. I might even become *the* authority on the work of Duncan Torrens.

As far as my mother was concerned, my day trip out to Dunkley was something akin to a solo expedition into the Amazonian jungle. She had no idea of where Dunkley was, and my insistence that it was only just outside the M25 and in one of the northern Home Counties did not reassure her. I stressed that I was taking my bike on the train and from the nearest station it was an easy ride along country lanes. She reminded me (three times) to wear my helmet, packed a Tupperware box with so many sandwiches it bloated and made sure my water bottle was full of weak lemon squash. And yes, I had my waterproof, my phone was fully charged and the lights on my bike were working, even though I insisted I would be back in time for dinner and long before I needed them.

At St Pancras, I stashed my trusty steed in what used, in better days, to be called the guard's van but is now known as a reserved space, and took the nearest available seat in order to keep an eye on it. On the stopping trains out to the suburbs and beyond, it's all too easy to 'de-train' (as they say) with a bicycle you didn't put on board, and I carefully checked out the passengers in my carriage for unsavoury characters. Five of them were looking at screens, but one was actually reading a book, even if it was a Lee Child.

At the town where Roly Wilkes lived, I left the train, consulted the map on my phone, saddled up and began to cycle the 9.68 miles (I had checked twice) to Dunkley. Although I hadn't planned it, my route took me past the town library, and I wondered if Wilkes was working today.

The picture of an idyllic ride through pastoral countryside which I had sold my mother turned out to be over-optimistic, as the suburbs seemed to go on forever and it was impossible to spot where London actually ended. But then I saw my first proper field and the first signpost pointing to Dunkley. I was gratified to note that it was an old-fashioned fingerpost sign, just the sort you would see on a map in a Golden Age detective story – and here was I, the detective arriving at the scene of the crime.

If, that is, there had been a crime other than Duncan Torrens' rather uninspiring plotting and prose.

The road into Dunkley ran alongside a meandering river and then up a hill on top of which sat All Saints, the village church. In a proper Golden Age village, the church would be in the centre of the village, but Dunkley seemed to have developed (or retreated from) All Saints, leaving it a good hundred yards from the nearest house. In the good old days, of course, it would have been called St Ethelreda's or St Aldheim's, not something as generic as All Saints. Still, it had a graveyard to one side and to the rear, and that seemed to be the perfect place to start my investigation. I was, after all, looking for a dead man. I was also hungry and ready to tackle the sandwiches my mother had insisted on packing for me.

The church was not only locked up, but there was also a notice on the doors saying that it was now redundant and was subject to an application to the Churches Conservation Trust, though to me it did not look to be of any particular historic value, though its grounds and the graveyard seemed well tended, with fresh flowers and potted plants on each grave.

I had brought my bike inside the rusty iron lychgate and sat on a patch of well-manicured grass rather than a gravestone to each my lunch, only to be rudely interrupted halfway through my first cheese-and-pickle doorstop. Had I been Lord Peter Wimsey, idling in a country churchyard, it would have been an ancient local bell-ringer who approached me. Had I been Albert Campion frisking among the gravestones looking for the most ludicrous inscription, it would probably have been a wizened village crone or an absent-minded professor hunting butterflies. Either would have been more welcome.

'I do hope you have no intention of leaving any litter,' she announced in a voice which carried across the churchyard and possibly into the next county. 'We might not use the church anymore, but we take pride in its appearance.'

She was through the lychgate and almost upon me before I had struggled to my feet, ready to defend myself.

'Naturally, I intend to leave no trace of my presence here,' I said, cringing at my own pomposity. 'It's a very nice graveyard.'

She nodded as if to acknowledge that I had given a correct answer, which gave me the chance to assess her. She was, I guessed, a woman the same age as my mother and yet so much *younger* – straw-blonde hair perfectly framing a face with eyes made wider with make-up and bright red, shiny lips. Around her neck was a string of pearls which drooped into a low-cut silky floral-print top tucked into skintight jeans and brown leather boots, and her perfume was so strong it was in danger of inducing a brain-swirl. Just in time, I remembered my manners.

'My name's Jacon Archer,' I said, holding out a hand which I hoped didn't smell of pickled onions. She did not take it, simply stared at me, but then I was probably staring at her and thinking that she had the poise of a classic Hollywood film noir. It seemed she was waiting for a supplementary answer, which I gave her in order to stop drooling. 'I've come to find a grave . . . I mean a burial . . . a gravestone, if one exists.'

'We have several to choose from,' she said in a cut-glass accent, still suspicious, 'and we try to keep them neat, though nobody's been buried here for a decade or more. Family history project is it? It usually is.'

'Not exactly. It's for my website.'

'I run the website here,' she said so sternly I felt I was back in school. 'The village website, Dunkley Direct,' she explained when she saw my confusion.

'Mine's nothing like that; my site is all about detective stories, vintage detective fiction, what we call the Golden Age.'

The woman put her hands on her hips, and I swear she made a thrusting movement towards me. 'That's what my husband says I'm in,' she drawled like a noir-film femme fatale, 'but it sounds more interesting than covering cake bakes, open gardens and endless campaigns against wind farms and pylons. Oh, and speed bumps. We get a lot of hits whenever we demand speed bumps in the village, not that anything has ever moved quickly in Dunkley. Detective stories sound much more interesting. My name's Cunningham, by the way.'

It felt too late to offer to shake hands again, and in any case my hand was slippery with sweat, so I smiled my best smile and tried to keep things professional, even though she seemed to have moved even closer.

'Does your site cover the graveyard, Mrs Cunningham?' I asked politely because I had noticed she wore a wedding ring, plus she had told me she had a husband.

98   Mike Ripley

'It's not a great source of news,' she said with what I suspected was sarcasm. 'The church was boarded up years ago and nobody's been buried here since.'

'Where could I find a list of who is buried here?'

'On Dunkley Direct, of course. There's a section on local history, not that anything much ever happened here, but, as I said, there's a growing interest in family histories. Can't think why. I've never felt the urge to trace my ancestors. Have you?'

'No, certainly not,' I said, perhaps too quickly. 'I'm only interested in dead writers.'

That didn't come out quite as I had meant it to, but it seemed to amuse Mrs Cunningham.

'Some people would say that's the only sort of writer worth being interested in, but if you're looking for a dead writer, we can offer you the late Alan Hibbert. There's not much to see, but he's the only one Dunkley ever had.'

'Duncan Torrens is exactly who I'm looking for!' I could have hugged her, but I had been warned about hugging women, whatever their age, and it must have been obvious because she took a half step backwards.

'I've no idea who that is.'

'It's the pen name of Alan Hibbert. I'm sorry, I thought you knew.'

'Why should I know?'

'Did you know him just as Hibbert?'

She pursed her lips as if she had been touched inappropriately. 'How old do you think I am?' Fortunately she did not expect an answer. 'I never said I knew him; I just know where his urn is.'

'His urn?'

Now I knew I was looking stupid.

'I don't make a habit of hanging around graveyards,' said Mrs Cunningham, 'or memorizing gravestones, but I know of Alan Hibbert because he's the only urn burial here. Somebody must have told me he was a writer. Is that not clear? You look confused.'

'I'm not sure what an urn burial is,' I said meekly.

'Someone who has been cremated but wanted his ashes placed somewhere. Perhaps somewhere on sacred ground. He got a plot about a foot square and a little brass plaque rather than the whole six-feet-and-a-headstone job.'

'Was he religious?'

'How the Dickens would I know? Go and ask him yourself if you're any good at seances. His plot's just down the path on the right, about ten feet from where you were picnicking, but it's easy to miss.'

She must have thought me rude because I turned on my heels and marched towards the church without a word, thinking that 'picnicking' was a lovely expression and wondering if it was possible to hold a seance with someone who'd been cremated.

Mrs Cunningham had been right: it was easy to miss the last resting place of Alan Hibbert as his plot was no more than a foot square edged by a frame of thin white tiles in the grass. A stone square fitted into the frame, and chiselled into it was the legend:

ALAN GEORGE HIBBERT
13 April 1913 – 14 July 1999

That was all. No family tributes, no 'in loving memory' and no mention of his alter ego Duncan Torrens. Still, I could take a photograph for the website and for Spencer Crow to show I was earning my corn.

I caught a whiff of Mrs Cunningham's perfume (though unlike a real detective I was unable to identify it) and realized she was hovering behind me.

'Not much to see, is there?'

I could have said that at least I had a date of death, but instead I vocalized the thought that had just popped into my head. 'Is there a sarcophagus anywhere in the graveyard?'

Once again, Mrs Cunningham moved away from me, looking alarmed. 'What?'

'It's like a stone coffin which rests on the ground rather than a wooden—'

'I know what *sarcophagi* are!' she snapped. 'I've seen them in Italy and Greece. And Egypt,' she added unnecessarily. 'And there's no such thing here at All Saints. What on earth made you think of that?'

'One of Torrens' books – I mean Hibbert's – *Buried Above Ground*, was about a body buried in clear sight in a stone coffin. I just wondered if he got the inspiration here.'

100 Mike Ripley

'I very much doubt that.' She looked around her, to the left then the right, not for a raised stone coffin but rather an excuse to leave. I had seen the same reaction in females before.

'Is there anyone in Dunkley who would remember him?' I tried.

'Can't think of a soul,' she said almost immediately. 'I've only ever met one person who knew we had a book writer in the village.'

Book writer. She said it the same way she would have said blacksmith or cobbler or greengrocer, giving the impression that Dunkley didn't do tradesmen anymore.

'I'd like to talk to her if I could.'

'There again, you're out of luck I'm afraid. Melanie was Hibbert's biggest fan, maybe his only one, and sometimes mentioned when he had a new book out in the village magazine, which became the website when I inherited the job.'

'Inherited?'

'About ten years ago, when Melanie died. She was the wife of the last vicar here, which is probably how she got Hibbert's ashes that tiny little plot. If you fancy trying to contact her, though, you're welcome to go and offer a prayer next to her grave. You'll find it just over there.' She flapped an arm vaguely to her right, a pair of gold bracelets chiming like a bell on her wrist. 'Can't miss it. Granite headstone engraved "in loving memory of the Reverend Andrew Crow and his beloved wife Melanie".'

Crow?

SIXTEEN

Even if I hadn't seen Mrs Cunningham drive off in a bright red BMW convertible, I knew that Dunkley was no longer a village which had tradesmen and hadn't had any for a while. Every house was detached with a manicured front lawn or carefully barbered hedge. Many were new builds, the older ones having been upgraded to mini-mansions, and none had a car parked outside older than three years or with an engine less than two litres, unless it was electric.

Except one. The one I was looking for.

Mrs Cunningham might not have known Alan Hibbert in life – how old *did* I think she was? – but she knew about his grave thanks to her role as the custodian of the Dunkley village website, though my perfunctory search for Hibbert's name there had produced no results.

The reason Hibbert was persona non grata on Dunkley Direct was his legacy to the village – not his reputation as a crime writer but the fact that in his will he'd left his house to the county council on condition it was used as a refuge for illegal immigrants. At the time Hibbert died, the newspapers had carried daily reports of desperate refugees hiding away on lorries crossing the Channel, or even trying to walk through the Channel Tunnel. Today, the problem was worse thanks to illegal 'small boats' crossing and leaving thousands needing somewhere to live while their asylum claims were processed. However much it was resented by the residents of Dunkley, as a possible drag on property prices, Alan Hibbert's old house was still serving a useful function.

The house, Mrs Cunningham had told me, was called Peacefals but she had no idea where that name had come from, and it sounded more appropriate to a hospice or a residential care home instead of a glorified Airbnb for foreign migrants.

'Safe places,' I said, determined to impress her. 'Peacefals is an anagram of safe places. Was the house always called that?'

'I have no idea. Does it matter?'

Mike Ripley

'Anagrams appeal to writers of detective stories. Maybe there's a clue in there.'

'A clue to what?'

She gave me that I'm-not-angry-just-disappointed stare which most, if not all, of my female teachers had given me.

'To what happened to him,' I said, realizing that wasn't helpful.

'He died,' she said, jangling her car keys as if ringing a bell to end the lesson. 'He lived alone, had no family and when he died, he left his one asset, his house, to what he thought was a good cause. Melanie Crow thought him something of a saint to get his ashes buried here, but she died more than ten years ago, before the flood of boat people arriving in a never-ending stream reached its peak and Hibbert's philanthropy became a bit of a millstone around the neck of the village – if you were trying to sell a property nearby. I mean, Christian charity and all that, but who wants refugees as neighbours? Still, it could have been worse, I suppose. It could have become a halfway house for paedophiles and rapists on probation.'

I nodded in what I thought was a sympathetic manner, sensing she was ready to mount a high horse and wanting to get back to the topic in hand.

'Mrs Crow died ten years ago, you said?'

She paused for thought. 'Twelve actually. Is *that* important?'

I shook my head. 'No, it's just that I got the impression that she had passed fairly recently.'

'Did you know her?'

'Not at all, but I think I've met her son.'

'Oh yes, Spencer.' She said it dreamily, her lips quivering slightly. 'The City whizz-kid. Came to the funeral in a flashy sports car but didn't hang around. I don't know if there's a male equivalent of being all fur coat and no knickers, but if there is, that would sum up Spencer.'

I sensed she was going off track again. 'Can I get to see Peacefals?'

'If you think you really must. It's the last house at the other end of the village, on the left mostly hidden by a hedge of leylandii which should have been grubbed out years ago but for the fact that they mask the goings-on there.'

'Goings-on?'

I was getting the feeling that I was tapping into some local resentment.

'Well, there must have been over the years. There's been a steady stream of foreigners in and out of there . . . but it's not for me to judge.' Which is exactly what she was doing. 'On the whole, they keep themselves to themselves, and it's unlikely that any of them have ever read anything written by Alan Hibbert – or anything in English, come to that.'

With that, she turned and sashayed down the path, offering a view of her rear aspect which would have reminded a music hall comedian that his watch needed winding. I gathered up my bag, lunch box and helmet, took a couple of pictures of Alan Hibbert's urn burial and collected my bicycle at the lychgate.

Mrs Cunningham was sat in her BMW examining her make-up in the vanity mirror in the driver's sun visor. I gave her a cheerful wave to which she did not respond, but the mirror enabled her to watch me head off into the village. When I looked over my shoulder, she had started the car and pulled away, disappearing down the hill towards the river.

SEVENTEEN

It was just as well I did not need to ask for directions to Peacefals as I did not see a single resident of Dunkley to ask as I passed through the village. Those not at work must have been inside checking their online banking balances.

Alan Hibbert's old house was not difficult to spot as it was by far the scruffiest property in the village and seemed to have been banished to the very edge of Dunkley as far away from the church as possible, as if the village was ashamed of it, which, given the attitude of Mrs Cunningham, it probably was.

I guessed it had been built in the twenties, a solid red-brick and tile detached house with an impressive garden, designed and built for a middle-class professional family. I wondered whether it had been commissioned for the Hibbert family or whether Alan Hibbert had bought it as his personal safe place in which to become a writer. I was sure there would be a way of finding out how long it had been called Peacefals or whether Hibbert had come up with that name. I could only add it to the long list of things I did not know about him.

On closer inspection, I could see that the house was in need of care and attention or at least a new paint job and some refreshed pointing. Each window had drawn curtains, probably to hide the view of the front garden, which was overgrown with weeds and littered with a variety of children's toys. There was nothing solid enough for me to secure the bike to, so I wheeled it up to the front door and pressed the doorbell.

I did not know what to expect, but I was on my best behaviour because I always feel self-conscious when being examined through a peephole or, in this case, the doorbell camera. I was kept waiting so long my right leg started to shake, as it always did in such situations – my mother used to say I suffered from St Vitus's dance – but then I heard several deadlocks being turned and a bolt pulled, and the door opened about six inches.

'Can I help you?'

'Probably not,' I said without thinking, 'but your house might.'

'If you're Border Force, HMRC or social services, you'd better have some ID. You're not a cop; they don't come on bikes anymore.'

'I'm nothing like that,' I said, but as the door opened wider and I saw the girl behind the voice, I was tempted to say that I was a private detective, but I didn't, as she did not seem the type to be easily impressed.

She was my age, possibly a bit younger, and small, so I looked down at her. She was difficult to miss, with long, unruly red hair – and I mean dyed bright red, not ginger. She wore a flowery top and tight jeans like Mrs Cunningham, except she filled neither as well as Mrs Cunningham did.

'So what are you exactly?'

She did have one thing in common with Dunkley's very own web maven (as I now thought of her) and that was the upper-middle-class accent and attitude.

'I'm doing some research into a family history.'

'I don't think you'll find any family members here,' she said, looking me up and down as if measuring me for a coffin, as my mother would have sneered.

'Not my family,' I said quickly. 'The previous owner of the house.'

'Alan Hibbert?'

I felt a jolt in my chest and a distinct trembling in my right leg. 'That's right. You know' – I remembered my mistake with Mrs Cunningham – 'of him?'

'Only what I was told at my induction about the history of Peacefals. It's a nice name, isn't it? Quite fitting, really.'

'It's now a refuge, isn't it?'

'It's a temporary home for asylum seekers. I'm sure you will appreciate this is a sensitive subject and why, unless you have specific permission, I cannot let you in.'

She made a move to close the door on me, and I could see opportunity slipping away.

'Wait!' It came out louder than I had intended. 'Please – just hear me out. Please. I've come all the way from London.'

'On your bike?'

'Train first, then bike. It was nice to get out into the countryside.'

'But apart from some exercise, what did you hope to gain by coming here?'

Her voice had softened somewhat, and I felt I was on my way to convincing her that no stranger arriving by bicycle ever meant any harm.

'Look, Miss, my name is Jacon Archer and I run a website dedicated to crime fiction.' I decided not to confuse her – she was young and a girl after all – by specifying Golden Age. 'What we do is research and write about forgotten authors, hoping to get some of their books back in print. Alan Hibbert was an established crime writer back in the day, but very little is known about him other than he lived in Dunkley and he left this house to the county council when he died in 1999. I'm trying to find out as much as I can about him.'

'He was a writer?'

Her eyes widened in surprise. They were rather attractive eyes, but mine were probably just as wide at her cheerfully admitted ignorance.

'He wrote dozens of novels under the name of Duncan Torrens and created a memorable detective duo in Inspector Seeley and Sergeant Grimes. They had a loyal following in the nineties.'

'I wasn't born in the nineties, so I haven't heard of them. Have they been on the telly?'

I felt my leg start to quiver, this time in anger, and I pulled my bike close so I could lean on it for support.

'No, and they never even made it into paperback,' I said through gritted teeth.

'No wonder I've never heard of them. They couldn't have been very good.'

I couldn't tell if she was being wilfully ignorant or was winding me up.

'Many' – I almost said experts – 'connoisseurs feel that Hibbert's books had considerable merit.'

'And that's you, is it? A connoisseur?'

'I'm a researcher just trying to find out as much as I can about a writer; a writer who lived here.'

She thought about this, then, as if taking pity on me, she stepped out on to the stoop to face me, letting the door close behind her with a click. I noticed that in her right hand, hanging down by her jeans, she was clutching a bunch of keys, two of which protruded from between her fingers – a self-defence measure used by females who had to walk home alone late at night.

'What did you say your name was?'

'It's Jacon Archer. That's Jacon with a "C". Do you need to see some photo ID?'

In my wallet in my back pocket, I had my British Library card for just such an emergency, though I had never been asked to produce it other than at the library itself.

She waved a hand with multicoloured fingernails – not the one holding her keys like a knuckleduster.

'Not necessary; I can't let you in. We have some traumatized families staying here, and they are not to be disturbed with questions about somebody they've never heard of in a language they don't understand.'

'But you said you'd heard the name Alan Hibbert.'

'In passing, in my induction when I was interviewed for this job.'

'Are you the warden here?'

She scoffed at that. 'No way. I'm a part-time assistant manager, and I'm doing this as part of my uni course in social work.'

I bridled at her use of 'uni' – if I had ever gone to university, I would not have denigrated the term, but I let it pass.

'Once I got the placement here, I was briefed about the local situation – that there was some antagonism in the village towards the house being used as a refuge and there was always a chance that a newspaper reporter would come sniffing around. So all we should say, which was all we actually knew, was that a local worthy – Alan Hibbert – had left the house for this specific purpose in his will back in 1999. That's it.'

'Nothing about his career as a writer?'

'Somebody may have mentioned that, but honestly it's never come up whilst I've been in Dunkley, and nothing in the house suggests it was a writer's home. No book-lined library, for instance; no books at all really, but of course the house isn't what it was in 1999. The interior must have been gutted to turn it into six family rooms.' She put her head on one side and studied me carefully. 'I'm not even supposed to tell people how many families we have here.'

108 Mike Ripley

'If there's nothing like an Alan Hibbert legacy in the house, then I'm not really interested,' I said, putting on my most trustworthy expression. 'I'll just take a picture of the place for my website and then I'll be out of your hair.'

'I can't allow that! No photographs – please. The people living here are refugees and have suffered enough. They are very sensitive and don't need any more publicity.'

I must have seemed bemused as it took me a minute to realize she was actually proposing a compromise.

'But if it's Hibbert's legacy you're interested in,' she went on rapidly, 'you could mention the rather daft conditions he imposed in his will: no dogs were to be allowed in the house or garden, and his shed was to remain locked up and untouched for ten years.'

'His shed?'

'Where he must have done his writing.'

'How do you know that?'

'Well, there's a typewriter still in there. Do you want to see it?'

Silly question.

EIGHTEEN

I t was around the back of the house at the bottom of a garden which had been turned into an unruly vegetable patch, and one blighted by some unspecified botanical disease or perhaps just left untended for a couple of years. It was a shed, a standard wooden garden shed of dark wood with a worn rubber fabric roof covering and a grimy window on one side.

'My name's Hannah, by the way, with two aitches,' she told me as she escorted me round the side of Peacefals to the back garden – and it did feel as if I was a prisoner under escort as she never left my side. It is never a comfort for a prisoner to be on first-name terms with his jailer, although it was probably fairer to say that Hannah was acting like a supermarket security guard and I was a well-known shoplifter. Not that there was anything to steal on our walk, and I carefully avoided trying to peep through the windows of the house.

The nearer we got to the shed, and further from the house, the more Hannah relaxed and indicated that I should go ahead of her, so I made a beeline for the window in the side of the shed, pressing my nose up against the cracked glass rimmed with green mould and festooned with cobwebs holding a larder of dead and desiccated flies.

I have to admit I was excited at peering in to the *sanctum sanctorum* of Duncan Torrens, if indeed that was what it was. There was a major clue to the fact that this was where somebody had done some writing in that I could make out the unmistakeable shape of a typewriter resting on a wooden table or bench. That was just about all I could make out through the gloom, and my hopes faded only to be instantly rekindled by Miss Hannah.

'Do you want to see inside?'

'I thought you said it was sealed in Hibbert's will.'

'For ten years it was. Then somebody remembered ten years must be up and smashed the padlock off so it could be used for the purpose God intended.'

'God?' I was confused. 'Was it a place of prayer?'

Hannah laughed and snorted as she did so. It was not her most attractive aspect, particularly as she was laughing at me.

'No, it was a garden shed! And so it became one again, though no one in my time here has shown any interest in doing any actual gardening.' She opened the door and held it for me. 'Go on – knock yourself out. There's not much to see. There used to be electricity laid on for lights, but that was disconnected when the house came to the council. That was a provision of the bequest I was told.'

I stepped inside, the wooden floorboards creaking under my weight. Hannah was right on both counts: there wasn't much to see and it had been used as a garden shed. It stank of rot and dirt and strongly of nicotine, and was stuffed to the gills with spades, trowels, seed trays, watering cans, a half-empty bag of peat-free compost and a leaning tower of plastic plant pots. The only evidence that it had been used for any other purpose was the typewriter, which sat on what turned out to be an old school desk, and a rusty metal filing cabinet with three drawers.

Without asking my guard's permission, I pulled open the top drawer of the cabinet, although I had expected it to be locked. The drawer came out with a teeth-jarring screech and a pungent whiff of mouldy vegetation to reveal dozens of opened packets of seeds and leaking bottles of plant food.

'Expecting to find something?' Hannah asked behind me.

'Not something *growing*. Were there any papers in here?'

'I don't know; I wasn't here when the shed was repossessed. There was no mention of papers in the house logbook.'

'What's that?'

'The manager here has to keep a record of what they call the fabric of the property, so that repairs and renovation can be ordered up. I was on night shift one night and so bored I actually read it, and I remember a reference to when they opened up the shed after ten years. It was a sort of inventory, but all that was listed as being in there was a metal chest of drawers and an Underwood typewriter. That was it. Why the shed had been off limits for ten years is a mystery.'

'Do you mind if I take a picture of the typewriter?'

'Don't see what harm it could do. Is it worth anything?'

Buried Above Ground   111

As an artefact connected to the work of Duncan Torrens, I doubted it other than that it might be an illustration for the Gadabout site, but I didn't say that.

'These old Underwoods are sold these days as ornaments or interior design accessories, but this one is in such poor shape it would cost a bomb to have it cleaned and restored.'

Hibbert's old Underwood had been, in its day, an impressive machine. As solid as a tractor and almost as heavy, it was clogged with grime and rust, the carriage and the metal margin tabs would not move, and I suspected the only part which might work would be the bell to signal carriage return. The single-colour black ribbon had been pulled from its spools and chewed, probably by the same rodent that had used several of the keys as a toilet. It was the sort of typewriter occasionally seen in 'the author at work' photographs from the late forties. The author in question would invariably be male and usually smoking a pipe. The classic detective story writer, of course, used a fountain pen and ink, and the really successful thriller writer would dictate to a secretary or typist, sometimes attempting to narrate two stories at the same time. The supremely confident thriller writer would order a gold-plated typewriter to celebrate the publication of his debut novel.

'Do you want a hand getting it out into the daylight?' Hannah asked as I got my phone out.

It might have been a chance to get her in the photograph – she was certainly pretty enough – but that wouldn't make much sense on the website as she'd never heard of Duncan Torrens.

'No, let's leave it where it is,' I said. 'It's too heavy and too dirty to move. This way, there'll be more atmosphere to the shot.'

'A rather weird atmosphere. It looks like a gravestone. Still, I suppose that's a fitting memorial for a dead writer.'

NINETEEN

There was nothing else to see or photograph in the shed and so, after taking a couple of photos of the exterior, Hannah offered to see me 'off the premises'. As we walked back to where I'd left my bike, she started to ask about Alan Hibbert's books but was probably just humouring me as she still held her bunch of keys poking out through the fingers of her right fist.

'So what sort of books did the late Mr Hibbert write, then?'

'Torrens,' I said automatically. 'He wrote as Duncan Torrens.'

'Why?'

'Why what?'

'Why did he choose the name Torrens? What was wrong with Hibbert?'

'I don't really know. Crime writers often adopted pseudonyms, and maybe he picked Duncan Torrens because it sounded Scottish. A lot of popular thriller writers had Scots-sounding names.'

'So his books were thrillers, were they?'

'Well, technically we'd call them police procedural crime novels.'

She frowned at that and then frowned at me watching her face. 'Procedural? You mean like *CSI* and all that forensic stuff?'

'No, not at all. There's very little about forensics or blood and gore. Very little about real police procedure actually. It really means that the hero, the detective, is a professional police officer and not a talented amateur sleuth as in' – I was going to say the Golden Age but thought that might complicate things – 'days gone by.'

'You mean like Hercule Poirot?'

'Well, technically he was a retired police officer who then began to work as a private detective.'

'Oh, I see,' she said unconvincingly. 'Still, he was good on the telly.'

Buried Above Ground 113

I had no idea whether she was taking the mickey or not, so I pretended I had not heard her.

'Most procedurals had partnerships of detectives,' I said, 'usually an inspector with a sergeant or detective constable to bounce ideas off. Every Sherlock Holmes has to have a Watson, and Torrens invented Inspector Seeley and Sergeant Grimes. He had them solving crimes . . .'

'Murders?'

'Invariably. The accepted format was discovery of a murdered body, followed by a second murder to cover up the first and then a third murder avoided by Seeley and Grimes cracking the case just in time.'

'And this formula worked, did it?'

Again, I could not tell if she was teasing.

'For more than thirty books.'

'Christ! How many trees had to die for that?'

Once more, I pointedly ignored her crass comment, which I had heard many times before when promoting obscure Golden Age authors.

'He must have done something right as his books kept getting published, at least one a year.'

'But were they any good?'

'There's a saying in crime-fiction publishing about certain authors – that what you see is what you get. In Torrens' case, that meant simple, straightforward prose with no bad language; a credible plot which had a minimum of explicit violence, even though the nub of the plot was always murder; and absolutely no explicit sex scenes. By the end, all crimes had to be resolved and justice seen to be done.'

'Were they all like that?'

'I haven't read them all,' I said, thinking she might regard me as a bit geeky if I told her how many crime novels I *had* read and that the entire Duncan Torrens canon would not represent a significant percentage. 'But that was the formula he stuck to. Familiarity rarely breeds contempt when it comes to fictional detectives.'

'But he must have rung the changes – varied things, otherwise he would have gone mad, wouldn't he?'

'Oh, he did change his style when he got a new editor about

ten years before he died. He started dropping in classical references, the idea being that Inspector Seeley, who had never been to university, was on an intellectual self-improvement kick. In one book, *Buried Above Ground*, Seeley found a body in a Roman sarcophagus. Goodness knows where Torrens got the idea from as there aren't any in Dunkley churchyard.'

We had turned the corner of the house and the garden was out of sight when I got the idea and foolishly blurted it out.

'When we were in the shed, you said the typewriter reminded you of a headstone from a grave.'

'Did I?'

'Something like that. Does the shed itself look something like a sarcophagus? From a distance, I mean, like the ones you find in graveyards?'

Hannah looked at me, her blue eyes moist with pity. 'It looks like a shed, for God's sake. You're not exactly selling this guy's books to me. Didn't he have anything else going for him? What was his USP – his unique selling point?'

I grimaced at her thinking she needed to explain USP to me but let it pass. 'Well, he had a quirk – I suppose you could call it that – which his readers seemed to like.'

'Let me guess,' Hannah said with a curled lip, 'his detective has a drink problem or a failed marriage or a phobia like vertigo which he's hiding from his superiors, or all three. Or . . . or' – she became quite animated – 'he sees dead people, like the ghosts of murder victims, and they help him solve the case.'

I resisted the urge to tell her not to be ridiculous. 'No, nothing like that. Inspector Seeley was a happily married man for the most part and an honest copper. The trick Duncan Torrens pulled was that he never identified *where* Seeley was a policeman. He never named the town where he was based.'

'Didn't that just annoy people?'

'No, his readers seemed to like it – or at least accepted it. Perhaps they enjoyed trying to guess where it was supposed to be. When writers make up a name for a town, or even a whole county, half the fun is guessing the place it's based upon, and there are usually clues in the descriptive passages.'

'Big on clues, was he? I could never do cryptic crossword puzzles, so they probably wouldn't be my thing.'

'Spotting the clues before the detective does is the great joy of reading crime fiction.'

'Really? I would have thought it would be the triumph of good over evil or the impact of crime on modern society, but what do I know? I live with real problems caused by crime. Everyone who comes to stay at Peacefals has been the victim of a crime of one sort or another. How would this Inspector Seeley deal with them?'

'Fairly and justly, I'm sure,' I said, knowing that it sounded trite and rather prim. 'After all, Alan Hibbert left his house as a refuge, so he must have had a social conscience.'

We reached my bicycle in silence, and I just knew she wasn't going to go back inside the house until she'd watched me go. As I kneeled to release the bike lock, I thought of something which might impress her.

'There was one trick Duncan Torrens had which might appeal, a very clever one.'

'I don't think you're going to convert me,' she said, 'but go on.'

'He'd written more than thirty Inspector Seeley books before he broke the secret about Sergeant Grimes.'

'His sidekick?'

'If you like. For all those books, it was always just "Sergeant Grimes", or "Gerry", which everyone assumed was short for Gerald, but in *Most Wretched of Deaths* the bombshell was dropped that Gerry was actually short for Geraldine, and Detective Sergeant Grimes had been a woman all along.'

Hannah remained determinedly unimpressed. 'That wouldn't exactly be front-page news these days. Was it really so shocking back then?'

'It would have been 1993 or '94.'

'Before I was born, and you couldn't have been very old.' I was sure she was being provocative, but I was not going to fall for it. 'Was that really such a big deal?'

'For the dedicated crime-fiction reader, it would have been startling,' I said, feeling the need to defend Torrens the writer. 'In a way, it was a wonderful piece of sleight of hand, disguising Gerry's sex for so many books by never using "he" or "she" – nobody had ever done that before.'

Hannah shrugged. 'Maybe he just forgot. Did anyone notice – or care?'

'The reviewers did.' Well, one had. 'And if I had been a regular Torrens reader, I would have gone back and read all his previous titles to try and spot the clues he planted about Gerry being female.'

She was quiet for a moment, watching me mount my bike. Then she said, 'Yes, I believe you would have. I hope you got what you wanted here; cycle safely.'

'If I can think of anything I might need, I can always pop back,' I said as I pulled on my safety helmet, which I knew made me look distinctly uncool.

'Better ring the county council press office before you do. I'll be back at uni.'

She seemed sure of that, even though I hadn't indicated when I might return. By the time I had decided to thank her for her help and wish her well in her studies, she had turned her back and was striding back to Peacefals, the bunch of keys jangling in her hand.

I pedalled across the road and stopped against the kerb. There was hardly any traffic, and it only took a moment for me to get a quick shot of Peacefals and the retreating red hair of Hannah-with-two-aitches on my phone.

Pedalling through Dunkley, I saw just as few of the residents as I had on my way in, although I did spot Mrs Cunningham unloading shopping from the boot of her BMW. The shopping bags were all labelled Waitrose, just as I could have guessed.

And then I was at the church again, the last resting place of Alan Hibbert and Duncan Torrens, and leaving Dunkley behind as I began to freewheel down the hill towards the main road.

Part Three

The Publisher

TWENTY

So maybe it wasn't clever to put young Jacon on the trail of the Torrens books, but I couldn't be seen to be sniffing round them myself, could I? And I sure as fuck couldn't go to Robina Robinson because she'd dob me in to Pabulator like a shot and then the sodding Vikings would get their noses in the trough.

Jacon never was the sharpest blade in the Sabatier knife block, but he was keen and, above all, malleable. Although he was blinkered towards the so-called Golden Age, he did have a pretty fair working knowledge of crime fiction as a whole and a good idea of who was who in the publishing pecking order. He had even recommended out-of-print titles for my Hooded Crow imprint, which we had done as ebooks priced at under £1. Nobody was ever going to get rich from them, but the authors were long dead and their agents grateful for miniscule royalty payments after fifty years of none at all, plus they made Jacon feel important, and he did help promote them through his unbelievably dull website.

I was actually looking for something else when I spotted Jacon's Gadabout piece on the Torrens manuscript he'd bought on eBay and it immediately rang a bell.

When I started Hooded Crow, my mother had pestered me to consider republishing the Inspector Seeley books, or at least the one she remembered reading, *Most Wretched of Deaths*, from the early nineties. In truth she didn't remember too much about the book, but then she never could remember plots, characters or titles. Cynics might say she would have made the perfect publisher!

Mother was not a great reader and generally not of crime fiction despite my father, being a vicar, having a fair collection of green Penguin detective stories, but she was much taken by the fact that there was a published author living in Dunkley. It was something to be proud of locally, as long as one didn't have to read his books, and she probably had some silly romantic notion of the lone, tormented artist starving to death in a garret – or in Hibbert's case, a garden shed. I have no idea how well, if at all, she actually knew Alan Hibbert, but she often referred to him as 'poor Mr Hibbert' and expressed concern that he lived a solitary life and probably wasn't getting enough to eat. My father would tell her not to be ridiculous as it was well known that Hibbert, who would at this time be in his eighties, had regular visits from 'care workers' – which he always said whilst clearing his throat – who were usually foreign, invariably female and occasionally 'statuesque'. As for his diet, had she not noticed the delivery van arriving every fortnight from the food section of that posh department store in the town?

Both gossip and actual news about Hibbert must have been thin on the ground in Dunkley, but Mother convinced herself that his hermit-like existence concealed some unspecified but fatal illness or syndrome. She was particularly worried by the fact that she had, on more than one occasion, whilst walking the dog late at night, seen a faint light glowing in Hibbert's garden shed while the house itself was in darkness. She thought it unnatural. My father put it down to artistic eccentricities, a touch of insomnia or the onset of dementia.

At some point in 1999, the natural inertia of Dunkley must have been momentarily disturbed by the arrival of paramedics and ambulances at Hibbert's home, though as I was away at university, it mercifully passed me by. I do not even remember my mother mentioning it at the time, but later she made sure that his ashes, unclaimed by any relative or friend, found a resting place in the churchyard. She had been horrified to find that, in her book, he had died virtually destitute – and him a published author! Knowing what I know now, that doesn't surprise me, plus the fact that he had given away his one major asset, his house.

Of course, that gesture of turning his house over to be a refuge for asylum seekers showed that Hibbert had been a stand-up Christian in Mother's eyes, and my father, being a Church of England vicar, could do nothing but second his wife's fulsome praise, though I well knew he had strong private opinions about immigrants, legal or otherwise, and after a rare visit to London,

Buried Above Ground 121

he had complained that he had heard eight languages being spoken on the Underground and the only English voice had been the speaker making platform announcements on the tannoy.

In one of her letters to me, Mother noted that the name of Hibbert's house had been changed from The End House to Peacefals, which was nice, but it was just a pity they had misspelled it. But I never heard how the majority of respectable residents of Dunkley took to their new neighbours. Perhaps they got used to the sound of eight (or more) languages being spoken in the village pub – not that Dunkley had such a plebeian thing as a pub – but no one actually organized an angry pitchfork-wielding mob to march on Peacefals by torchlight. I am sure mother would have mentioned it in a letter or during the obligatory monthly telephone call.

But then, she did have other things on her mind. Within two years of Alan Hibbert being filed as a discarded remainder, my father also died, which gave me one less reason to visit Dunkley. On the plus side, I did inherit his collection of crime novels, which gave me the idea to start up Hooded Crow, though significantly none were by Duncan Torrens.

Clearly it was my mother who was the fan, at least of local author Hibbert if not his literary alter ego, for she often mentioned him in passing in her letters, which grew more and more rambling after my father died.

Hibbert was dead and gone, of course, but she remembered him every time she passed on news about the village, or rather the comings and goings at Peacefals, which was essentially the only interesting thing happening in Dunkley. Every time she thought it worth reporting that Mrs So-and-So had been taken ill due to 'the smell of foreign food' coming from Peacefals, or that another Mrs So-and-So had suffered, as my father had on the Central Line, after finding herself surrounded at the bus stop by strange people laughing and talking in languages she couldn't identify let alone understand, Mother would reflect that surely this wasn't what that nice Mr Hibbert had wished on the village. I could almost hear her sighing as she covered the Basildon Bond in her delicate handwriting, always done with an italic nib fountain pen.

There was even a wonderfully sly reference to a 'very busy'

village incomer called Mrs Cunningham, who seemed determined to get a petition going to press the county council to close down Peacefals and move its transient residents elsewhere. This, she thought, was downright un-Christian and would never gain support as Dunkley was essentially a Christian village, even if All Saints was being made redundant and would no longer be a working church, a regular incumbent never having been appointed after my father's death.

I never discovered if Mrs Cunningham's petition got off the ground because Mother's health began to fail and her letters became infrequent and even more rambling. As it happens, I met Mrs Cunningham at Mum's funeral and could almost have been tempted to hang around Dunkley because I think we could have hit it off. She was, for her age, really fit, and just the sort of woman my mother would not approve of.

In Mother's will I was left the house, which I sold quickly in order to give Hooded Crow the cash injection it needed to really get established. I had left all the details to an estate agent. It was one of the minions there, in charge of house clearance – there was nothing there I needed or wanted – who found the copy of *Most Wretched of Deaths* secreted in a bedside-table drawer. Clearly, after I had relieved her of my father's collection of detective stories, my mother had been of the opinion that crime fiction may be read but not seen. Folded into the book, a first-edition hardback, was a sheet of notepaper with handwritten instructions that 'This book is for my son, Spencer' and her wishes were observed, post-mortem as it were.

I would like to think that was a sign, but I don't believe in such things, and to be honest, I put the book on a shelf and forgot about it for several years until Hugo Cottrell-Gore came sniffing around trying to find Inspector Seeley – or rather, Sergeant Grimes.

TWENTY-ONE

I knew Hugo from our Cambridge days together when we had shared more than one girlfriend, many a bottle of wine and several grammes of cocaine, which he always referred to as his 'marching powder'. He was a trust-fund kid from a posh family and I would have trusted him with anything except my money. After three years of party-giving instead of studying for whatever subject he eventually scraped a degree in, Hugo took a year off, married a Chanel model on a beach on Mauritius – the sand got *everywhere* – and then settled down to the job he had been born to, or rather promised by friends of his father, as a BBC producer. He had started on documentaries, including a couple on aspects of World War II, which can still be seen today on PBS America, then, tempted by the budgets offered by Netflix, he decided to move into drama.

He invited me to lunch at The Ivy under the impression that it was still a dining hub for television executives and agents, and was rather put out to find that two of the waitresses knew my name. I had arrived ten minutes early and ordered a bottle of their most expensive Vermentino to keep me company, knowing that Hugo could afford it, and if he couldn't, I could.

'Getting a head start as usual, I see, Spencer,' he said as he flopped down on the chair opposite. 'We always said you were the only one of us in Trinity who could hear a cork being pulled in Peterhouse. Independent Publisher of the Year again, I hear.'

'Merely shortlisted – again. How many BAFTAs so far, Hugo?'

'They are like buses, old boy. Nothing for half an hour, then three come along at once.'

'When were you ever on a bus?'

Hugo grinned the grin he had perfected at public school and helped himself to a glass of wine. 'Seriously, how is the Emperor of Pulp Fiction?'

'Not at all offended by that spurious title, Hugo, and doing very well indeed, thank you very much.'

Mike Ripley

'I always knew you would fall on your feet.'

'Good thing I never had far to fall,' I said, concluding the social niceties. 'To what do I owe the pleasure of this free lunch?'

'It's not *exactly* free, I'm afraid.'

'They never are, but let's order some food to go with some of the very chuggable Bordeaux they keep here.'

'Chuggable?' Hugo's eyebrows rose half an inch. 'You haven't changed, have you?'

'Why would I? Now what's on your mind? Nothing rocking the domestic boat is there? You know I would never come between a man and his trophy wife, so no taking sides or offering bedroom advice.'

Hugo chuckled. 'As if I would come to you – as if anyone would come to you – for advice on marriage. No, I wanted to ask you about something you actually know about. But let's order first and get the boring eating bit out of the way.'

We both went for twelve-ounce rib-eyes because the beef Wellington took forty-five minutes, by which time we would probably be too pissed to appreciate it, and Hugo deferred to my choice of the most expensive Bordeaux without turning a hair.

As we ate, Hugo brought me up to date – not that I had asked – on the health and achievements of his wife (Fiona, I remembered just in time) and their two children (so difficult finding a decent preschool), and then, as we were starting on that dangerous third bottle, he got down to business, and for once Hugo managed to surprise me.

'What do you know about Duncan Torrens?'

'Who?' I said automatically.

'Come on,' Hugo encouraged, 'you're supposed to be the expert on pulp fiction.'

'Oh, Duncan Torrens the crime writer?'

'The very same.'

'I'd hardly class him as pulp fiction, and I'm actually surprised you've ever heard of him. Not that many people had when he was alive.'

'So he's dead, then? But he did write *Most Wretched of Deaths*, didn't he?'

'When he was alive, back in 1993 or thereabouts.'

'Christ on a donkey, I didn't realize it was that old.' Hugo was beginning to slur his words, the wine finally starting to kick in. 'Still, that gives the option to go for a costume piece and we can say the nineties are the new seventies or suchlike. What was the music like in the nineties? No, how would you know? What was the economy like?'

'Pretty good, I think. Lots of people in the City made their money then, but it was before my time. We were at Cambridge if you remember.'

'Frankly, I don't remember too much about the nineties and I count that as a blessing, but the rule of thumb is that if the economy was booming, the music was shite.'

'And what's that got to do with Duncan Torrens?' I said, trying to put a brake on Hugo's rambling.

'Nothing directly, just about the background scenario . . . the *vibe* we give off . . . the filter we see this through . . .'

I filled his glass from a half-empty bottle, determined to shut him up one way or another. 'Hugo, you're speaking in tongues again and this time, in fluent pure bollocks. I therefore assume that it's got something to do with a television project.'

'Better than that.' He lowered his voice as if the restaurant was full of people who listened to other people's conversations rather than the sound of their own voices. 'A Netflix series, and you know what that means: the sky's the limit and so's the budget.'

'And you can rely on me to be here to help you drink it, Hugo, but where does Duncan Torrens come in?'

'Source material, Spencer my lad, source material. It helps with the pitch to have a published book behind you.'

'Even one thirty years old, which few people read then and even fewer have done so since?'

'But that's your thing, isn't it? Bringing old books back into print. A new book is simply one you haven't read yet, isn't that your mantra?'

'Don't quote my own sales pitch back at me, Hugo. Hooded Crow revives crime fiction which doesn't deserve to be forgotten and presents it in new formats to modern readers.'

'Now who's reading from their prospectus? You've republished hundreds of books, but you've never done any Duncan Torrens, have you?'

126   Mike Ripley

'Nobody has, and there are good reasons for that. He didn't have the recognition among our core audience demographics. He was simply not that popular.'

'Not that good, you mean?' Hugo seemed suddenly sober.

'No, I don't. He was a good enough writer to get published year after year for God knows how long, but he was always a "midlist" author and never made the big time. He was up against four or five hundred other British crime writers churning out a crime novel a year at the same time and increasingly competing against the Americans, who arrived big time in the nineties.'

'And then we had the Scandi-noir craze,' Hugo said to prove he had been listening, 'and all those dreary, badly lit detective dramas where the most colour came from those jumpers knitted on the Faroe Isles.'

'Well, that was a bit later, after Torrens was dead and gone, but you could say he was a victim of a Nordic invasion.'

'You mean the takeover by Pabulator?'

Hugo was not only well informed, but he also seemed to be sobering up.

'He died just in time to avoid the humiliation of being dropped in the new owner's great rationalization.'

'So they had no interest in his Inspector Seeley books?'

'Seems not. They didn't even publish his last novel post-humously, which is often a good marketing ploy. Perhaps it wasn't any good; he was getting on by then and probably losing it, but either way, it was rejected and literally thrown in the bin.'

'You know that for a fact?'

'I wouldn't know if it was any good or not, but the manuscript was rescued from a skip and sold on eBay a while back.'

'So it was never under contract?'

'Doubt it. There would have been the usual clause in the contract for his last published one, which gave the publisher first right of refusal on his next. Obviously, they didn't take up that option.'

'So Pabulator has no interest in Torrens' books?'

'They've not made any attempt to keep them in print as far as I know, and it's been twenty-odd years now since they took over his publisher. If the rights weren't reverted or claimed by

Buried Above Ground

his literary executors, then technically I suppose they still reside with Boothby and Briggs, though he might have had a ten-year expiry clause in his contract.'

'You've never been tempted?'

'I'm always being tempted, Hugo – you know that. But I take it you mean by the books.'

Hugo nodded in agreement, the effort clearly threatening to affect his sense of balance. 'For your Hooded Crow business,' he said, his head still bobbing like one of those ridiculous nodding-dog ornaments you see on the dashboards of mid-range Vauxhalls. 'I would have thought the Inspector Seeley books were right up your street: a forgotten detective, out of print and going cheap.'

'I have no problem with out-of-print titles, and I do like ones I can get cheap. We don't offer any advance, so you could say we get them free; of course, we have to cover the cost of setting, printing and digitalization, not to mention promotion and exposure through social media. But' – I brandished my glass to emphasize the point – 'the key word here is "forgotten". Hooded Crow revives authors who are *not quite* forgotten. We have a huge database of customers, and we keep in touch with them on a weekly basis. They love it when we ask their opinions on books and authors and what books they remembered reading in the past. All of them will list an Agatha Christie or a Minette Walters or a Len Deighton, all of which are still in print and way out of our league, but we do get the occasional gem, usually a suggestion from a reader who can't remember the title or the author but does remember a particular detective – or a particular quirk.'

'Quirk? Such as?'

'It could be geographical location – a series set in Scotland, for instance, or in Cornwall or even abroad, in Spain or Japan perhaps. Readers can be quite parochial in where they like their crimes committed, especially the Scots. Others favour detectives to do their detecting in historical settings. World War II is popular at the moment, but there are lots of examples of Edwardian and Victorian detectives, Georgian Bow Street runners, Elizabethan detectives who all seemed to have known Shakespeare and all the way back to any amount of Ancient Roman investigators. Somebody worked out that there were more crime novels set in fourteenth-century monasteries than there were books actually produced in them. And again, it could be a trademark quirk. I can think of one modern crime writer who always had something bad happen to animals in his first two books and readers came to expect similar in all his others.'

'So what was Torrens' quirk?' Hugo asked, pushing his wine glass out of reach, which was always a bad sign. 'Or should that be his USP – his unique selling point?'

'I know what it means,' I said tetchily, 'and his particular quirk was that his books didn't have one. They were solid, reliable police procedurals which didn't stand out from the hundreds of similar ones being published at the same time.'

'But what about the revelation in *Most Wretched of Deaths*?'

I gave him my best stare of bemused disinterest until he felt it necessary to continue.

'When it was revealed that Sergeant Gerry Grimes was a woman. You have read the damned book, haven't you?'

TWENTY-TWO

At the time I hadn't, and I was frankly astonished that Hugo had. Senior 'creatives' in television rarely read books as they had all bought into the Hollywood myth that all film scripts are not allowed to be longer than eighty pages. It's not true, but they take it as gospel and simply scale it down if doing a sixty-minute TV drama. Of course, the more senior, or self-important, television bigshots can muster an army of script editors and writers to do their reading for them.

'According to my people,' Hugo said, confirming my suspicions, 'those books Torrens wrote in the nineties provide good topical plots – for the period, that is – and would give us great opportunities to raid the music back catalogue for the soundtrack. Think about it: Spice Girls, Fatboy Slim, Suede, Blur, Oasis . . .'

'Bryan Adams.' I sighed.

'Yes, but it's all instant nostalgia, along with getting the clothes and the cars right, and we'll make the nineties fashionable again.'

'Was it fashionable the first time round?'

'Doesn't matter. We create the image . . . the vibe.'

'If you'd put a gun to my head, the last thing I would have said about the Inspector Seeley books was that they were fashionable.'

'Maybe they weren't in their day, but they could be now. My researchers tell me that those last few books of his showed a nice touch of cynical realism. It was a time when politicians were stressing family values but not practising them themselves, and that things could only get better, but they didn't. The later books were also better written than his earlier stuff.'

'You've read them all? Or rather, got somebody to read them for you?' I couldn't resist.

'Of course not. Some of the early ones are impossible to find now, and my people had to scour every second-hand bookshop in the country for the more recent ones.' I let Hugo have that one as he probably wasn't aware that his minions had just done a quick internet search. 'But I'm only really interested in the later ones which set the scene, as it were. We don't actually need all the books, just one and the character rights. We could use some of Torrens' plots where they touch on topical matters – there's one about a violent group of fox-hunt saboteurs and another about homeless people living in camps made out of cardboard boxes – but the writers can always provide plotlines. I mean, how hard can it be to write a cop show? All you need is a murder early on and then the characters take over.'

'Let me get this straight, Hugo: you want to make the nineties interesting through books featuring one of the least-interesting detectives in crime fiction?'

'Come on, Spencer, you know that television can put a shine on the dullest source material.'

'Just as it can make a pig's ear out of a silk purse.'

'OK, I get it – you don't think much of the books, but I always had you pegged as someone who knew what they didn't like but still knew its value.'

'If I thought there was a market for the Inspector Seeley books, I would have republished them in Hooded Crow editions.'

'You might want to revisit that particular business decision in the future, so by helping me now, you could be helping yourself.'

Here it comes. It had taken three bottles and a good piece of meat to get here, but here we were. 'Help you how?'

'You can do something I cannot.'

'I've always known that,' I sniped, but he ignored me.

'As a publisher specializing in old thrillers, no one will turn a hair if you start sniffing around the rights to the Seeley books, but if a television producer with a Netflix budget does, prices go up and God knows who come out of the woodwork trying to get in on the action. If you actually did end up republishing the books, we could do a deal on the covers – use stills from the production. Television companies usually charge the earth for those.'

'And then some,' I agreed, 'and they date the book immediately.'

'That hardly matters with your list at Hooded Crow, does it? All your titles are dated.'

'We prefer to say nostalgic, and I never saw anything nostalgic about Inspector Seeley.'

'There probably wasn't – or should that be isn't? Anyway, it's not Seeley I'm really interested in.'

'But you want my help getting the rights to the Seeley books.'

'Just one specifically: *Most Wretched of Deaths*. We have to secure the rights to that one; the lawyers insist on that, so we have to do due diligence and all that crap.'

'Because . . .'

'That's the one where we have proven source material for the story of how Sergeant Gerald Grimes transitions into Sergeant Geraldine Grimes.'

I reached for the bottle Hugo seemed to have abandoned. 'I don't think that's what Torrens had in mind when he wrote it back in 1993 or whenever.'

I doubted that anyone in Dunkley had that topic in mind back then; surely my mother would have told me in one of her letters.

'Of course he didn't, but for years he never made it clear whether Gerry Grimes was male or female, always avoiding "he" and "she" until *Most Wretched of Deaths*.'

'I can't believe he had an agenda as such; maybe he just forgot.'

'Really? Can you think of any other crime writer who had a character without a defined gender?'

'You're treading on very thin ice if you're going where I think you're going, Hugo. Dealing with trans issues is the social media equivalent of carrying a wasps' nest into the middle of a minefield while blindfolded.'

'But that's the beauty of *Most Wretched of Deaths*. By setting it in the nineties, we're sanitized from the current debate. History gives us a firewall, and we can explore the issues through characters who didn't know the importance of those issues.'

'Whilst solving crime.'

'Well, yes – you have to have a hook to bring the viewers in, but we'll be using a cop show as a sort of Trojan horse, to examine a more serious issue. This could be big, Spencer, and a sure thing in the awards season, but you've got to help me get the rights to that book. That's the source, the Holy Grail. Once we have that, our writers can do the rest. They've got tons of ideas.'

132   Mike Ripley

'Writers can be dangerous,' I said, but I knew Hugo of old and was certain he had no intention of heeding my warning.

I had no doubt that Hugo's overambitious plans would end in tears if they ever came to fruition, but then outraged headlines and questions in parliament could be good for viewing figures. And that might be good for book sales, so having ignored Duncan Torrens' backlist (mainly because my mother recommended him), I agreed to help Hugo track down the rights.

But I was not going to get directly involved. If Pabulator learned that Hooded Crow were sniffing around titles they might consider to be inherently theirs – and we had in the past republished books which Boothby & Briggs had let go out of print – then they would make acquiring the rights as difficult and expensive as possible, especially if there was a whisper of a sensational television drama, and I had little faith in Hugo being able to keep such a project secret in the gossipy world of television.

I needed a gundog, a ferret, a researcher – and remembering the stuff I'd read online about the guy who had bought the 'found' manuscript of that last Duncan Torrens book, I was sure I had a candidate.

TWENTY-THREE

'No, Jacon Archer doesn't work here.'

'That's not the information we've been given, sir.'

'He was doing a job for me, a piece of research, but he was not an employee of Hooded Crow.'

'And would this piece of research have anything to do with a place called Dunkley?'

'It might have . . . why? Why are you asking about Dunkley?'

'Because that's where Mr Archer's body was found yesterday.'

TWENTY-FOUR

Since Covid, I had encouraged the staff of Hooded Crow to work remotely from home. They seemed to like it (one of our copy editors lives in Vienna with a boyfriend, and our main cover designer works from above a gay sports bar in Berlin) and I had been able to sublet more than half our floor area to, ironically, a firm of estate agents who couldn't find office space.

Consequently, if the front door was unlocked, it was quite easy for a visitor to negotiate the maze of shoulder-high privacy screens, step over the snakes' nests of cables loosely attached to the carpet with black gaffer tape, turn left at the bank of photo-copiers and find themselves at the heart of Hooded Crow Books: me, sitting behind a plain desk in a leather executive chair which cost more than all the other furniture combined. Most unexpected visitors usually look around bemused and say something inane like 'I expected there to be more books for a publisher', and a surprising number would be hopefully carrying plastic bags containing between two and five hundred sheets of paper bearing their deathless prose. Intruders like that were relatively easy to dispose of, and it was the duty of the most recently appointed editorial assistant to show them the exit with a charming smile and a heart hardened to any sob story deployed against them.

This latest unexpected visitor – young and sharp-suited – wandered straight in and, apart from flashing the occupants a winning smile, sailed by all the Hooded Crow workstations until he was in my face, or at least close enough to flash a warrant card, though not close enough for me to read it properly.

'Spencer Crow? I'm DC Holland here on behalf of Hertfordshire Police.'

Hertfordshire. That should have been a warning sign, but I was sure my conscience was clear. I may have passed through it, but I hadn't properly been back there since my mother's funeral. Then he started to ask about Jacon Archer and Dunkley, and alarm bells started to clang.

'Found?' I said stupidly, trying to process.

'By a local resident out walking their dog according to my information,' said the police officer, as if following a script.

'Oh, that old cliché.'

'I'm sorry, sir?'

'Sorry, that just slipped out. I didn't mean anything; it's just what they always say on the news: dog walker finds body.'

'It happens quite a lot out in the countryside, sir – you might be surprised,' the police officer said politely. 'Though there again you might not be, publishing all those detective stories like you do.'

'Funnily enough, it's not something which turns up very often in crime fiction,' I said, conscious of the fact that most police officers are fairly agnostic when it comes to crime fiction. 'But that's fiction – it's all made up. We don't have to deal with the nasty realities, like you guys do,' I added limply. 'What happened to Jacon?'

'It looked like a road traffic accident at first sight,' he said after pulling up a chair, undoing his single-button jacket before sitting and crossing his legs. I had no idea whether he was going to be good cop or bad cop. 'He was on his bicycle coming out of Dunkley down that steep hill, so probably travelling at speed. Near the bottom of the hill, the road does a nasty turn and runs along the side of the river – or that's what it looks like on Google Earth.'

I nodded in agreement, picturing the hill down from the church as I remembered it from a depressing childhood. I even recalled cycling down that hill at breakneck speed and using some very unsuitable language for the son of a vicar on the slow ride back up it.

'Seems Mr Archer misjudged the corner, ran off the road and crashed into the trees on the riverbank. Apparently there's no barrier or fencing there.'

'And the crash killed him?'

'We're still waiting for the results of the autopsy. The body was hidden by the grass and foliage' – he said it as if it was distasteful to him – 'and not found until the next morning.'

'By the traditional dog walker.'

He narrowed his eyes at me for that. 'Weather was fine, conditions dry.'

'So an accident,' I said with a nasty feeling that more was coming.

'Hertfordshire hasn't ruled out the involvement of another vehicle,' said the constable, sticking to his brief. 'Sadly, there's no CCTV coverage out there.'

'Nudging him off the road? That would still make it a road traffic accident,' I prompted.

'Except for some other suspicious factors, such as the body being moved after death and Mr Archer's bicycle being thrown into the river.'

Detective Constable Holland was studying my face for a reaction and allowing himself a tight little smile.

'Is this where I throw my hands up and scream "Are you saying he was *murdered*, Officer?" or something am-dram like that?'

'Isn't that how it goes in all those books you publish?'

'Not all of them, but one character usually says something like "Surely I'm not a suspect". Well, am I?'

'You tell me, sir – or at least tell me about your relationship with the late Mr Archer.' He pulled a small black notebook from inside his jacket as if he kept it in a shoulder holster, but as he didn't seem anxious to clap me in handcuffs, I saw no reason not to comply, albeit carefully.

'Of course I will, but can I ask how you came to call on me?'

'Jacon Archer was found with plenty of ID with his address on his body. When we informed his mother, she told us he was working for you and very excited about his job.' He squinted down at his notebook and flipped a page. 'Is that really Jacon with a "C"?'

'I'm afraid so. He was an unusual young man.'

'In what way?'

'He was a great lover of detective stories.'

'So a big fan of what you publish.'

'Not exactly. Jacon had found his tribe among devotees of what is called the Golden Age of English detective fiction, stuff from the twenties and thirties: locked-room murders, country houses, butlers doing it, that sort of thing. Not a common hobby for someone of his age.'

'He was twenty-three.'

Buried Above Ground   137

'Really? I'm surprised at that. Still, I knew he was deep into crime fiction and had a website about it, which I'd even consulted in the past, and so he seemed just the guy to help me track down a writer.'

'I wouldn't have thought that was difficult in this day and age,' said Holland. 'Aren't they all on TikTok or Instagram or Facebook?'

'Does anyone use Facebook these days? In any case, the writer in question died a little over twenty-five years ago.'

'Did he live in Dunkley by any chance?'

'Yes, Alan Hibbert did – that was his real name – but he wrote as Duncan Torrens.'

'Was that for tax reasons?'

I suppressed a giggle. 'I doubt that very much; he wasn't that well known or successful.'

'Why were you tracking him down then – if he was unsuccessful and dead, that is?'

'What we do here at Hooded Crow is revive books, specifically crime novels as they are the most popular genre, which do not deserve to be forgotten. We can scan them and digitize them to bring them to a new readership by doing them as ebooks and maybe audio versions as well as paperbacks. The Duncan Torrens books never made it into paperback in their day, and their readership was confined to library borrowers.'

My detective looked confused. 'Libraries? Are there any left?'

'One or two,' I said, 'but who needs a library when you can read a good book on your phone or your tablet or listen to one on your earbuds?'

'So Jacon Archer was out in the sticks looking for books for you?'

'Not books exactly. I set him a little research task to find out about the author, Torrens – or rather, Hibbert – who lived in Dunkley.' I got the standard police officer's thousand-yard stare to urge me to carry on. 'But I had no idea Jacon would go out there.'

'Can you think of any reason he would go there?'

'Background, perhaps. I had hoped he would write an introduction to the Torrens books if we ever did them here at Hooded

138   Mike Ripley

Crow. In his own rather specialized field, he was quite an
expert.'
'An expert in crime?'
'Crime fiction, Officer. *Fiction.*'

TWENTY-FIVE

I thought for a moment that DC Holland was going to tell me not to leave town. He certainly looked as if he wanted to, but instead he told me that someone from Hertfordshire Police would be in touch within the week. As he stood and his suit straightened itself, I waved a hand towards the eye-level shelf which held one copy of every paperback title we had published that financial year (just to prove we could use real paper and ink) and asked him if he would like a book to take with him.

'No, thanks,' he said with a half-smile, 'I've read one.'

I had no idea if he was joking.

He was not when it came to the follow-up visit a week later when I was politely asked to report to Bishopsgate police station to be interviewed by an officer investigating the death of Jacon Archer. Would that be convenient for me? I supposed it had to be, and I had done nothing wrong after all. I hadn't told Jacon to go haring off into the wild beyond the M25 – and on a push bike?

Consequently, I did not think it necessary to have a lawyer with me, nor tell Hugo, who would instantly have made plans for a true-crime documentary about the making of his controversial cop show. There was nothing in the London papers about Jacon's death and nothing new on the Gadabout website, so I trotted round to the steel-fronted cop shop on Bishopsgate with a relatively clear conscience and announced myself at the front desk to be told that Inspector Tony Walker was expecting me in Interview Room B.

In my head, I was rehearsing how many times I could say 'no comment' like they do in the television dramas but instantly decided to behave myself when I saw that Inspector Tony Walker was actually Inspector *Toni* Walker.

I'm sure Hugo would have been delighted at the similarity with the Gerald/Geraldine Grimes revelation which he intended to make the unique selling point of his proposed drama, but I

140 Mike Ripley

also thought that Duncan Torrens had simply been ironic, pointing out that the reader really shouldn't be surprised that it had been a woman doing that job all along.

'Do sit down, Mr Crow,' she said from the other side of a metal table on which rested a smart, burgundy red vegan leather shoulder bag, which I doubted was official issue. It was a production note I determined to pass on to Hugo.

I also took note that there was no double-headed tape recorder set up on the table, the one prop no actor can refuse using, saying 'interview terminated' and giving the precise time, all of which suggested that this was not going to be a formal interview.

'This is not a formal interview,' said Inspector Walker, putting my mind at ease. 'I am seeking clarification on a number of points concerning the death of Jacon Archer.'

'Jacon with a "C",' I said, instantly regretting it, as she withered me with the look she likely reserved for cheeky young shoplifters, then silently began to unpack several thin cardboard files from her bag.

In her smart dark-blue trouser suit and crisp white shirt with the top three buttons undone she reminded me of a very strict, very snooty human resources officer who once actually had interviewed me for a job in the City. I didn't get that job, but I wasn't going to hold that against Toni Walker.

'You've been advised of the circumstances surrounding the death of Mr Archer,' she said formally.

'A traffic accident I was told, on Clingo Hill in Dunkley. It's a dangerous bit of road.'

She was instantly, and very obviously, alert. 'You know it?'

I knew perfectly well that I was pre-empting one of her surprise questions. 'My father was the vicar of Dunkley for a while, and as a kid, me and my friends would race down that hill on our bikes – or sledge down it if it snowed.'

All that was perfectly true, apart from the bit about having friends.

'So you know the area.' It wasn't a question.

'I did as a child, but I haven't lived there for over twenty-five years.'

'Did you know Alan Hibbert?' She chose one of the cardboard files she had taken from her bag and carefully straightened it on the table in front of her before opening it and taking out a series of photographs.

'No.'

'That's odd, isn't it? A successful, published crime writer living in the village you grew up in and you making a career in publishing crime novels.'

'Very few crime writers are successful, and the vast majority wouldn't be recognized in the street. When I lived in Dunkley, all I could think about was getting out of the place, first to university, then into the city. Only after I made my pile there did I start up Hooded Crow.'

'Where you publish old crime novels,' she repeated in case I'd forgotten.

'Favourite stories which do not deserve to be forgotten, we like to say.'

'But not the books of Duncan Torrens – until now.'

She was speaking without looking at notes, which meant she'd either done her homework well or I had had the misfortune to come up against the one police officer who actually read crime fiction.

'I was thinking about it, which is why I asked Jacon to do some background research on Duncan Torrens, as he is something of an enigma.'

She rapped on the file with her fingernails. It was the gesture of a card player waiting to reveal an ace in the hole or at least a jack.

'An enigma in what way?'

'Perhaps that's the wrong word – recluse might be a better one. Most midlist crime writers, at least English ones, seem happy to keep their lights under bushels – though I was never terribly sure what a bushel was.'

'And you the son of a vicar,' she said, straight-faced, so I ignored her.

'As a rule, they are fairly modest about their achievements, perhaps because their achievements are fairly modest. They don't make the bestseller lists, their books rarely get reviewed and often don't make it into paperback, so they rarely get stocked in bookshops.'

'But they can get exposure through social media, can't they?'

'Now they can, but back when Duncan Torrens was writing, there was no such thing; hardly even an internet. The majority of titles we publish at Hooded Crow have never appeared before in paperback or as an ebook.'

'So how did Duncan Torrens – Alan Hibbert – make his money?'

'As a crime writer, I can't imagine he made much. His books would have only made one edition and gone mostly to libraries. He would have got a bit of PLR but, again, not much.'

'PLR?'

'Public lending right. It's a sort of compensation scheme for British authors who might have sold a few more books if people couldn't get them for nothing out of the local library. They estimate how many times your books have been borrowed, and you get a couple of pence or fractions of a penny per borrowing, but only a minority of published authors register enough borrowings to qualify for any cash.'

The inspector looked interested in that but not interested enough to take notes, and she still had not shown me the photographs in the file.

'His books were never made into television, were they?'

'No, they weren't.' This was an avenue I didn't want her to explore. 'I would have thought you would have been consulted if they'd been filmed on your patch.'

She wrinkled her nose dismissively, and I knew why: location productions of cop shows tend to be a pain for the local police force and never provided the good public relations the chief constable hoped for.

'He may not have been a bestseller,' she said, fingering the file before her, 'but he had a nice house, which you must have been aware of even as a child.'

She dealt one of the photographs across the tabletop. It was a slightly off-centre shot of a red-brick detached house which, frankly, could have been anywhere. On a garden gate, slightly out of focus, was a sign declaring 'Peacefals'.

'I suppose I was aware of it, but that's about all. It was at the far end of the village, and it wasn't called Peacefals when I was a kid.'

'You sound as if you were well aware of it.'

Buried Above Ground 143

'I got all the village news in letters from my late mother. She was quite proud of the fact that Dunkley had a writer in residence, even bought one of his books, though I doubt that she ever read it. She said he'd caused quite a stir by dying.'

'Excuse me?' She was quickly suspicious.

'I meant when he left his house as a refuge for asylum seekers. There was nothing funny about his death, was there? I wasn't living there back in . . . whenever it was.'

'1999,' she said and smoothly slid another photograph out of the file. This one showed a close-up of a headstone claiming that the plot it guarded belonged to Alan George Hibbert and his dates, 1913–1999. 'He was eighty-six and it was natural causes apparently. He was found by his care worker when she called to get him his breakfast, but it seems he went in his sleep. Local officers attended, but no suspicious circumstances were recorded. It was said his health had been failing and he was very weak.'

'Good thing he managed to finish his last book then, even though it never got published.'

Toni Walker gave me the look she probably reserved for men who tried to chat her up by asking if she wore black stockings when in uniform.

'His final Inspector Seeley story,' I continued quickly, '*The Missing Fabergé*, was submitted to his publisher but rejected, and the manuscript was thrown out only to be found years later and put on eBay. Jacon Archer bought it and wrote a piece about it on his website.'

'Why was it rejected? I would have thought there was some value as a – what do they call it on television – a season finale?'

'Hibbert's publisher was in the process of being taken over at exactly that time,' I said, steering her away from any idea of television, 'and the new owners clearly didn't fancy books by Duncan Torrens. Or maybe it just wasn't any good. It was a bit unusual by all accounts, about a missing Fabergé egg taken from Russia during their civil war, with flashbacks to Russia in 1920.'

'You've read it?'

'No, and I don't think anyone has apart from Jacon Archer. I'm only going by what he put on his website.'

'Would you say Jacon was an expert on Duncan Torrens?'

'Not especially. His field was earlier stuff, classic English whodunits from what is sometimes called the Golden Age, and his expertise was researching dead authors and forgotten books. When he came across that last Torrens manuscript, it got his juices flowing, and I set him a challenge to discover as much as he could about Hibbert – or rather Torrens.'

'Why?'

'Well, if we ever decided to republish the Inspector Seeley books at Hooded Crow, he would be ideally placed to write the introductions to them.'

'So that's why you employed him.'

'Not exactly employed; I merely offered him a freelance opportunity. I had no idea he would go haring off to Dunkley because there can't be anything to find there after all this time.'

'He found the house.' She tapped the photo of Peacefals with a fingernail. 'And also the last resting place of Alan Hibbert – or at least his ashes.' The finger stabbed again. 'And then this. Any ideas?'

She slid two more pictures out of the file. One showed a dark brown wooden hut with a grimy window, the other a close-up on the window which held a blurry reflection of a hand holding a camera phone and some vague outlines of the interior.

'It looks like a garden shed,' I said. 'I'm guessing these are from Jacon's phone.'

'Correct. Why was he interested in this shed?'

'I'd guess it had some connection to Hibbert, if only on the basis that Jacon was boring enough without having a sideline cataloguing garden sheds. Was it where he did his writing? Lots of writers work in garden sheds or summer houses if only to get away from the wife and kids.'

'That wasn't a problem for Alan Hibbert,' she said primly, 'but it seems this is where he did his writing. Here's an interior shot.' She slid another photo across. 'It's a bit murky, but you can just make out the shape of an old typewriter in there.'

'Must be an antique,' I said, then did some mental arithmetic. 'It was probably an antique when Torrens wrote his books on it – if he did, that is.'

'You don't know anything about the shed?'

'Never seen it before. I take it that it's in the garden of Hibbert's house, otherwise Jacon wouldn't have snapped it and you

Buried Above Ground 145

wouldn't be showing me it, but I've never been inside that house, let alone the garden.'

'You're not aware that the shed featured in Hibbert's will?'

'Why should I be? He didn't leave me anything in his will, but, to be fair, I'd never met him. What was so special about the shed?'

'When he made his' – she struggled to find the right word – 'bequest of the house, he put two specific conditions on it. One was that the shed remain locked and unused for ten years, and the other was that there should be no dogs in the house or garden.'

She tilted her head as if she expected an answer.

'Don't look at me. Maybe he saw the shed as a shrine to his writing career, and maybe he just didn't like dogs. From what I gathered from my mother, he was a bit of a recluse.'

'It looks that way. I hope your boy Jacon had more luck finding things out about him than I did.'

'Jacon wasn't my boy, and I don't know what he found at Dunkley – like I said, I didn't even know he was going there. He was supposed to be researching the Duncan Torrens books, not the life and times of Alan Hibbert.'

Inspector Toni began to shuffle the photographs back into her file. 'Are the books any good?'

'Depends on your tastes in reading. Do you like detective stories?'

'No. Still, I might try a Duncan Torrens if I can find one.'

'Good luck with that,' I said, and she smiled, and then she made my day.

'You're not likely to be going away over the next week or so, are you?' she said. 'In case we need to speak to you again.'

'Don't worry – I don't intend to leave town.'

TWENTY-SIX

For another week, I avoided Hugo's calls demanding an update because I had nothing to tell him, and if I had mentioned that I had met an Inspector Toni/Tony, he would have claimed it supported his idea of the Gerry/Geraldine scenario being the 'Wow!' factor in his proposed drama and would have started commissioning scripts immediately.

Thing was, I wasn't any further forward on ascertaining who had the rights to the Inspector Seeley books, unless Jacon had left some notes somewhere on his progress before his hit-and-run accident. If he had, he would have left them at home with his mother, and the fact that he still lived with his mother did not surprise me.

I realized I didn't actually know where he lived, though I could have found out by phoning Toni Walker – who had given me an official police visiting card with a direct-line number – and saying that I wanted to send flowers to his mother. But would that look suspicious or, even worse, suggest that I had a conscience?

I decided to keep my head down, screen all my incoming phone calls and concentrate on Hooded Crow, where, I was delighted to say, the ebooks were going out and the money was coming in.

It was the long arm of the law, as they used to say, which dragged me back into the story of Jacon Archer, when my presence was again requested in the Bishopsgate nick. This time, they came mob-handed, with DC Holland acting as the local guide and translator for Inspector Toni, who he almost certainly thought of as a country cousin up from the sticks. There was no doubt who was in charge though, with Toni Walker the one with the files and the remote control for the twin-headed tape recorder they had set up this time, which probably meant this was more serious.

'We meet again, Mr Crow,' she said, trying not to sound like a Bond villain, while DC Holland merely nodded and indicated I take a chair on the other side of the table.

'Thank you for coming in voluntarily, Mr Crow,' said the boss lady. 'I want to reassure you that this is still an informal interview. There are no charges being made against you.'

'As yet,' said Holland to show he was the muscle of the duo, just in case the lack of name badges prevented me from guessing which was the good cop and which the bad.

'We do, however, want to take a statement from you, and I thought it best, with your agreement, if we recorded this meeting. We'll have a statement typed up for you to sign, and you can have a copy of the tape to check it against.'

'Fine by me,' I said. 'Be just like doing a podcast.'

She raised an eyebrow ever so slightly at that then pressed the remote, and the two cassettes began to turn and a small green light came on. She went through the formalities of stating my full name – Spencer Gideon Crow – and address to show she had done her homework, and stating, for the tape, that I was happy to be taped.

'An interesting name, Gideon, Mr Crow,' which was not what I was expecting as an opening gambit.

'Perhaps to some,' I said carefully. 'I regard it as so uncool I'm glad it's relegated to a rarely used middle name.'

She twitched at 'uncool' and I wondered what her reaction would have been if I had told her that I'd gone through Cambridge telling fellow students that the 'G' stood for Goebbels and thanked God we hadn't been on Twitter back then.

'You weren't named after Inspector Gideon Seeley by any chance?' Now her face was pure 'mischievous emoji'.

'I hadn't thought of that,' I said honestly, having totally forgotten the Christian name of Torrens' bloody detective – if I had ever really registered it or read more than one of his damned books. 'But I doubt it, though my mother was a fan – or had probably read one of them.'

'Do you know which one?' asked Inspector Toni, continuing what was a diversion if not a detour.

'*Most Wretched of Deaths*, from 1992 or '93. I inherited her copy after she died. I would have been at school when it was written, so I doubt it inspired my baptism. I suspect my father being a vicar had more to do with it.'

'Did you read it?'

148   Mike Ripley

'I've skimmed it.'

'What does that mean?'

'It means I've read it professionally, as a commissioning editor would.' I hoped she wouldn't test me on it, so I changed tack. 'How about you? You said you'd try one of his books. Did you find one?'

'I did, and I want to pick your brains about that, but first I ought to get you up to speed with our investigation.'

I ignored her use of the plural, suspecting some sort of trap, and opted for the ignorant bluster of the average taxpayer.

'You guys seem to be going to an awful lot of trouble over a road traffic accident . . . a tragic one, of course.'

'The thing is, Mr Crow, we are now concerned that Jacon Archer's death was no accident. It's just possible that somebody in a vehicle ran him off the road hoping he'd crash into a tree or go straight into the river.'

'Don't look at me; I didn't know he was going to Dunkley and certainly not on a bicycle. You're not suggesting I followed him out there, are you?'

'You do own a car though, Mr Crow.' This from good lady cop.

'Yes, I do, though I mostly take Ubers around town. I keep my car in a lock-up in Dalston near where I live.'

'A Mercedes E-class Cabriolet,' said bad cop. 'Nice.'

'You've checked up on me.'

'It wasn't difficult.'

'Want to check it for Jacon-shaped indentations?'

'Should we?'

'Boys, boys, let's stick to the matter in hand,' soothed Inspector Toni, mostly for the benefit of the tape. 'Mr Crow, you remember those photographs I showed you at our first interview, which we took from Jacon Archer's phone?'

'The ones of Hibbert's old house, now a refuge? Yes, of course.'

'And of his garden shed.'

'Them too. If that's where Duncan Torrens did his writing, then I get why Jacon wanted a picture for his website. There's lots of useless nuggets about his favourite writers on there; he was a bit of a magpie when it came to the ephemera of crime writing and crime writers.'

Buried Above Ground
149

I was delighted to see DC Holland's brow crease at the word 'ephemera'. No doubt whoever typed up the transcript of the tapes would explain it to him.

'We've spoken to the assistant manager at Peacefals,' said Inspector Toni, looking at her notes. 'She met Jacon when he turned up at the refuge unannounced and tried to discover what he was after. As you might imagine, a sanctuary for asylum seekers is not the most popular of tourist attractions with the locals, and the house gets some funny visitors at times.'

'Angry villagers with torches and pitchforks? Sounds like the Dunkley I remember.'

Toni Walker ignored me, but DC Holland smirked as if he might agree with the idea.

'She engaged with Jacon Archer and said he seemed interested only in Alan Hibbert the person rather than the bequest of his house and made no request or demand to enter.'

'I can't see Jacon demanding anything. He was the sort who would apologize in advance to a goose before saying "Boo!" to it.'

'He seemed more keen to examine the garden shed – hence the photographs he took. Any idea why?'

'He was a nerd who loved trivia. Finding Duncan Torrens' writing shed would be like finding Ian Fleming's golden typewriter in an Oxfam shop. Well, maybe not quite the same, but it would be good copy for his website. I can imagine him drooling over the prospect.'

'He asked the assistant manager if the shed reminded her of a sarcophagus. What do you make of that?'

I shrugged and held my hands out palms up, then remembered the tapes were rolling. 'Jacon had a very vivid imagination, wilder than I would have given him credit for.'

Inspector Toni gave me a pitying sideways glance. 'You do know what a sarcophagus is, don't you?' No more Mrs Nice Cop.

'Of course I do.'

DC Holland leaned in to his colleague but didn't lower his voice. 'He went to Cambridge, you know.'

'Or visited the British Museum, like I did,' said Inspector Toni into Holland's face. 'School trip, when I was a girl,' she added

150   Mike Ripley

before turning back on me. 'It's a bit ghoulish, don't you think, Mr Crow? Not the normal thing to think of when you see a garden shed, is it?'

'Bit of a leap of faith. Garden sheds aren't normally made of stone, but I suppose they could be roughly the right size to take a laid-out body, though without the prospect of preserving the remains for all eternity. With creepers growing over it, moonlight and a rolling mist, you could, from a distance and without your glasses on, mistake a shed for a sarcophagus, but only if you were on the set of an old Hammer horror film and you added a howling wolf on the soundtrack.'

'Didn't you think it odd that in his bequest of the house Hibbert stressed no dogs?'

'You've asked me that before, and I told you I didn't know Hibbert or any of his little idiosyncrasies. Perhaps he was a cat person.'

'You said that maybe Hibbert fancied the shed as a shrine to his writing, but he also insisted that no one enter the shed for ten years after his death.'

'Sounds like he didn't want anyone, or anything, sniffing around,' said DC Holland with more than a hint of malice.

'Where's this going, Inspector?' I almost called her Toni but stopped myself just in time. 'I thought we were here to talk about Jacon Archer's accident.'

'I thought we'd made it clear, Mr Crow, that we suspect Mr Archer's death was not an accident. If he was run off the road and that didn't kill him, he could have been finished off with a blow from a blunt instrument and his body dragged out of sight of the road. His bicycle could have been thrown into the river, but rather strangely, his phone and his ID were left on the body. This is shaping up to be a murder investigation.'

'You may have glossed over a few of those details,' I sniped. 'Is this where I ask if I need a lawyer?'

DC Holland increased the size of the smirk on his face. 'You tell us – you're the one who publishes all those detective stories.'

'You're not under caution, Mr Crow,' said good cop.

'But am I under suspicion?'

'Not yet,' said bad cop.

'Officially, you are continuing to help us with our enquiries,

Mr Crow,' soothed the good cop. 'So tell me: have you ever read *Buried Above Ground*?'

'What?' I almost swore, if only for the benefit of the tape.

'*Buried Above Ground* by Duncan Torrens, first published in 1990.'

'It's a book,' said Holland helpfully.

'No, I've never read it.'

'I have,' said Inspector Toni, 'and I think Jacon Archer had.'

TWENTY-SEVEN

This may not have been a formal police interview, but my brain felt as if it had been well whacked by multiple truncheons.

I wasn't prepared for the way things were going; I wasn't really prepared at all, which was unusual for me, as I had always worked on the basis that one went into any meeting only to agree the minutes you had written the night before.

I had been determined not to draw attention to *Most Wretched of Deaths* due to Hugo's interest in adapting it for television, but I hadn't expected to be quizzed on an earlier Torrens title which I hadn't read. Fortunately, as Toni Walker had guessed, Jacon had, and being the nerd he was, he had blogged about it on the Gadabout website as a follow-on piece from his great scoop of rescuing that typescript from the refuse collectors.

Although not technically within his chosen time frame, the acquisition of an unpublished Duncan Torrens manuscript had clearly got Jacon excited and willing to give the author the same treatment, if not the same space, as his heroes and heroines from the Golden Age. To avoid complaints and sniping from his readers – seriously dedicated fans of the 'fair play whodunit' were known to be vicious in their comments – Jacon had actually listed Duncan Torrens in a subsection labelled 'Other Authors of Interest'.

He had adopted much the same approach as with the other authors featured: a detailed biography followed by a summary of the plots of each book in chronological order of publication. In the case of Duncan Torrens, there was little biographical information, stating simply that Torrens was the main writing name of Alan Hibbert and he had been 'active' in the years 1970 to 1999, and that his series characters had been Gideon Seeley and Gerry Grimes. Presumably, he had turned up more, at least I hoped he had, because that wasn't three hundred quids' worth, but had never got round to writing up his notes.

Buried Above Ground   153

In the section describing Torrens' books, there was a list of more than two dozen titles, which surprised me, but only the plots of two were described in any detail, keeping strictly to the Gadabout credo of not providing plot spoilers.

The Missing Fabergé was described as: thought to be the last completed Seeley novel and unusual because of multiple and very detailed flashbacks to the Russian Civil War of 1920. A bejewelled Fabergé egg of great value, if genuine, turns up on Seeley's patch and murder follows. The solution is eminently guessable, and the book was, understandably, never published.

Which I thought was a bit harsh, but the only other completed entry was for a book which Jacon clearly thought more interesting, though wasn't going so far as to say he actually liked it, and went something like:

> *Buried Above Ground* [Boothby & Briggs, 1990, £12.95] was Torrens' first book under new editor Roland Wilkes and originally had the more intriguing title *A Catafalque for Cynthia*. The plot revolves around the murder of a young woman (name changed from Cynthia to Kirstie in the book), a member of a potholing club (so lots of reference to being underground) whose body is hidden in the previously empty stone sarcophagus now being used as a decorative feature in the garden of a local country house (i.e. *above* ground). Clues fairly laid, and although some knowledge of gardening is required, it is not too difficult to spot whodunit before Seeley does.

'I've never read it,' I repeated, 'but I know of it.'

I was not going to comment on the working title of *A Catafalque for Cynthia* as DC Holland would only ask me if I knew what a catafalque was, which of course I did. I had not only been to Cambridge, but I was the son of a vicar who did funerals for a living.

'Does the title suggest anything to you?' asked the not-quite-so-good-anymore cop.

'I don't like where this is going, Inspector. I think you're leading me to talk about a book I have not read,' I said for the benefit of the tape, wanting to get my alibi, if I needed one, in first.

154   Mike Ripley

'Only the title, Mr Crow. If it was, say, a Hooded Crow book, what would you expect to find inside the covers?'

'A crime story – obviously – almost certainly a murder case.'

'And the significance of being buried above ground?'

'I suppose the body in a sarcophagus is technically buried above ground – or should that be laid to rest, as the coffin isn't actually buried; it stands on the earth, not in it.'

'In plain sight, would you say?'

'Of course; that was the whole point: you stood out from all the poor oiks who were put six feet under. In Torrens' book, as I understand it, a fresh body is found in an antique sarcophagus that's being used as a garden feature.'

'Doesn't that strike you as weird?'

'Not for a crime writer. They have bodies turning up everywhere. One of Jacon's favourite Golden Age mysteries, according to his website, involved a victim being boiled to death in a copper vat in a country brewery. You wouldn't believe some of the scenarios.'

'We might,' said DC Holland, as if it was a threat.

Toni Walker did not wait for my reaction. 'Where do you think Torrens got the idea?'

'How would I know? I was still in nappies, or thereabouts, when he wrote that book.'

'Jacon Archer seemed fascinated by the plot. We have statements from two people he spoke to in Dunkley and he mentioned sarcophagi to both of them.' She consulted her notebook. 'The assistant manager at the Peacefals refuge and a Mrs Cunningham, a local resident.'

I remembered Mrs Cunningham from my mother's letters and from my mother's funeral, where she gave both me and my car a come-on look whilst undoing the top button of her blouse and trying half-heartedly to smooth down a skirt far too short for her age. If she'd met with Jacon, I was surprised he had got out of Dunkley alive – but then he hadn't.

'Mr Crow?'

'What?' I had drifted for a moment.

'Do you see any connection between Mr Archer's interest in sarcophagi and his photographs of Alan Hibbert's garden shed?'

'I've told you he was a nerd and finding an author's secret writing shed would have got his juices flowing.'

'I meant physically. As you yourself said, a sarcophagus and a garden shed share a common property. They're both . . .'

'Above ground,' I finished for her.

'Knew he'd get there in the end,' muttered DC Holland.

'Wait a minute . . . ' I said over the alarm bells ringing in my head. 'Are you saying that Hibbert's garden shed is a sort of sarcophagus and that there's a body inside?'

'Yes, we are, and yes, there is,' said the good cop.

TWENTY-EIGHT

'**Y**ou look rather relieved, Mr Crow.'

I was.

'I am, Inspector. If you've found a body where there shouldn't be one, then you're looking for someone to blame, and I've read, and published, enough police procedurals that if you had me in your sights, then you wouldn't be telling me this without an official caution and my brief being present to make sure all I said was "no comment".'

'Quite right, Mr Crow, you are not being treated as a suspect,' said Toni.

'Not yet,' muttered DC Holland.

'Hey, hold the phone,' I said as my brain caught up with the latest news. 'Are you thinking that Jacon's interest in the shed, and those photographs he took, means he knew there was a body in there?'

'No, we're not saying that. It is possible that Archer somehow knew or suspected there was a corpse in the shed, though he gave no indication of that to the assistant manager he talked to at the house. We have more or less ruled him out of being responsible for placing the body as the initial forensic report suggests that it has been *in situ* for around thirty years.'

'Which would rule me out also. I like to think I was a precocious child but not *that* precocious. We are talking murder, aren't we?'

'We have to wait for lab results and further forensics to be sure, but at the very least we are looking at the unlawful disposal of a body.'

'And not one found by a dog walker for once,' I said, remembering my first session with DC Holland.

The look on Toni Walker's face suggested she was not amused, which was fair enough. After all, murder is always a tricky business.

'Funny you should say that,' she said and left it hanging in the air between us.

'Why?' I was genuinely perplexed.

'When Alan Hibbert left his house to the county council to be used as a refuge, he stipulated that his shed be untouched for ten years and that no dogs be kept on the property. At the time, those were probably thought to be the whims of an eccentric old man who had no family or friends. The council got a useful property, which will have increased in value considerably by now, and so didn't ask too many questions at the time.'

'No dogs; no sniffer dogs, no dog walkers,' I said, joining the dots. 'Clever.'

'If you've hidden a body.'

'Do we know whose body?'

'No, we have been unable to make an identification so far, but we're hopeful. All we know so far is the body is female, around twenty-five years old and possibly non-British.'

'Foreign dental work,' I said, feeling part of the team.

'How the fuck did you know that?'

Inspector Toni silenced her colleague with a laser-beam stare, but whether for his tacit admission or his language, I wasn't sure.

'It's a common trope in the books I publish. Russian spies are spotted by their dental repairs, and our spies going in to Russia have to have their teeth doctored to pass muster. I've no idea whether that's true, by the way, and I've no time for police officers – fictional officers – who identify bodies by their "dental records". I mean, if they've no idea who somebody is, how do they know who their dentist was?'

'Fair point, Mr Crow, but we are not dealing in fiction here. We have two bodies in Dunkley – two very real, dead bodies to deal with.'

'And you're sure they're connected?'

'If nothing else, there's a connection to Alan Hibbert's shed, in which Jacon Archer seemed remarkably interested. Did he not mention this to you? He was working for you after all.'

'He was doing research for me, but as I've said, I had no idea he was even going out to Dunkley. If he thought he'd discovered a crime writer who had hidden a body, he would have creamed his jeans – if you'll pardon my French. It would have been gold dust for his website and got him on to a million podcasts.'

'What *exactly* was Jacon researching for you?'

'He was looking into the situation regarding the rights to some of the Inspector Seeley books for me, with a view to me reissuing them at Hooded Crow.'

'Including *Buried Above Ground*?'

'Not especially; I was more interested in the later titles,' I said, which was slightly true.

'And what did Jacon uncover for you?'

'Very little – or rather I should say he reported back to me on very little.'

'Anything on Alan Hibbert's private life?'

'I didn't know he had one. My mother mentioned him occasionally in her letters when I was at uni, but I can't honestly remember much. I got the impression he was a bit of a recluse, but I never paid that much attention to Mother's ramblings, and back then I wasn't interested in publishing crime fiction or crime writers.'

'Was he married?'

'I wouldn't know, but I guess not. My mother would not have missed a chance to slag off a Mrs Hibbert if there had been one . . .'

I felt myself faltering in mid-thought and then having a light-bulb moment, though it's often wiser not to turn on the lights.

'Just a tick, are you telling me that the body in Hibbert's shed is his wife?'

'No, we are not saying that because we do not have a firm identity yet, but it's interesting that you thought of it.'

I shrugged. 'Automatic response. Aren't most murder victims killed by someone they know and love? Well, maybe not loved that much.'

'Clearly because of the timeline, we have to assume that Hibbert knew the body. It was his house, his shed and then there was that codicil to his will which stipulated that no one go into the shed for ten years and no dogs be allowed on the property.'

'And you think Jacon's interest in the shed indicates that he suspected there was something nasty in there? How could he have known? I mean he's younger than me so couldn't have been around Dunkley thirty years ago, could he? Did he see something when he took his pictures?'

Buried Above Ground 159

'Probably not,' said Toni Walker, and I felt both officers studying my face closely. 'According to our information, the only thing Jacon Archer was interested in photographing inside the shed was that typewriter. The decomposed body was found in a shallow grave under the floorboards during a sweep by our forensics people. It couldn't be seen by anyone looking in through the window, but we are working on the hypothesis that Jacon knew, or suspected, it was there.'

'Why?'

'Because it gives somebody a reason, a motive, for killing him almost immediately after he started sniffing around the shed,' offered DC Holland gleefully.

Toni had the good taste to wince when he said 'sniffing' given what had been said about sniffer dogs and decomposing bodies.

I shook my head to clear it. 'I don't get it. Are you saying that Jacon was bumped off by someone trying to protect the reputation of Alan Hibbert, who's been dead for a quarter of a century?'

Inspector Toni widened her eyes and tilted her head to one side in a you-tell-me gesture.

'You're the crime-writing expert,' said Holland quietly. 'Was it a reputation worth defending?'

'Absolutely not. I can think of hundreds of crime writers superior to Duncan Torrens.'

'Yet you were thinking of publishing his old books.' I had the feeling that Toni Walker had been waiting to slip that one in. 'That's why Jacon was researching for you.'

'Jacon was good at ferreting stuff out, stuff about dead crime writers. He'd got hold of that manuscript of the last Inspector Seeley book and that sparked a bit of interest on his website. It also got him interested in Duncan Torrens, so he seemed just the guy to do some digging.' I realized I was now choosing my words badly. 'Not that he did any actual digging – as in digging up a body – did he?'

'No. I got our scenes of crime officers to do that because Jacon Archer had shown such an interest in it.'

'But Jacon couldn't have known there was a body in there.'

'Not unless he'd read the book.'

160   Mike Ripley

'What book?'

'*Buried Above Ground*,' said the helpful cop. 'You really should read it.'

TWENTY-NINE

'One other thing,' she said, channelling the Columbo technique of interviewing a suspect as she shuffled and stacked her files like a newsreader at the end of a bulletin.

'Yes?' I was wary but confident that I wasn't an actual suspect. Well, fairly confident.

'You said that Jacon Archer was researching the rights to Duncan Torrens' books for you.'

'As well as general background information, yes.'

'Even though he's dead?'

Now I felt on safer ground.

'A writer's copyright lasts for seventy years after his or her death, and that copyright could be held by a literary estate, a relative, a trust, a charity or an agent. To republish the books, we have to get the agreement of the rights holder.'

'Why didn't you ask his last known publisher?'

'His only publisher, as far as I am aware, was Boothby and Briggs and they got taken over in 1999. If they still have the rights, they've done nothing with them, and if they thought Hooded Crow was after them, they might make life difficult.'

'And what? Stop you getting some thirty-year-old books back into print? I would have thought that could only be good for the reading public.'

I stifled a laugh. 'Welcome to the world of publishing. But you've got a point.'

'I have? Do tell.'

'Boothby and Briggs were devoured by a multinational company, but they still keep the imprint going for certain titles, such as crime fiction. There may be somebody still there who remembers the books of Duncan Torrens; maybe somebody who remembers Alan Hibbert. I would certainly think Jacon tried them first.'

I crossed my fingers.

162   Mike Ripley

'Would you have a contact there?'

Bingo.

I waited until DC Holland had his notebook out and his ballpoint clicked.

'Robina Robinson. She's been with Boothby and Briggs forever and I believe is quite senior. She was certainly there in Alan Hibbert's time. It couldn't hurt to have a word with her.'

Of course, knowing Robina, I was hoping it would hurt, and if nothing else it would take the heat off me.

Part Four

The Editor

THIRTY

D uncan Torrens? Christ, there's a blast from the past. He was one of Edward Jesser's favourites and got away with murder when it came to some of the ropey books he turned in. I don't know how Edward put up with him, apart from the fact he was a guaranteed seller to the libraries, which was Boothby & Briggs' main bread and butter after all, and Torrens wasn't that much trouble as far as authors go, I suppose.

He was unlike most writers who get a book published. Even one where the entire print run goes straight to libraries or the remainder dealers, they start calling themselves authors, even have visiting cards printed saying so, and they think they're God's gift. Then the pleading starts. Why aren't my books in bookshops – or even WH Smith? You did send out review copies, didn't you? Any progress on selling the American rights or translations? Has it been entered for the Crime Writers' Association awards? Should I be doing talks in libraries? Would having an agent help?

Torrens wasn't that sort of writer at all; in fact, he was a small publisher's dream in that he didn't complain, not even about the size of his advances, didn't crave publicity or promotional activity, didn't demand his photograph on the back of his jackets, never argued about copy-editing corrections or when we changed the bloody awful titles he came up with. Biggest plus point of all, he never turned up at the office unannounced demanding a free lunch – you'd be surprised how many do that. In fact, once Edward stopped being his editor, he started communicating by fax, so there was no personal contact at all, though funnily enough, the books improved.

Torrens had done about thirty books for B & B under Edward. In fact, Edward Jesser was his first publisher, maybe his only one, though he might have written under other pen names. Writers who can churn out two books a year can easily manage to spew out four, going all out for quantity over quality. These days, with ebooks and self-publishing, it's even worse, and I've come across

166 Mike Ripley

not one but two crime writers who each have produced thirty books in the last five years. At least, being mostly electronic, only a few trees had to die thanks to them.

Torrens got his break into print thanks to Edward Jesser back in the seventies, and Edward always said it was a classic case of 'the old boys' network' rather than him spotting the merit of a debut author. He meant it quite literally, as Torrens, or rather Hibbert, and he had been at the same all-boys' school. Not as pupils, of course; Hibbert was Edward's English teacher and helped get him into Cambridge. They kept in touch, and when Hibbert tried his hand at writing a murder mystery, he offered it to Boothby & Briggs, where Edward had his feet well and truly under the editorial desk.

He published it very much as a favour to an old friend – you could get away with that in those days – although he didn't expect it to do much. He once told me that *The Body at Starling Junction* was the author ranting about the closure of his local branch line station rather than a crime novel, but it did introduce Inspector Seeley and Sergeant Grimes – those two characters seemed to have legs and were worth a series.

For years, Edward wouldn't let anyone else at Boothby & Briggs touch the Seeley books; they were his pet project, and he guarded them – and the author – closely. Behind his back, we used to say this was because the books weren't very good and required a lot of rewriting, which may have been true, but I think it was simply a question of loyalty. Never mind the old boys' network – Edward was truly old school, a proper gentleman. He always said that Alan Hibbert had inspired him in the classroom, and he felt obliged to repay that debt.

Not that he talked much about him as an author. Torrens' books were very much a private venture for Edward Jesser, and without his support there would probably not have been so many of them – any other author writing that badly would have been dropped like a hot brick. But, to be fair, his detective duo did pick up quite a few fans as the series went on.

I started at Boothby & Briggs as Edward's secretary in the days when there were still such things as secretaries – the twilight era of the shorthand typist before there were emails – and I know that Edward would write to Mr Hibbert – it was always

'Mr Hibbert' – after he received the manuscript of the next Duncan Torrens. Occasionally, he would tell him of the changes he had had to make to the text, almost apologizing for having to do so. Hibbert never complained and always accepted Edward's judgement.

Edward always said Alan Hibbert was the ideal author, happy to keep out of sight and out of mind, and I got the impression that their relationship was a close, though very private, one. Edward rarely let anything slip in his letters, but it was clear Hibbert lived alone and was someone of whom the obituary writers – had he merited an obituary – would have coyly said 'never married'. I do remember one letter when Edward offered him his condolences on the fact that Hibbert's teaching career had 'ended far too soon', but he never explained what he meant by that, and I was in no position to ask.

No one ever saw Alan Hibbert at the office; everything was done by snail mail in those days, though I know Edward would drive out to Dunkley to visit him. He even asked me if I could suggest a home help agency as Hibbert, who was getting on, lived alone and was not doing too well on it.

Things came to a head in 1989. Alan Hibbert would have been seventy-six. The book he'd turned in for that year was a bit of a dud, and the synopsis he submitted for the next one was batshit crazy. Edward Jesser had had enough.

I remember the title – you couldn't forget it: *A Catafalque for Cynthia*, and if I had to look up what a catafalque was, what chance had the average borrower from a public library? The plot involved the murder of a domestic servant, a scullery maid – and this was 1989! – whose body is concealed in an ornate catafalque, the wooden box used to hold or move a coffin at posh funerals. Hibbert's plot revolved around the fact that a coffin was a scary image and you knew what would be inside one, but a catafalque was basically a box, kept in plain sight, not six feet underground. You might expect a coffin to be in one if you knew what it was but not a body, freshly murdered. Such a thing you could walk past for days until you smelled something fishy, so to speak.

It was ridiculous and a bit disgusting, so Edward decided it was time to do what publishers had always done with problem authors – pass them on to someone else.

168   Mike Ripley

I had been doing a fair amount of copy-editing on several
B & B series, and Edward clearly thought I was ready for the
step up to associate editor, but I knew it would be a poisoned
chalice given Edward's personal connection to Alan Hibbert.
Consequently, I did the sensible thing and suggested that one of
our brightest young editors – both 'bright' and 'young' being
relative terms at B & B – Roly Wilkes would be a better choice
to supervise the ongoing career of Inspector Seeley.

Edward did not take too much persuading. Wilkes would be
a safe pair of hands and, most importantly, they would be male
hands, which Edward admitted might be a consideration, as he
had convinced himself that behind the plot of *A Catafalque for
Cynthia* was the fact that Alan Hibbert was 'not getting on' with
his current home help, who was, wouldn't you just know, called
Cynthia.

I admit that when Edward told me that, I thought he was
suggesting that Alan Hibbert, and an unwilling Cynthia, had acted
out the plot of his next novel. That wasn't the case, of course
– Cynthia was alive and well and far more likely to murder Alan
Hibbert than he was to put her in a catafalque.

And I can't say I would have blamed her from what I saw of
the way he treated her.

It was the one and only time I saw Duncan Torrens in the
flesh.

THIRTY-ONE

There was plenty of rumour and gossip in the B & B offices when word got around that the boss was taking his 'secretary' on a jolly into the countryside – not that anyone said anything to his face, and they wouldn't have dared say anything to mine. It was anything but a fun away day from the office; Edward Jesser was too much of a gentleman to play fast and loose with his female staff – I don't think the thought ever crossed his mind in all his years in the business. Publishing really is, or was, a fairly straight-laced and well-behaved industry in those days. And if Edward was taking his (much) younger secretary out of the office for a bit of hanky-panky, then surely to God he would have taken her somewhere more exciting than Dunkley and Alan Hibbert's grotty garden shed.

The house was bad enough, clearly the home of a man who lived alone and who had abandoned all hope of rectifying the situation. There were open books lying stranded on every flat surface, many layered with dust, and the whole place reeked of ingrained cigarette smoke, which did little to mask the pervading smell of damp and mould. Hibbert's home help, the very-much-not-in-a-coffin Cynthia, had declared a work to rule and refused to deal with anything that was not directly concerned with cooking his meals or doing his laundry. It turned out that this was due to the barrage of shouted abuse hurled at her by her employer should she even contemplate touching his 'sacred volumes' – and he actually called them that, though from what I could see they were mainly ancient reference works or old school textbooks. There was even an old Philip's School Atlas which had a Flags of the World page and Germany's was a swastika! A decent Oxfam shop would have turned its nose up at them.

Hibbert greeted Edward Jesser like the old friend he was, totally ignored me and shouted for Cynthia to get off her fat arse and make tea and crumpets for their guests. I had just enough time to exchange looks with Cynthia, who was standing in the

170   Mike Ripley

kitchen doorway slowly shaking her head, then I was following
Hibbert and Edward, who were already out of the French windows
and marching across the garden to a wooden shed which wouldn't
need a Kansas tornado to blow it away.

'So this is where the magic happens,' said Edward as Hibbert
ushered him inside.

It is a cliché which has always made me squirm, just as any
writer with a grasp on reality (and there are few of those left)
would squirm and have forbidden its use at Boothby & Briggs
should any of the staff find themselves in one of our author's
homes where the spare bedroom has been converted into a 'study'
or, pretentiously, 'the office'.

Alan Hibbert was even more pretentious and announced, in a
voice which could have called the faithful to prayer: 'Welcome
to my humble *scriptorium*.'

Humble it certainly was. After all, it was just a shed which
reeked of nicotine and compost – at least I hoped it was compost
– with a single light bulb dangling from a flex and one garden
chair in front of an old-fashioned school desk, the type which
had a hole for an inkwell and where the lid lifts up to reveal
cheerful obscenities carved with a penknife. On the desk was a
huge, ancient typewriter that from a distance could resemble a
North Sea oil rig, which was where Hibbert bashed out his potboilers. Next to it was a wire in tray with a stack of typewritten
pages – typewritten on foolscap sheets, not standard A4 size,
which were clearly far too modern a concept for a scriptorium.
I knew from having seen a previous manuscript that Tippex was
also an undiscovered country. Instead, ever the schoolmaster, he
used a pen with red ink to correct his mistakes, but only rare
mistakes of punctuation or mistyping. Correcting his plots, his
superfluous descriptive passages, his antiquated dialogue and his
narrative structure was all left to Edward.

If he was a favoured author because he never complained about
alterations made by his publisher, he was certainly typical of
most authors who insist that their next book will be their break-
through novel and certain bestseller. (An unsubtle and certainly
not foolproof way of asking for a bigger advance.)

Consequently, as we stood in his cramped and dingy shed,
Hibbert waved a sheaf of paper under Edward's nose and went

into a long and animated exposition about Inspector Seeley's latest case, which involved a catafalque, whatever that was. To be honest, I zoned out within the first five minutes and found myself more interested in the ants and various bugs creepy-crawling over the floorboards, but it was clear that I was surplus to requirements in that little love-in between author and editor.

I doubt either of them noticed that I excused myself and returned to the house just in time to find Cynthia coming out of the kitchen, putting her coat on. Though we had not been introduced, I knew instantly what was going on.

'I'm off,' she said as if no other explanation was necessary, and I knew she wasn't talking about the end of a shift. 'I've had enough, so I'm taking my fat arse out of this nuthouse and it won't be coming back.'

I don't remember exactly what I said but probably something along the lines of how it couldn't be that bad. But of course I didn't know the half of it, though Cynthia was more than willing to enlighten me.

Nowadays, we would probably describe it as early onset dementia, but back then Cynthia had a more basic medical assessment: Alan Hibbert was a nasty, vicious old git whose memory was shot to pieces along with any sense of personal hygiene. Only the fact that he lived alone, virtually as a recluse, stopped him being locked away as a danger to himself or the population at large. It was only a matter of time before he was shouting at people waiting at the bus stop in the village, hopefully having remembered to put his trousers on.

There was no arguing with Cynthia, who, having told me that her resignation letter was attached by magnet to the fridge, flounced out. The letter wasn't sealed in an envelope, just a folded sheet of paper, so naturally I took a peek. Whilst Cynthia complained so violently about Hibbert's bad language that her biro had gone through the paper, she demonstrated that she could turn a colourful phrase of her own, especially when describing her employer as reeking of sweaty secretions with a personal hygiene rating lower than that of a pig in a sewer.

When Hibbert and Edward came in from the garden, he asked where that 'stupid bitch' was – or rather where was his tea and why wasn't that stupid bitch making it? Although he was not

172   Mike Ripley

talking to me directly, I helpfully pointed to the note pinned to the fridge. Hibbert snatched at it, read it, then flung it to the floor and said that he supposed I would have to 'do the honours', to which I stupidly said I would.

That was my only conversation with Alan Hibbert, and I can't honestly say I'm sorry about that.

THIRTY-TWO

On the drive back to London – and I couldn't get out of Dunkley fast enough – Edward apologized profusely for Alan Hibbert's behaviour.

He was old, had no immediate family (and probably no distant one willing to acknowledge him) and had lived a solitary life since leaving (for reasons unclear) the public school where he had taught Edward. Clearly, he was less and less able to look after himself – the overriding stale stench of the house as well as his personal body odour bore testimony to that – and Edward suspected Hibbert had suffered a minor stroke, possibly two. Most importantly, his books were requiring more and more work before they were fit to publish.

The obvious answer was to reject *A Catafalque for Cynthia* and drop Duncan Torrens as a B & B author, but there was no way Edward would do that, although he did admit that he could no longer face the prospect of editing his books. He left that hanging for far too long before he popped the question, so I was ready with a surprised yet humble expression, my eyes as wide as they would go, when I said that whilst I was flattered, I was far too inexperienced to be Duncan Torrens' editor, a stalwart of the firm's crime-fiction list. Naturally, I had ambitions in that direction, but the long-running Inspector Seeley book series was, as yet, above my pay grade.

I knew that any mention of 'pay grade' would put Edward in a panic, and so I offered him an immediate way out by pointing out in all innocence – and I was good at innocence in those days – that Roly Wilkes was well versed in crime fiction and an editor who could rise to the challenge of handling Duncan Torrens.

I think he murmured, 'Yes, bright chap,' and I knew that I had, as the Americans might say, avoided the very bad bullet.

But not quite.

He drove in silence for ten minutes, mulling things over, then he sighed loudly, as if having come to a decision on which the whole future of Boothby & Briggs depended.

'Roly can handle the editorial side,' he said at last, 'but Alan clearly can't be left on his own. I'm relying on you to find a replacement for Cynthia.'

'Of course,' I said immediately before considering what I might be letting myself in for. But as it turned out, it was quicker and easier than I expected.

Back then, before the internet, there were lots of small employment agencies, especially in Soho, who could provide temporary staff, sometimes highly specialized staff, if you know what I mean, on very short notice. Shorthand typists had been their bread and butter, but they also handled waitresses, butlers, bodyguards, nurses, extras for crowd scenes in films, cleaners, language tutors and even nurses. In Victorian times, they would have had a couple of hundred governesses on their books, perhaps a dominatrix or two. Surely one of them could supply a reasonably honest home help who could cook a bit and put up with an irascible old man. She – I knew it would have to be a female – would get board and lodgings as well as minimum pay but would have to settle for being out in the sticks, out of London. The job would ideally suit a woman escaping a violent marriage or one on the run from Holloway.

The vacancy was filled almost immediately thanks to the Berlin Wall coming down and Gorbachev loosening the chains on Soviet Russia. Suddenly, there were hordes of young East Germans and Russians seeking job opportunities in the West. It was a strange time, and the end of the Cold War threatened to put all our spy fiction writers out of business. One of them even started a spoof campaign against Gorbachev for threatening his livelihood!

The most attractive females, almost always the blondes, soon found work as 'models' or 'escorts' in Soho and began to advertise their services on postcards stuck up in telephone boxes – when there used to be public telephone boxes. They were rather disparagingly known as 'KGB Wives', but some of them had nursing skills and passable English, even if they didn't have the right visas and work permits.

That was how we found Alice.

Buried Above Ground

She was a pretty nineteen-year-old (she said) who had done three years' training as a physiotherapist in some unpronounceable place east of Poland. She was small but muscular with the build of an athlete, which she needed to support that bosom, a snub nose on which she balanced a pair of big round glasses, which turned out to be plain glass and only there to make her look more intelligent, and wore her hair – blonde, of course – scraped back into a loose ponytail. Her English was excellent, and she had no qualms about working for an elderly gentleman living out in the countryside, though she had absolutely no idea where Dunkley was.

Edward Jesser, who had insisted on interviewing her, said he did not hold that against her because hardly anybody in England did, and she had laughed politely at that, which had probably got her the job. The clincher was that she was happy to work for a very modest wage as long as she could live in with 'the client'. She was from a small village and preferred the country to the hustle and bustle of London. (She actually said 'bustle and hustle' which endeared her even more to Edward.)

I should have been suspicious, I suppose, a girl of that age with those looks off the leash in London, footloose and fancy-free, yet she was happy to be trapped without a car out in the wilds with a crotchety old git like Alan Hibbert. I gave her a week, assuming she got through her second interview with our not-so-famous, far-from-bestselling author.

I would have quite liked to have sat in on that first meeting between Alice and Alan, but I wasn't invited. Edward drove her out to Dunkley, having picked her up from an unsavoury bed-and-breakfast place off the Tottenham Court Road, and, according to his post-match report, Alan was quite smitten with Alice and wanted her to start immediately. Perhaps he had run out of clean underwear.

Bizarrely, Alice seemed equally keen and enquired about trains and buses out to Dunkley the next day. Knowing there were no direct trains anymore and the bus service had probably been privatized, Edward played the gentleman again and offered to transport her and her luggage. I was not allowed to go on that trip either, so I never saw Alice's triumphal arrival at her Manderley. All I learned was that Edward had been required to

176 Mike Ripley

make an initial detour to a Polish delicatessen on the Edgeware Road so that Alice could stock up on various pickles and an obscure brand of vodka which she was sure were not going to be available in Dunkley, and she was right about that.

Edward spent the better part of a week commuting to Dunkley to make sure his favourite author was 'settling in' – not, you'll note, that Alice was settling in – and I was left in the office to break the news to Roland Wilkes that he was now the editor of the Inspector Seeley series.

It felt like the start of a new era, as if Edward Jesser had freed himself from some obligation and a weight had been lifted from his shoulders. He seemed to enjoy work more; certainly he began to entertain authors, fellow publishers and even agents lavishly. Perhaps too lavishly.

Modern technology began to impinge even in Boothby & Briggs as computers came in to replace electric typewriters and emails began to replace secretaries. I moved over to editorial, initially as a copy editor, quite smoothly and without any undue influence from Edward Jesser, despite what the office gossips whispered. Edward didn't really need a secretary anymore, and with no one to keep him under control, his business lunches became more frequent and longer. He even began to attend the growing number of crime-writing conventions and conferences which sprang up in the nineties, sent a small sales team to the Frankfurt Book Fair and hosted a modest drinks reception at the London Book Fair.

When he died – suddenly but quietly and undramatically – he was, in a sense, living his best life and had become something of a standard bearer for the independent publisher. That didn't last long, of course, as the other shareholders in Boothby & Briggs, including Edward's widow, couldn't wait to sell out to the first multinational that came calling.

Passing on the burden of editing Duncan Torrens made those last eight or nine years easy and enjoyable – as if Edward had finally been able to get on with his life. Amazingly, the Inspector Seeley books seemed to get better.

THIRTY-THREE

It wasn't that they stormed the bestseller lists or started getting rave reviews or anything, but library sales not only held up but pre-orders actually increased over the next four or five books. Nobody was going to get rich, but it suggested that Inspector Seeley was maintaining a loyal fanbase at a time when all library borrowings were declining until Harry Potter came to the rescue.

I had nothing to do with Duncan Torrens' books; I had authors of my own to edit and, like Edward Jesser, I was quite happy to leave them to Roly Wilkes. I have no idea if Roly reported to Edward on Alan Hibbert's health – he certainly looked pretty sickly that one time I saw him – and if Edward enquired after him, he didn't do it through me because I was no longer a mere secretary.

I never read any of those Inspector Seeley stories when they were published, and after Edward died and Pabulator took over, there were not going to be any more, as Alan Hibbert had luckily died before the new corporate broom could sweep him clean. Any unsold stock was discounted massively to clear the warehouses, and the office file copies went to charity shops. Nobody missed them, and I don't think I heard the name Duncan Torrens mentioned for twenty years, until now.

In view of recent events, I thought it best to find out what all the fuss was about, which normally would mean talking to his editor – which was out of the question as Roly Wilkes had long since been let go – or reading the books – and who has the time for that, even if copies were available? Fortunately, in the clear-out which followed the Pabulator buyout, I had tucked away a complete set of the biannual Boothby & Briggs catalogue – or at least the catalogues which covered my time as an editor there. After all, if things hadn't worked out with Pabulator, I might have needed them to bolster my curriculum vitae.

Each catalogue, aimed mainly at the trade rather than genuine

178   Mike Ripley

readers, listed recent and forthcoming titles with a paragraph or two describing the new (or sometimes new*ish*) books to be published in the relevant six-month period and half a paragraph about the author. In the case of Duncan Torrens, the biographical note was short and not particularly sweet. It said, and it was the same in all those catalogues, that Torrens was the creator of the 'much-loved' Inspector Gideon Seeley mysteries and had written more than two dozen novels. That was it, and I recognized the B & B touch in the reference to 'two dozen', which was office shorthand for the fact that no one knew for certain how many books Torrens had published and no one could be bothered to count them.

When it came to his books and last ten titles after Edward Jesser bequeathed him to Roland Wilkes, there was just enough information alongside a picture of the jacket to hopefully tempt a library buyer or a bookseller into placing an order. No great imaginative effort had been put into the copy, and the clear assumption was that this was another 'in the popular Inspector Seeley series', which was either an imprimatur of quality or code for saying 'more of the same'.

A book a year followed until the catalogue for the second half of 1998 (all the Torrens titles being published in October), the entry for 1990 being *Buried Above Ground*, which I remembered as being the positively awful *Cynthia's Catafalque* or some such daftness.

Roly Wilkes had persuaded Torrens to drop 'Cynthia' and that stupid title. The female who got herself murdered – and it usually was a female in the Seeley books – had become Kirstie, which was a popular enough name then; certainly there weren't many Cynthias about. Her body (though you didn't know it was hers from the catalogue) was found in a fake sarcophagus in the gardens of a country house. She had been a member of a pothole and caving club, whose gruesome motto was that the members all hoped to be buried above ground, rather than die in the dark in some subterranean cavern in the Peak District. Placing the victim's body in a sarcophagus above ground was a nice tie-in to that club motto and no doubt a clue which led Inspector Seeley to the murderer, for he invariably got his man, and his loyal library readership would have it no other way.

Buried Above Ground

The 1991 Seeley, *The Herb Border*, according to the catalogue blurb, was 'a traditional English village mystery' – and whoever wrote that clearly fought hard not to add the words *like so many others*. All the traditional elements were there: a village horticultural society with the usual parochial rivalries about who takes first prize in flower arranging or who can grow the most obscene root vegetable, a campaign of sabotage of the annual flower and produce show, and a fatal poisoning of its guest judge – the local vicar. (A couple of years later, that vicar could have been a woman. If only Torrens had waited.)

The next three books were unusual, although I didn't notice at the time, in that their titles all came from something called the *Meditations* of Marcus Aurelius, who was a Roman emperor, as everybody who saw *Gladiator* knows. I have no idea what prompted Hibbert to turn to the classics; perhaps he also taught Latin or Greek at the posh school where Edward went.

Not that those three books had anything to do with Ancient Rome, at least not from their catalogue entries, which had them down as fairly standard Seeley mysteries.

Most Wretched of Deaths revolved around threats to kill local journalist Anne Divine, who had reported on previous Seeley cases but now found herself at the centre of the mystery. *Small Is the Span* apparently featured another minor character from Seeley's world – his boss, Superintendent "Grumpy" George Sixsmith, who is devastated by his son's suicide and calls on Inspector Seeley to undertake an unofficial investigation. The catalogue adds that this is 'Gideon Seeley's saddest and most sensitive case to date' – and that was meant as a recommendation.

The title listed for 1994, *One Who Is Afraid of Death*, was notable for 'finally going behind the scenes of a police detective's domestic life' and promised to show the stresses and strains of fighting crime on a previously blissful marriage. Now this was something new, as Mrs Seeley – I'm sure she must have had a first name – had previously been securely in the background of the book, there only to make sure Seeley had a clean shirt every morning and to complain (gently) that another dinner had been ruined by Seeley working late. If the novel was a portrait of a marriage under stress, then Hibbert must have had some vestige

180   Mike Ripley

of an imagination, as he wasn't drawing on personal experience, was he?

The next three books had more conventional titles and owed nothing to Marcus Aurelius according to their thumbnail descriptions in the catalogue. In *Unlawful and Premeditated*, Inspector Seeley has to solve a murder 'twenty years in the careful planning' whilst *Seamless Death* saw Seeley and Grimes – Sergeant Grimes getting a dynamic duo credit for once – investigating the death of a village seamstress who may have left the name of her killer hidden in a piece of embroidery. For *The House Guest Who Never Left*, it was as if the title was self-explanatory and the catalogue entry said merely that this was another case for Inspector Seeley.

The last catalogue listing for Duncan Torrens was for October 1998 for *The Attainder*, and it would be the last Inspector Seeley book to be published by Boothby & Briggs. That title was not only out of whack with the rest of the series but pretty meaningless to the general public, and the catalogue write-up didn't exactly help, claiming that it was 'a legal conundrum which Seeley and Grimes have to solve to prevent a murder'. I had to look up what an attainder was, and it's a medieval thing where land and property is confiscated from a person, usually a man, under sentence of death and given to the state or the king or the local sheriff.

It wasn't billed as the last Inspector Seeley, so I'm thinking Alan Hibbert hadn't checked out by then and, technically, the last one was *The Missing Fabergé*, which was never published. Duncan Torrens was definitely no more by the time that manuscript was delivered, but neither was Edward Jesser or – once Pabulator took over a few months later – Roly Wilkes. I do remember reading it when Roly left – or at least part of it, as I don't think it passed the S-Point. That's the standard criteria used by crime-fiction reviewers: you give a book up to page fifty and if you don't give a shit about the plot or any of the characters, then the book hits the wall. Or in this case, the skip at the back of the office.

It was a terrible book, lots of backstory about the Russian Civil War and a fake Fabergé egg, neither of which seemed natural territory for Inspector Seeley and Sergeant Grimes, who by this time was known to be Geraldine, not Gerald.

That had been quite an innovation – or a massive mistake – in *Most Wretched of Deaths* and will probably be the thing Duncan Torrens is remembered for, if he's remembered at all.

THIRTY-FOUR

'Jacon Archer remembered him. Tell me about him.'

I had agreed to see Inspector Toni Walker in my office once I realized it would be Toni and not Tony. It was perfectly in line with Pabulator policy to promote the role of female detectives in crime fiction, and if in fiction, why not in reality? As long as senior management was aware of my stance, it couldn't do me any harm career-wise, assuming, of course, that she wasn't here to arrest me. Which was clearly not the case as she had combined an official trip to the big city with some shopping on the side, and turned up for our meeting with a Selfridges bag and a box from Irregular Choice on Carnaby Street, which showed she had a whacky taste in shoes when off duty. Those impressed me far more than the sight of her police warrant card. She didn't ask me if I minded her parking her shopping while we talked, but if she had, I would have said, 'You go, girl!'

'Ah yes, Jacon with a "C" not an "S". The strange little man who runs a website dedicated to detective stories which went out of print when his granny was a virgin. An unusual obsession for someone his age but not unknown. He's probably somewhere on a spectrum.'

'Was,' she said, wrinkling her nose in reproach. 'He's dead and the reason I've come to London to see you.'

I checked out her shopping bags but held my tongue. 'I don't see how I can help; I never had anything to do with him.'

'But you had a meeting with him. He had it logged and high-lighted on the laptop we recovered from his home.'

'It was hardly a meeting,' I said after pretending to think for a while. 'More an ambush.'

Now an un-plucked eyebrow went up at the word 'ambush', and I thought I had better play it straight.

'It wasn't planned, that meeting. At least not on my part. It was at a launch for one of my authors in a bookshop off the Charing Cross Road. We don't normally do book launches,' I said as if I had to explain, 'but the author was a wealthy lady who didn't write for the royalties, which was just as well as she would have starved, but she took great pride in being a published author and loved to show off in front of her friends. So when she insisted on a launch and offered to pay for the Prosecco and peanuts, we supplied some of her books. We may even have sold a couple to friends and family. You look surprised.'

'I didn't know authors paid for their own book launches,' she said with a shrug, as if it really wasn't important.

'Not the big ones, the ones who insist on going on tour and demand a first-class ticket and a car to meet them at the station, even if they're only booked to appear at a garden centre in Sidcup. But only the top sellers get that. A small imprint with a lot of midlist authors can't afford it.'

'But you're a massive multinational. Don't you own Sweden or somewhere?'

I had to laugh at that. 'The parent company is certainly a global business, but Boothby and Briggs is a specialist imprint within that. We don't make much money, but we don't lose any. It's my job to make sure that continues.'

Inspector Walker looked up from the notebook resting on her crossed legs and surveyed the office, its furniture, the wall hangings and general decor, which I had helped design. She stared at the big window overlooking Soho Square before speaking again.

'You must be good at it . . . your job, I mean.'

She knew I had registered the definite pause in that sentence.

'I am, but B and B is only one of the imprints I am responsible for within Pabulator. I am a senior editor on several others which publish science fiction, horror, fantasy and women's fiction.'

'Chick lit?'

'We don't like that cliché, unless it helps with marketing.'

'But nothing that would appeal to Jacon Archer.'

'I guess not, but he wasn't at that launch for the author; he was there to waylay me.'

'So how did he get invited?'

Now she was back concentrating on her notebook, her ballpoint poised.

'A general email invite went out to reviewers, bloggers, librarians and basically anyone we could think of. It costs us nothing

184 Mike Ripley

and shows support for our author. Amazing who turns up when you say there will be drinks and canapés, even if the canapés are a jumbo bag of salted peanuts and not even dry roasted.'

'So Jacon did have an invite?'

'Well, yes, but only really to make up the numbers. Nobody wants a book launch where nobody turns up – that just looks sad. I intended just to show my face, say hello to my author, knock back a couple of Proseccos – I remember the days when it was always bad Algerian red at these events – and then bugger off home and put my feet up. A couple of the girls from Pabulator's publicity department were on duty to supervise the party, so all I had to do was be nice to any reviewers from the national papers if they'd bothered to turn up – which they hadn't. Last thing I expected was to get pinned up against a mountain of Richard Osman novels and be given the third degree by a creep like Jacon Archer.'

'Creep?'

'Oh, definitely creepy. I don't think he even introduced himself, just launched into Duncan Torrens this, Duncan Torrens that, like he was obsessed. It didn't matter to him that there was supposed to be a party going on – or that I was flashing warning signals telling him to piss off in no uncertain terms.'

'I can see you'd be good at that,' said Inspector Walker cheekily.

'Oh, I am – that's how I've survived so long. Over twenty years working for our Viking overlords at Pabulator.'

'Weren't the Vikings a rough crew? When I was at school, they were famous for raping and pillaging.'

I couldn't fail to spot the twinkle in young Toni's eye. 'Well, they've calmed down a bit in recent times and now restrict their pillaging to old-fashioned publishing companies like Boothby and Briggs. As for their penchant for rape, I've never noticed it, and in any case, we have a huge HR department should anyone even suggest it.'

'Would you describe Jacon Archer's approach as aggressive?'

'Good Lord, no. He was annoying, but he didn't frighten me. To be honest, he didn't look as if he could take the top off a yoghurt without help, and he wasn't drinking; that's usually where the trouble starts at a book launch. He was persistent and totally

Buried Above Ground   185

unaware of what was going on around him, totally lacking in social awareness. All he wanted to talk about was Duncan bloody Torrens and what a shame it was that it's no longer possible to buy his books.'

'And you didn't?'

'A mediocre author who died in the last century? Give me a break! My last dealing with Duncan Torrens was rejecting his book about Russia and Fabergé eggs.'

I must have curled a lip at the thought, which Inspector Toni picked up on.

'Did that annoy you?'

'Almost everything about Jacon annoyed me, but that didn't at the time.'

'But it did later?'

'The next morning, just out of interest because he'd niggled me, I checked out Jacon's Gadabout website and found the piece he'd written about buying Torrens' manuscript from some geek who'd found it in a skip, which is where it should have stayed and where it belonged. Jacon hadn't mentioned that small fact or that he was asking Gadabout readers, or subscribers or whatever they call themselves in the fan world, for info on Duncan Torrens.'

'And you were suspicious?'

'Curious. I mean the Inspector Seeley books were not Jacon's drug of choice when it came to crime fiction. He was clearly stuck in the "fair play" Golden Age school; Duncan Torrens would be far too modern for his taste.'

'You mean he didn't play by those rules I've read about?'

I was impressed that she'd done her homework, but I wasn't going to tell her that.

'The famous Golden Rules of writing detective stories as laid down by the Detection Club in the twenties, which said that nothing supernatural was allowed, and you couldn't have more than one secret passage per book? No, that was all tongue-in-cheek bollocks, and I don't think anyone ever took them seriously – well, maybe Dorothy L. Sayers – but Torrens did stick to some of the unwritten rules of crime writing, the accepted tropes of the genre.'

'Such as?'

186   Mike Ripley

'Such as giving a character who appears early on in the story the means and motive to do the murder, but of course he's not the killer, which becomes clear when there's a second murder – and there usually is. And then of course there's the resolution where the murderer is caught and punished – that's very important. Crime-fiction readers must see justice done, and you can't have the murderer getting away with it.'

'Doesn't sound much like real life,' Inspector Toni said as if genuinely interested.

'It's completely artificial, but we're in the entertainment business.'

'There's nothing entertaining about crime.'

'It's a living.' I shrugged and smiled sweetly.

'You mean there's money in it.' Suddenly she'd pulled on her judgy knickers.

'I've no complaints about my career in publishing crime fiction,' I said. 'It's been good to me and I will miss it when I retire . . . in a few years' time.'

I didn't mention the fact that my well-planned retirement would take place in a converted water mill in a small Tuscan village with an excellent gelateria and hot and cold running Chianti. I didn't want to rub it in.

'I'm sorry' – though she didn't look sorry at all – 'I was thinking out loud. There must be money involved somewhere in Jacon's interest in Duncan Torrens.'

'I like your cynicism,' I said, 'and you might be right. Was there something in that manuscript I dumped all those years ago or some added value in the Inspector Seeley books that I'd missed?'

'Added value?'

'An extra income stream becoming available: audiobooks, downloads, ebooks, that sort of thing. These days, any and all income streams are exploited; something to do with marginal gains of profitability – they all add up, and it's always better that we have them than our competitors.'

'Television rights?' she asked with a big sigh.

'I feel your pain,' I said. 'I know you guys want another cop show on your telly bots like you want a hole in the head. Frankly, at the level of the vast majority of our authors, the very idea is a pain in the arse. Books do get optioned for telly, but very few actually make it to the small screen, and more options run out of time than ever get taken into production. If you think publishing is slow and ponderous, we're positively jet-propelled compared to television drama. The big problem is with our authors. Just the mention of a television option and they get the vapours and start playing the fantasy casting game – you'd be amazed just how many English detective inspectors George Clooney has been suggested for.'

'I'd watch that,' said Inspector Toni.

'So would I,' I admitted, 'but for most it remains a fantasy. It's a lucky, lucky few who get picked out of the slush pile. There have been cases when a popular actor has been instrumental in getting a crime novel turned into successful television, but it is really rather rare.'

'Surely the Seeley books have past their sell-by date as television fodder?'

'Not necessarily. Television producers don't read much and because they've never heard of a forty-year-old novel, they assume it's new to everyone. I can think of several crime series that took more than twenty-five years to make it to television and one which took over fifty, finally appearing two years after the death of the author, though I doubt the author would have recognized his original characters.'

'So Inspector Seeley could still be a viable proposition for television?'

'It's unlikely but just possible. Telly can make a silk purse out of a sow's ear, though it mostly does the exact opposite. Still, it got me thinking about the current status of the rights to the books. I mean, I had to if someone else was sniffing around them, even a nerd like Jacon Archer, so I put one of our interns on to it.'

'Intern?'

'They were called Youth Opportunities back in my day, but now they're unpaid interns trying to get a year's work experience in publishing to put on their CVs. Mostly they're chinless wonders keeping busy after uni until they can access their trust funds, or they're would-be influencers waiting for their Instagram sites to get a million followers. Still, we have one called Jake who's not totally dim, and I set him to digging up what he could on Duncan

188 Mike Ripley

Torrens and the rights to his books – particularly ebooks. I may have given him a bit of a vague brief – in fact I'm not sure he even realized Torrens was dead, but it got him out of the office and out of my sight.'

'Annoying is he?'

'Not really; more *distracting* and disgustingly young.' I tried to exchange knowing, girl-to-girl looks, but she kept her eyes on her notebook. 'So I told him to go and see Roly Wilkes, the last editor to have handled Duncan Torrens. If anybody knew anything about that last decade of Inspector Seeley books, it would be him. I told Jacon Archer that too, just to get him out of my hair.'

'Why didn't you contact Roland Wilkes yourself, directly?'

'That would have been difficult. Well, uncomfortable and difficult.'

'Because he was made redundant when the Pabulator takeover happened?'

'That didn't help, and Roly probably blamed me for it – still does – but that was business. Roland and I had *history*.'

THIRTY-FIVE

I didn't see any harm in telling my friendly local police detective; I mean I'd never done anything wrong. Well, not criminal. It had been over thirty years ago and couldn't possibly reflect on Pabulator in any way, so my approaching retirement age and subsequent chunky pension were not in danger.

'Back in the old Boothby and Briggs days, everyone assumed that Edward Jesser was knocking off his much younger secretary – me.' I was slightly disappointed that Toni did not look shocked, nor was she taking notes. 'Which of course he was, or rather I was having an affair with him. We kept it very discreet, and I'm sure his wife never knew or suspected. The odd thing about our affair was Edward's enthusiasm . . .'

The inspector looked up, startled.

'. . . which suddenly waned, at exactly the time we dropped Duncan Torrens on to Roly Wilkes from a great height. I thought Edward, free of that burden, would perk up a bit.'

I was enjoying Inspector Toni's unease; after all, one doesn't get the chance to intimidate someone younger and slimmer without being reported these days.

'But instead, he lost interest, at least in me. Distancing himself from Duncan Torrens, or at least the editing of him, gave Edward a new lease of life, just not with me. He began to really enjoy his role as a veteran publisher and industry commentator, always doing bits and pieces for *The Bookseller* and *Publishing News* and getting on juries for literary prizes. He was even the guest speaker at the Crime Writers' Association annual awards – and gave more or less the same speech at the Romantic Novelists' shindig, which he said was a far scarier event.'

'So your affair with the boss ended when he passed the Duncan Torrens books over to Roland Wilkes?'

'It started to taper off then,' I admitted, 'but that wasn't the main reason for Edward's waning interest.'

I waited until she looked up from her notebook again, as I wanted to see her face.

'I think Edward realized that I was also sleeping with Roly Wilkes.' I paused for the dramatic effect I always encourage my authors to add at the end of chapters. 'I told you we had history.'

She was still not taking notes, but at least I had her attention.

'He was nowhere near the accomplished lover Edward Jesser was, but he was certainly grateful . . .'

Inspector Toni stabbed her notebook with her biro.

'Interesting as this is, Miss Robinson' – I noted the 'Miss'– 'I'm really here to find out about Alan Hibbert. How is this personal background relevant?'

'It's relevant,' I said in the tone I usually reserve for the sales department, 'because Hibbert was Duncan Torrens the writer as far as we were concerned, and when the torch of being his editor passed from Edward to Roly, it affected them both; changed their behaviour you might say. Edward became more relaxed and began to enjoy life more, and Roly, well, Roly came out of his shell and seemed to really enjoy working at B & B, even though we'd passed him what we'd thought was a poisoned chalice in Alan Hibbert. He couldn't dump the Seeley books because of Hibbert's relationship with Edward, so he had to make them better, which by all accounts he did. I can't say I read them; I had enough on my plate progressing my own career.'

'Were you Roland Wilkes's boss at this time?' She poised her pen above her notebook.

'Not then but soon after. I was going up; Roly was going nowhere.'

She made a quick scribble. I guessed it was the word 'grateful', probably underlined.

'So Roland Wilkes got on well with Alan Hibbert?'

'I've no idea.'

'But he was his editor, and you said the books improved.'

'Both those things are true, but neither means the editor has to be bosom buddies with the writer. Quite often, an editor improving a writer's books leads to a straining of relations. Some writers rely heavily on their editors; most probably see them as a necessary evil standing between them and seeing their names on the cover of a book.'

Buried Above Ground 191

'But they worked together well, didn't they?'

'If they did, it didn't mean they went down the pub or picked out curtains together, but the manuscripts came in on time and passed muster – all bar that last one – so, yes, they seemed to work well together.'

'The normal editor/writer relationship?'

'I don't think there's anything normal about those relationships, but Roly seemed to have the ideal one with Alan Hibbert. There was no agent to get in the way, and he kept Hibbert at the other end of a fax machine.'

'What's a fax machine?' she asked with a smirk – the bitch.

'The thing before email – go Google it. The beauty of it, back then, was that you could send corrections and changes back and forth without having to suffer the whining author on the phone or even, God forbid, in person. For a while, it seemed a clever way of keeping authors at arm's length, but then everybody got email, and nowadays some are demanding to have Zoom calls to defend their precious prose, for Christ's sake.'

'So they weren't close?'

'Not as far as I know, but I didn't take much interest. The books kept getting published on time, and that's what mattered.'

'And Roland Wilkes never talked to you about Hibbert, given your relationship?'

'You mean as in pillow talk? Not likely! We didn't waste time talking, certainly not talking shop.' I wasn't keen on the look she was giving me. Back then, I was her age now and footloose and fancy-free. 'In any case, our relationship was not much more than a fling. Edward Jesser didn't like playing second fiddle to a junior employee, and he was always a better option than Roly, who, to everyone's surprise, went off to plough pastures new, to coin a phrase from one of Pabulator's bestsellers this year.'

'So he never mentioned Hibbert's health deteriorating?'

'Can't remember that ever came up. When I met him, he was clearly a bit doolally – or experiencing a form of cognitive impairment, as we're supposed to say these days. I guess he could have got worse over the years – he certainly got older. What was he when he died? Eighty-six? Still, he kept churning out the Inspector Seeley books, right up to the end.'

192 Mike Ripley

Inspector Walker flipped a page in her notebook and cleared her throat to show she was being serious.

'We've spoken to several doctors and social workers who saw Alan Hibbert in the last ten years of his life, including the doctor who signed the death certificate.'

'Any suspicious circumstances? Sorry, occupational habit. I read too many crime novels.'

'Not about that death,' she said pointedly. 'That was natural causes. Hibbert had been ill for a while. Early onset dementia aggravated by two or possibly three minor strokes. He was recommended for an assisted living place but refused to consider it and had his solicitor write to his doctor to say he would violently resist any attempt to hospitalize him.'

'Could he do that?'

'A solicitor would write you a letter staking a claim to one of the moons of Jupiter if you paid their bill. Hibbert was described as a good client.'

I laughed. 'There's an old saying in publishing: always beware of the author who says he doesn't need an agent because he has a good lawyer. Not that Hibbert was a troublesome author. He kept himself to himself, or at least he did when Roly was looking after him.'

'And Roland Wilkes never reported any problems with Hibbert?'

'Not that I can recall. If there were issues about the books, they were sorted out by fax. We never saw Hibbert at the office, and he never did public events; I doubt he ever got invited to any. Out of sight and blissfully out of mind.'

'So no concerns about his health or well-being?'

'Why would we have? Sure, he lived alone, and he didn't have family or any relatives, but he had housekeepers and carers and doctors and social workers, or district nurses if they still existed back then – you said that yourself.'

'You found one of those live-in carers for him, didn't you, back in . . . 1989?' She had looked at her notebook for the date, but then she gave me both barrels with her eyes. 'A girl called Alisa Bulova.'

'Ah yes, Alice.'

'Tell me about Alice.'

'You should be asking Roly Wilkes; he married her.'

THIRTY-SIX

I explained that Alice had been a stop-gap measure. When Edward Jesser and I had visited Hibbert out in Dunkley, Cynthia, his housekeeper, walked out leaving the miserable old sod all alone. She certainly had good reason to want to see the back of him and probably got out just in time. Remember, he'd written the first draft of *A Catafalque for Cynthia*, and it wasn't just the rubbish title that upset Edward; it was Hibbert telling him how he was researching the plot and how he was going to dig a grave in the garden and then build another garden shed over it.

He did all his writing out in the garden shed he already had, so it was clear where the idea came from, but what was disturbing was he was telling us how he'd dispose of 'Cynthia' whilst there was a real Cynthia in earshot, making us a cup of tea. God knows how she felt, but it worried Edward, who already feared for Hibbert's sanity, though neither of us really thought Hibbert would actually do the deed – he was just plotting out loud.

Cynthia quitting whilst we were on the premises prompted us to take action. After all, Edward not only had a long-standing relationship with Hibbert and that strange notion of loyalty that affects men more than women, but Hibbert was one of our authors with a book due on which an advance had been paid, so it was a question of protecting one of the company's assets.

We needed a replacement who could handle Hibbert and his moods – or at least run faster than him. Actually, Alice could have floored him if the need arose. She was a tough cookie who wasn't going to be easily intimidated by bad language and erratic behaviour – common traits among crime writers, I'm afraid. Edward, being a sensitive soul, feared for her well-being stuck out there in the sticks with Hibbert and doubted she would last a month, but I'd looked into her eyes and seen the steel. I even told Edward not to worry as her KGB training would kick in, which he thought was me being bitchy and jealous.

194   Mike Ripley

Not that I saw Alice as a threat to my relationship with Edward. She was pretty enough and lively enough, though far too young for him, and she knew nothing about crime fiction. What stumped me was what she ever saw in Roly Wilkes, apart from the obvious: a passport.

To be fair, Roly was probably the most normal person she came into contact with in Dunkley. When he became Hibbert's editor, he would have gone out there to meet him as Hibbert didn't travel – all his fictional settings for the Inspector Seeley books he got from reference books, not that Seeley often left his regular patch, which was never properly identified anyway. That's an old trick of crime writers. Rather than be caught out making mistakes of geography, they keep things vague and often make up fake names for real towns or just gloss over where they actually are.

I know Edward asked Roly how Alice was getting on with Hibbert, the subtext being whether they had killed each other yet, but Roly always reported that things were going smoothly, as far as he knew. The Seeley books continued to be written, getting better if anything, and Hibbert had got himself a fax machine so there was no need for any personal contact, which was a relief to all concerned; out of sight, out of mind, so to speak.

I don't know how or when Roly hooked up with Alice. Maybe it was at weekends, as he certainly didn't make trips to see Hibbert from the office. That would have been suspicious; no editor wants to see an author more than once a year if it's avoidable. And Roly always was a secretive sod, so it was a bit of a bombshell when he asked to see Edward one morning to tell him that Alice was leaving Hibbert's employ – he even used that word, 'employ' – in order to get married. Second bombshell: married to him.

I do know that it had happened quickly. The relationship between Roly and I had gone off the boil, not that it was ever volcano hot, and I was seeing less and less of him at work. There was no big break-up or blazing row – we just drifted apart. Both of us saw it coming and neither of us could be bothered to do anything about it, and nobody at the office ever suspected anything had happened between us. Roly was now a proper editor and taking his job seriously, and I was working my way up the B & B

Buried Above Ground

corporate ladder; plus, with Roly taking on Duncan Torrens' books, Edward was enjoying life more, and there were opportunities for trips abroad to book fairs and conferences, which he had convinced his wife were boring, boozy events where publishers of the old school bragged about deals they wished they had done.

Then Roly took our breath away with his announcement. Only Edward and I at B & B knew who Alice was – most of the staff knew little and cared less about Duncan Torrens – so it didn't cause that much of a stir in the office. Not enough people there admitted to being friends with Roly, so there was no stag do that I was aware of, and if Alice had a hen night somewhere, I wasn't invited.

She couldn't have been with Hibbert for much more than a year, and according to Edward, who still phoned the old sod occasionally, he was very happy with her and had been impressed by the fact that she never asked for holiday or time off. Now that was suspicious to me for a girl her age, and I was sure she was happy out at Dunkley because she was lying low, hiding from someone or something. Still, that wasn't my problem – it was now Roly's. To be fair, he got Hibbert registered with social services and hired some home helps, although Hibbert refused point-blank to employ a gardener, even though he could well afford it.

Roly and Alice got married in a registry office somewhere up Camden way. I wasn't invited – like I minded – but Edward and his wife went and said it was a dismal affair. The only bit of gossip was that the happy couple were buying a detached, new-build house in Watford, despite soaring house prices and the awful mortgage rate, and the assumption was that Alice must have brought some cash to the table as Roly's B & B salary certainly wouldn't stretch that far.

That would have been 1992 because it was the year *Most Wretched of Deaths* came out; the one where Sergeant Gerry Grimes is revealed to be a woman. That got Inspector Seeley into the review sections, and Roly was riding high on it, though it was not a break-through book for Duncan Torrens. The next book wasn't reviewed at all, and library orders slipped back to their normal level.

Such is the transience of success in publishing – and in marriage too. By the time *One Who Is Afraid of Death* came out in '94, Roly and Alice were getting divorced.

196 Mike Ripley

I heard about it on the office grapevine – not that it was a big topic for gossip. Roly's private life, unlike mine, was never of much interest to his work colleagues. He kept himself to himself and as far as I know had never introduced Alice to anyone in the office. It was one of the girls in Finance who told me, at that year's Christmas party, that Roly had changed his address because he was having to sell his house, despite a massive amount of negative equity. We all tut-tutted and muttered something sympathetic and then promptly forgot about it. Roly carried on at work as if nothing had happened, and Duncan Torrens continued to turn out a book a year, and I don't think anyone mentioned the name Alice Wilkes.

When Edward died, we all turned out for the funeral, and there was no suggestion that Roly would come with a 'plus one' unless it was Alan Hibbert, but he was too ill, too old and too addled to attend. He died shortly after Edward did, and then Boothby & Briggs went through the shitstorm of the Pabulator takeover, and very quickly both Roly and Duncan Torrens were history.

It must be twenty-five years since I heard Alice's name or even thought about her. Until now.

THIRTY-SEVEN

'You've found a body, haven't you?'

I don't know why I felt so nervous about saying that. My conscience was clear, and it was a scene I'd read in a hundred crime novels.

'Yes, we have.'

Inspector Toni was cool. She had obviously done the Breaking Bad News course; a seminar many crime writers wished their editors had taken.

'And you think it might be Alice?'

'We have been unable to definitely identify the body yet, I'm afraid. That it might be that of Alisa Bulova or Alice Wilkes is just one theory we are working on.'

'But it's definitely female?'

It felt good to be asking the questions, almost like being the detective in one of the crime novels I had to edit. If I had been more familiar with Duncan Torrens' output, I might have adopted the interviewing tactics of Inspector Seeley – or should that be Sergeant Gerry Grimes?

'Certainly female,' said the real police officer, tight-lipped, 'age estimated as early twenties.'

'And certainly murdered?'

'Oh yes. We didn't need an autopsy, or an archaeologist, to tell us that. Probably strangled is my guess at the official verdict. And such a method rules out suicide, apart from the fact that she took all her clothes off, dug a grave and buried herself, before you ask.'

Inspector Walker was clearly not in a playful mood.

'She wasn't found in a sarcophagus or a catafalque or whatever it was in the Duncan Torrens book, was she?'

'Not quite, but there are certain similarities to the plot of *Buried Above Ground*, as I'm sure you'll be aware.'

'It's a long time since I read it,' I admitted, hoping that wouldn't count as perjury, 'and then only a rough first draft.'

198   Mike Ripley

'Well, and I hope I'm not teaching granny how to suck eggs here' – *Granny?* The cheeky cow! – 'but in that story, the murder victim is buried in a shallow grave over which the murderer erects a garden shed. In this case – this real case – the grave was dug under the floorboards of an existing garden shed and then the floorboards replaced.'

'Hold the phone, sister!' The inspector gave me a look which suggested the last thing she wanted to be was my sister. 'Are you saying that Hibbert killed Alice, buried her in the shed he did his writing in and then went on to calmly write another five or six more novels with a body rotting away under his feet?'

'I'm saying nothing of the sort, unless you have additional information which may clarify the situation.'

'I certainly do not!'

'Pity. I thought you might have been able to offer an insight, given your long experience of crime fiction.'

'When did the police ever listen to a crime writer or editor? Not that there's any reason they should; we deal in fiction, make-believe. Real police officers usually say they can't stand crime fiction because it's not realistic. It's not supposed to be! And when retired officers try and write crime novels, they might be realistic, but usually they're pretty boring and badly written.'

'I wasn't looking for literary criticism, merely an insight, if you had one, on the mental state of one of your authors.'

'He wasn't *my* author; I wasn't his editor.'

'But you were his publisher.'

'We publish hundreds of authors and very few, far fewer than you might think, turn out to be criminals of any ilk, certainly not homicidal maniacs. Anyway, you don't have definite proof that it is Alice in, or under, Hibbert's shed?'

'Not yet, but we have yet to find anyone who has seen her alive since 1994.'

'Jesus! Did nobody report her missing? Like her husband?'

'Ex-husband. She and Roly Wilkes got divorced, remember?'

'What about her employer?'

'We can find no record of Alice working anywhere after she left the employ of Alan Hibbert.'

'Which would be when she got married.'

'Married and then disappeared. A common-enough experience for a lot of women, so I've been told.'

'You're not wrong there, sister,' I agreed, 'but from what I can recall, Alice did not strike me as a girl who would go quietly into that dark night. She struck me as one tough cookie who could take care of herself. Have you considered the possibility that Alice wanted to disappear? I mean, she was a young woman looking for a life of fun this side of the Iron Curtain and she opts to go out to Dunkley to look after a grumpy old git like Hibbert, miles from anywhere and with no car.'

'But she flew the nest, so to speak, by marrying Mr Wilkes, and escaped Dunkley.'

'For a new-build semi in Watford with Roly? That's hardly jumping the Berlin Wall for a life of decadence in the liberal West, is it? If you ask me, that was Alice changing one safe house with an unfashionable writer for another with a boring partner and a massive mortgage, neither of which were likely to offer her the high life.'

'Are you suggesting Alice was determined to keep a low profile? Talking about safe houses makes her sound like a spy.'

'Perhaps she was, though God knows what she was spying on out at Dunkley, and I can't imagine Roly Wilkes had any secrets worth stealing. I always suspected she came with some sort of baggage.'

'But you never got a hint of what that might be?'

'I didn't know her and had no inclination to engage in girl talk with her. As far as Edward and I were concerned, as long as she was prepared to put up with Alan Hibbert and all his moods, and not go mental and kill him, she was the girl for us.'

I caught Inspector Toni's expression. She was urging me to state the unasked but obvious, so I did.

'But we know Alice didn't kill Hibbert, don't we, because he went on living and writing after 1994 or whenever she disappeared. So the no-brainer question must be did Hibbert kill her and bury her under his shed?'

Inspector Toni tapped the end of her pen against her teeth as if this was a theory worth considering. She wasn't fooling anyone, certainly not someone who had read this fictional scene a million times. She had a bombshell and was keen to drop it.

200   Mike Ripley

'That would seem to be the logical conclusion, but if Alan Hibbert murdered and buried Alisa Bulova in or around 1994, why did he change his will in 1997 and leave her just over £11,000?'

Part Five

The Writer

THIRTY-EIGHT

had felt guilty about lying to young Jake Philbin, though not much. If I had misled him, it had been partly out of pique because he had constantly referred to Duncan Torrens, not having bothered to do the basic research and find his real name, and partly because I was damned if I was going to do anything to help Boothby & Briggs and their Scandinavian overlords after the way they had treated me.

Everything I had told him about 'Duncan Torrens' was, technically, more or less true. My dealings with Torrens, mostly by fax, were professional and devoid of the innate suspicion and histrionics which are the usual background music when editor meets author over a manuscript rather than lunch. I cannot say I ever had a casual conversation with Torrens the author and certainly not what might be considered social contact.

When I had dealings with Duncan Torrens, I was dealing with a fax machine or a typewriter. It was an unemotional, civilized, totally professional relationship which produced nine serviceable crime novels and could have produced a (posthumous) tenth if Robina Robinson had not been so keen to bend the knee to B & B's new owners.

With the person behind the Duncan Torrens brand name, it was another matter. I had pretended not to have known, or even met, Duncan Torrens in person, which in a way was true. But dear, precious young Jake's life was never going to be troubled by any misdirection or downright lies on my part. If he did decide to pursue a career in publishing crime fiction, which I personally doubted, he would soon become familiar – all too familiar these days – with the concept of the unreliable narrator.

If Jake had taken his errand, or me, seriously and done a modicum of basic research, then he would have asked about my relationship with Alan Hibbert, which was anything but unemotional and civilized – or even legal.

THIRTY-NINE

I must have realized at the time – I certainly hope I did – that in becoming Alan Hibbert's editor I was grasping a poisoned chalice with both hands. For me, it was a promotion, but he would almost certainly see it as a demotion, as for years he had enjoyed the undivided attention of Boothby & Briggs' most senior editorial executive, Edward Jesser.

Quite what Edward's relationship was with Hibbert I never discovered and knew only that it dated back to Edward's school-days, but I had no inclination to pursue the matter. There was enough gossip floating around the office – there always was – without adding to it; gossip about me and Robina Robinson for a start.

I suppose I should have been more suspicious about why Edward was so keen to hand over the editing of the Inspector Seeley books, especially as he always maintained, at least at meetings in-house, that Seeley and Grimes were his favourite fictional duo and how he enjoyed their investigations more than those of Dalziel and Pascoe and even Morse and Lewis, though few in the firm, especially not in the sales team, agreed with him publicly. When I was offered the job as Hibbert's editor, I rapidly read a clutch of his more recent novels and began to glimpse the problem. His plots were becoming more outlandish, their resolutions more slapdash, and his dialogue veered from the clichéd to the surreal. The pending novel which he had submitted for publication in 1990, and for which Edward had authorized the advance, was, frankly, awful and needed a lot of blue pencil.

It was clear to me that Hibbert was losing his powers of concentration and Edward Jesser was no doubt losing patience with him, but where the usual publishing maxim of 'who will rid me of this troublesome author?' did not seem to apply in this case, a Plan B was needed, and I was it.

Edward was very clear with his instructions. I was to do what I could to improve the prose and coherence of the manuscript

Hibbert had submitted, and do it without damaging the author's ego. I was also, as a personal favour to Jesser, to keep a watchful eye on Hibbert's well-being, which he defined as being the writer's health and sanity, both of which were growing matters of concern.

At this point, Hibbert must have been seventy-six or seventy-seven, and my understanding was that he was a lifelong bachelor who had lived alone and isolated for twenty-five years or more since 'leaving' the teaching profession. I got the distinct impression that his departure from teaching was far from voluntary but thought it wise not to ask for any details.

Edward was worried that Hibbert was not eating enough and possibly drinking too much. I knew even back then that a good editor should never come between an author and their alcohol consumption and suggested, rather timorously, that I did not see myself in the role of nursemaid. Jesser reassured me that Hibbert was to have live-in help, and indeed he and Robina Robinson were currently interviewing suitable candidates. Hibbert could afford it, Edward reassured me, as even without his meagre royalties, he had enough funds for such things plus private healthcare if needed. He had little else, said Edward, to spend his money on, having no pastimes or vices, or at least no known ones. All I had to do was check in on him occasionally to make sure he was not being taken advantage of by the home help, assuming any home help they hired could put up with his outbursts of temper, forgetfulness and increasingly voluble Tourette's syndrome.

Hibbert had chosen the life of a hermit because he was aware of his mental and physical failings, and Edward Jesser insisted that I respect this decision and on no account allow 'Duncan Torrens' to make any public appearances at libraries, book clubs, village fetes and such like, and certainly not let him give any media interviews, not even to the weekly gardening segment on Radio Three Counties.

Whilst most of this came across as useful advice, this last injunction was clearly an order from on high, and I was left in no doubt that it carried the threat of instant dismissal. I accepted it as I assumed that Edward Jesser was trying to protect his old friend or mentor from embarrassing himself in public rather than prevent him from public utterances which might damage

206   Mike Ripley

Boothby & Briggs – not that public outbursts by crime writers
have ever shocked the nation, at least not since Conan Doyle
claimed there were fairies at the bottom of the garden.

Not that Alan Hibbert showed any sign that he was seeking a
public audience of any kind. He never, to my knowledge, had
any visitors other than his domestic help or health professionals,
his larder (he called it that) was regularly restocked by a grocer
with a van in the next village, and the local brewery in Hertford
supplied him, year round, with a particularly nasty Spanish Rioja,
the odd crate of light ale in summer, and bottles of eggnog and
sherry in time for Christmas – which I can only assume he drank
himself to make the lonely season slightly more festive.

Was he lonely? It really was difficult to tell. He seemed neither
to crave or seek the company of others. He had thousands of
books – there were books all over that house – a radio tuned to
Radio 4, which he shouted at randomly, and a television, which
he watched mostly in silence but with a permanent scowl on his
face, but never expressed a desire to go beyond his front door.
Unless, of course, that was to his shed.

That shed was a ritual for him, something of an obsession; it
was his refuge and his place of work, and he would spend seven
or eight hours a day shut in there, bashing away on an antique
typewriter the size and weight of a small panzer. The shed was
not just a hiding place; he hardly needed one, as his house, the
last in the village, was free of nosey neighbours, and Dunkley
itself was so far off the beaten track it only featured on the
largest-scale Ordnance Survey maps.

But if the shed was his sanctum, it was not a secret sanctum,
as Hibbert's rare visitors were escorted there whether they wanted
to go or not, to the place where he received his 'inspiration' for
the Inspector Seeley books. I was treated to the guided tour on
my first visit to Dunkley, and it was clear that Hibbert expected
me to admire the shed as a sort of shrine where the holy muse
of crime writing descended upon him. Even on a cursory exami-
nation, I had more faith in the scattered maps, dictionaries,
medical texts and reference books on subjects ranging from law
enforcement and sociology to drug abuse and small arms that
littered the dank interior as being the more practical sources of
his inspiration.

Buried Above Ground 207

The shed was not a place where guests could be entertained. It was badly lit with only a single bare light bulb; it reeked of damp and cigarette smoke, and I was convinced there were nicotine stains on the impressive cobwebs strung across every right angle. There was only one chair strategically placed in front of that juggernaut of a typewriter, and the wooden floorboards creaked loudly under the least pressure, as if complaining if more than two people stood on it – not that it was likely that the shed would ever host more than two.

I remember asking Hibbert if he only used the shed in summer, as it must be like working in a fridge in winter. He seemed surprised at my question and lifted a stack of old AA Handbooks from the top of an ancient paraffin heater, the sort which used to be recommended for greenhouses. Although the health and safety of an author is not usually the responsibility of their editor, I thought it necessary to point out that the fumes from those things in an unventilated space could be fatal. Alan Hibbert merely smiled at my concern and said, 'Well, that would be a peaceful way to go.'

As he said that, I looked for a sparkle or twinkle in his eyes which might indicate that a plot point had just occurred to him and which he would mentally file for future use, but there was nothing. I was quickly to learn that where his fiction was concerned, Hibbert was not so much secretive – many crime writers are paranoid that other crime writers will steal the plots they are working on – as somehow *distanced*. It was almost as if Duncan Torrens was not merely a pseudonym but a different person entirely.

Before that first meeting with Hibbert, Edward Jesser had briefed me on this, but I had not taken his warning too seriously, as I knew that writers, especially crime writers, could be Jekyll and Hyde characters. Alan Hibbert might come across as a loner with little small talk, no sense of humour and few social graces, but get him in Duncan Torrens mode and talking about his fiction – then he became gregarious, animated and enthusiastic.

I discovered two things immediately. Firstly, on meeting Hibbert in his house, he did initially make me feel as if my visit was both unexpected and unwelcome. He provided coffee, almost as if it was a penance, and studiously avoided any conversation

Mike Ripley

about his books or his long relationship with Boothby & Briggs. When I said how proud and pleased I was to be his new editor, he looked no more impressed or interested than if I had said it wasn't raining outside. It was only later that I realized it should have surprised if not impressed him, as Edward Jesser had not had the courage to tell him of my promotion to that exalted position.

My second discovery was confirmation of Edward's diagnosis that Duncan Torrens was a different personality, if not a different person, to Alan Hibbert, at least when he was in his shed surrounded by his reference books, packs of foolscap paper, an overflowing ashtray the size of a fruit bowl and that mechanical monster on which he typed his masterpieces. I am sure the transformation happened as he escorted me out of the house and into the garden with the invitation, delivered deadpan, that 'we'd better get down to some work', and by the time he was creaking open the shed's wooden door, he was in full flight describing the plot of what he thought was going to be called *A Catafalque for Cynthia*.

Squeezing into that shed with him, trying not to breathe in the swarming dust particles and now so close to my new author I was getting a headache from the strong whiff of stale smoke coming from his clothing, I proceeded, as diplomatically as possible, to explain that there were certain 'structural' flaws in his latest manuscript. 'Structural flaws' being the useful, all-purpose term used by editors to tell an author their book was rubbish.

Edward Jesser had made it clear that I had to persuade Hibbert to remove 'Cynthia' from the title, out of respect for his former housekeeper and the avoidance of litigation, and that there was no way on God's earth that the word 'catafalque' would feature in a Boothby & Briggs title. It was a brief I followed as best I could, and I am sure I would have rehearsed a script before driving out to Dunkley, but I have no memory of what I actually said – or most likely gabbled rapidly as I tend to do when nervous.

Hibbert's reaction disconcerted me more than anything I had anticipated, and I had thought I had imagined every possible scenario. I was well aware of the many legends within crime-fiction publishing of what transpired when an author was told that their latest book was 'not good enough', even if that verdict

Buried Above Ground 209

was couched in the softest, most diplomatic terms. Authors had been known to scream, burst into tears, shout, throw things, offer violence, even set fire to a manuscript in their editor's office. (One notoriously unstable writer always carried a tin of lighter fluid and a box of matches when delivering a new novel to his publisher.) Some had – successfully – played the self-effacing card and instantly agreed that their latest offering was 'not up to snuff' and if only the editor could work their usual magic with a few suggested improvements, then the quality of the book could surely be improved. This approach, when accompanied by a down-casting of the eyes and a wringing of the hands, was often quite effective and might result in minimal changes to the book, especially if every editorial 'improvement' no matter how minor was greeted with gushing gratitude by the humble author.

Alan Hibbert's reaction to the dreaded news that *A Catafalque for Cynthia* was not up to snuff fell into neither of these camps.

His face went blank – no, not blank but suddenly totally *empty* – and for a moment, I thought it could presage a storm brewing behind those dead eyes, but there was no explosion. Instead, Hibbert dropped to his knees, and I half-expected he was playing the self-effacing card and was about to beg for editorial assistance, but grovelling was the last thing on his mind.

'But it would work,' he challenged me. 'Move your damn feet and I'll prove it to you.'

And then he began to take up the floorboards to show me the grave he had prepared.

FORTY

When I met Alan Hibbert that day out in Dunkley, my first impression was that he had stepped out of a black-and-white Ealing comedy. He was a slight, probably once dapper figure with a pencil moustache, now white and nicotine stained, thinning white hair and a slightly florid complexion. At his present age, he would have been perfect for the officious golf club steward, ten years younger he would have been a verger or even a vicar, and twenty years younger would have been perfect as the local assistant bank manager. The characters he would have played would always have been uptight, humourless and suspicious of anyone perceived as having fun.

Even in his seventies, long retired from any proper job and in his own home, he wore a suit and tie that morning. At first, I thought it was a mark of respect when greeting his new editor. It was only later that I discovered that he dressed formally before going to work in his shed, at least when he intended to write. I assumed he had adopted more casual, garden-friendly clothing when he was busy digging graves because he had indeed dug what the lazy crime writer might call a shallow grave but a pedantic archaeologist would argue was a burial chamber.

I stood there speechless, looking down at the back of Alan Hibbert's head. He had put down a foam rubber garden kneeler to protect his suit trousers and had levered up a floorboard with a penknife blade. I shuffled backwards until pressed against the side of the shed as adjoining planks followed easily to reveal a rectangular cavity about five feet long, two feet wide and three feet deep.

When he looked up at me, Hibbert's eyes were shining with excitement. 'You see, it would work, once the floorboards were nailed back down,' he said. 'From the outside, there would be no sign of anything untoward, not even if someone got inside and looked around. The soil I dug out is piled round the back

Buried Above Ground 211

under some grass cuttings and clippings, so it looks like a compost heap. Some of it would go back in, of course, and any surplus scattered around the garden. What usually gives a grave away? A bump in the landscape or disturbed ground, but here, nothing to see but everything in plain sight.'

'Ingenious,' I said, simply because he required an answer.

'I got the idea from an article on wooden catafalques used to disguise coffins. Hence the title.'

'About that . . .'

'Though thinking about it' – he paused and held his chin as if conjuring the thought – '*Buried in Plain Sight* could be a good title.' Then he shook his head. 'No, I like catafalque – it adds to the mystery.'

'I'm afraid we don't.' It was time to bite the bullet and give him the bad news – and few editors could ever be better placed to announce bad news than to an author kneeling over an open grave. 'The considered view at B and B is that your title would simply confuse readers and even a few librarians. I'm instructed to tell you that is non-negotiable.'

I thought he was going to ask if his old friend and mentor Edward Jesser had issued that edict, but he merely looked up at me, rather pathetically, with any twinkle now gone from his eyes.

'But I do like your overall thinking,' I said, improvising quickly, 'and *Buried Above Ground* is an excellent alternative.'

He got slowly to his feet, brushed dirt from his knees and then looked me in the face without any visible emotion. 'Yes, that would work.' He said it as if handing back homework to a pupil.

I counted the fact that he was not screaming any objection or even showing disappointment as a small victory and decided to press home my advantage.

'There are some structural changes we also feel would improve the book, and the murder victim, Cynthia . . . we think a name change might be appropriate there.'

I could not tell what he thought about that, or if he had even registered what I had said. He simply nodded once, which could have meant agreement or dismissal – or both.

'Then you'd better get on with it. Now, the next Seeley will be all about poisons . . .'

And that, genuinely, was all Duncan Torrens had to say about his novel *Buried Above Ground*. He never mentioned the new title again, nor enquired about what structural changes were being proposed to his manuscript.

On the walk back to the house, all he talked about was the next Inspector Seeley novel, which he intended to call *Inspector Seeley's Poison Parsnip* – a title which I knew, though I said nothing at the time, would not be acceptable at B & B (it was eventually published as *The Herb Border*). Once inside the house, he made it clear that he was expecting me to collect my things and leave him in peace to get on with his new project on murderous vegetables.

I had brought with me Hibbert's manuscript, almost 200 sheets of typed foolscap pages held together with thick rubber bands, but it now felt like the elephant in the room. I offered it to him gingerly.

'I'm suggesting quite a few changes . . .' I stumbled.

His top lip curled slightly. It was, I was to learn, the nearest his face came to a smile.

'Then you'd better get on with it,' he said again.

'Will you want to see the copy-edited version before we go to proofs?'

'Not really. I'm far too busy to look back either in anger or admiration. I'll read it on publication. No doubt with the pleasure that always comes with the second half of the advance.'

I was at a loss about how to take that. Was he joking, or was he really one of that rare breed of writers who were quite happy to have their work rewritten by an editor or, even worse – a real nightmare scenario – by a publisher's committee?

When I reported my misgivings back at the office, Edward Jesser looked totally non-plussed. In fact, if anything, he seemed quite relieved that the pressure had come off.

'There's a considerable amount of rewriting involved,' I said.

'Not looking for a pay rise, are we?' said Edward, not expecting an answer. 'I have every confidence in you, Roly. You've read enough of his stuff to match his style. Make sure you can meet the printer's deadline and try not to let your other works suffer. Alan was quite happy with the change of title, was he?'

'Yes, I'm sure of that.'

'And what about changing the character of Cynthia?' Robina had asked me. 'How did he react to that?'

'Very favourably actually,' I lied. 'He said he didn't mind losing a Cynthia because now he had an Alice.'

FORTY-ONE

To say Alisa Bulova made an immediate impression on me would be an understatement; I was positively *smitten*, to use the romantic novelist's favourite expression.

That day when I first met Alan Hibbert, he had offered coffee, which I realized later must have been made by Alice, but I had no memory of her serving it, if she did, as I must have been transfixed, though certainly not smitten, by the author I had to deliver bad news to.

The real first impression came as I was leaving Hibbert's house, clutching the manuscript of *A Catafalque for Cynthia* – with copious (unseen) notes in the margins – and heading for my car.

'Hey, Mr Nice Man! Wait up a moment,' was the voice from behind which stopped me in my tracks.

I had never before understood the term 'pocket rocket'; in fact, I had always suspected it was slightly obscene, but it fitted perfectly the young woman who skipped towards me, the huge smile on her face radiating a dynamic energy.

She was, as they say, small but perfectly formed, with long blonde hair lassoed into a swishing ponytail, and she wore glasses with big round lenses and steel rims perched on an upturned nose. She was dressed in very tight blue jeans and a sleeveless T-shirt cut short to show off a ribbon of pink flesh.

'Please. A favour is what I need.'

If her fresh-faced appearance didn't snare me instantly, then her accent did. I recognized it immediately from my student days. I am not a spontaneous person, but it seemed only natural to acknowledge it.

'Anything for a pretty lady,' I said.

She stopped dead in her tracks and squealed. 'You speak Russian!'

'Just a little.'

'But I must speak English and always look to be corrected. So you must correct me. Promise.'

Buried Above Ground   215

I was never any good at recognizing flirting signals, not that I've had much experience, but I thought it appropriate to switch back to boringly formal English.

'I promise, though I doubt the need will arise, and your English is far superior to my Russian. It's Alisa, isn't it? I'm Roland Wilkes.'

'In England, I am Alice, the girl who goes through the looking glass.' We shook hands, her grip surprisingly strong, and I could see the muscles tense in her bare forearm. 'And I know you are Mr Wilkes, as Mr Alan told me you were coming. You are his copy editor I think he said. For his books.'

I decided not to try and explain my recent promotion. 'Yes, I help him with his books, at his publishing house in London.'

'Has Mr Alan written many books?' she asked with innocent curiosity.

'Yes, lots. He writes one a year' – I hefted the bundle of sheets I was holding – 'and this is the latest, or it will be when we publish next year.'

'Should I read one?'

I tried a non-committal shrug. 'Why not? You might like them if you like detective stories.'

She pulled a face, wrinkling her nose so that her glasses bobbed up and down, making her look slightly owlish, but a cute owl for all that.

'Like Sherlock Holmes? We had to read Sherlock Holmes at school in English lessons. Two imperialist old men talking and smoking pipes.'

'Crime fiction's come a long way since then,' I said. 'Look for books by Duncan Torrens – that's the name Mr Hibbert writes under, though I'm sure he has lots of other detective stories to choose from.'

She nodded enthusiastically, the ponytail landing over her right shoulder, caressing her cheek. 'Oh yes, he sure has a lot of books in the house.'

He did but surprisingly few crime novels, just a handful of worn paperbacks, none of them recent titles or new editions. I had scanned the shelves as soon as I had arrived, as I always did in a new location, and had been staggered that he did not seem interested in the current competition within the genre, not even

216   Mike Ripley

the Boothby & Briggs titles which I knew he was sent for free by Edward Jesser.

'You're slipping into American,' I said with a smile. When she frowned, I explained, 'You asked me to correct you. When you said "he sure has", that sounded American. A polite young English lady would say "he certainly has".'

She leaned in closer and looked up at me through fluttering eyelashes, and even I could tell she was now definitely flirting. 'I never said I was a polite English lady, but thank you for the correction. It is . . . certainly most welcome.'

'My pleasure. Now, what was the favour you wanted?'

She pretended to look as if she had totally forgotten about her opening pitch and clearly had talent as an actress, as she made a show of patting the back pockets of her jeans until she extracted a folded piece of paper and offered it to me.

'I have no car or bicycle,' she said sweetly, 'and the shops are far away. If you come back here again—'

'Oh, I will be coming back,' I said, possibly too quickly.

'Could you bring me this, please? I will give you the money.' She trained her big blue eyes behind those big round lenses directly on my face as I read her note. 'Perhaps I should have written it in Russian for you.'

Her shopping list consisted of a single item: a bottle of Stolichnaya, blue label.

The words 'blue label' were underlined twice.

Here was a girl who knew exactly what she wanted, so naturally she got it. I returned that afternoon, guessing correctly that Hibbert would be hard at work in his shed, after a lengthy detour to find an off-licence which stocked her favoured brand of vodka.

Father Christmas arriving early could not have been made more welcome, nor greeted with such a passionate kiss, but I resisted her offer to crack open the bottle there and then – even though it had not been stored in the freezer for the required twenty-four hours. I declined on the grounds that I was driving and had to get back to London, said that I did not want payment for the vodka and she should treat it as a gift from Hibbert's publisher. I discovered that she had Saturdays and Sundays as days off, but weekends were terribly boring out in Dunkley.

No one at B & B ever asked what I did with my weekends,

as in publishing it is expected that an editor or copy editor uses any out-of-office time to catch up on their reading of the never-ending flow of manuscripts, but I made a point of telling Edward Jesser that the latest Duncan Torrens would require a lot of rewriting, which would mean further trips out to Dunkley to consult the reclusive author. These I would happily undertake at weekends, and Edward was not only grateful for my dedication to one of his favourite authors but even agreed to authorize my petty-cash claims for petrol money, at thirty pence a mile if I remember correctly.

Robina Robinson didn't mention my extra-curricular activities at all. As far as she was concerned, Duncan Torrens/Alan Hibbert had been a problem for Edward which had now been boxed up and delivered on to my desk. As far as Alice being the reason I was now showing a new interest in my work, if she suspected, she didn't show it. Not that she cared much, as by then our brief office fling – which had started, cliché of all clichés, with a fumble in the stationery cupboard – had petered out. If she thought of me at all, it would have been smugly, considering that she had put one over by lumbering me with Alan Hibbert, giving Edward Jesser more time to concentrate on her.

I don't think there was any office gossip about Alice and me. Very few people knew she existed and even less cared if Alan Hibbert did, though some in the sales team might miss the annual Duncan Torrens if it failed to appear. Certainly there was no gossip in Dunkley as far as I knew, as we were very discreet, aided and abetted by Alan Hibbert, not out of deference to his reputation in the village but because he despised his neighbours, wanted as little contact with them as possible and certainly did not want to provide them with any juicy morsels of scandal.

Though where was the scandal? We were both adults and had no intention of doing anything to frighten the horses in Dunkley; in fact, we spent much of our time elsewhere. Alice liked nothing better than a trip to Watford or even Cambridge, though she was curiously reluctant to go back to London, to avoid going stir-crazy in Dunkley.

My visits there became regular events, and I was always greeted with polite indifference by the master of the house, who would wish us a good day out before retreating to his shed. The first

218   Mike Ripley

time I called, I brought with me fifty corrected pages of what was to become *Buried Above Ground*, but Hibbert made no move to take them from me, and so I left them prominently on the small, lacquered table on which rested the house phone. (Not, according to Alice, that it ever rang.) They were still there, untouched, a week later when I called to take Alice for a country pub lunch, and she confirmed that Alan Hibbert was too busy being Duncan Torrens in his shed and writing a new book without worrying about one that he considered finished.

After a month of affectionate but innocent contact, Alice took our relationship to a higher, or at least more physical, level. She suggested it in no uncertain terms in a sultry whisper in my ear during a goodnight clinch in my car as I delivered her back to Dunkley. The language she used, throaty English interspersed with some choice Russian, was forthright and quite obscene, dialogue which could have graced a soft porn film – or so I imagined – and which would certainly not have been allowed in any Boothby & Briggs title, not even in the romantic-fiction imprint.

She had never shown any interest in visiting, let alone staying over at my place in London, and it had never occurred to me that we might consummate our relationship in Alan Hibbert's house, but Alice assured me that not only was it possible, it seemed we had the owner's blessing. In that wide-eyed and rather angelic way she had, especially when discussing matters sexual, she swore that Hibbert had given her permission to invite 'a boyfriend or two' back to her bedroom providing she did not 'make too much noise'.

At the time, I was too surprised to comment on the fact that Alice might be expected to have plural boyfriends, and I was soon to learn that Hibbert's concern about the domestic noise level was well justified. I have long held the view that, in my editorial opinion, the action in a crime novel should stop at the bedroom door. Such a consideration had never worried Alice, at least in terms of volume control. To say she was demonstrative in the bedroom would be an understatement, not to mention innovative, experimental and above all curious about the minute details of the sex act, and in addition, she felt the need to provide a running commentary in two languages on its progress.

Buried Above Ground 219

Not that, in the moment, I had anything to complain about. I learned a lot, and my Russian vocabulary was significantly enlarged.

Amazingly, Alan Hibbert never complained about my 'sleepovers' on Saturday nights, and after an initial frosty encounter one Sunday morning, he seemed to accept my presence, where I would nurse a mug of coffee at the kitchen table as he prepared his breakfast – always a bowl of instant porridge. Not that these morning-after-the-night-before encounters could be described as anything other than strange. Beyond a perfunctory 'good morning', he never spoke to me; he would eat his porridge then make a fresh pot of tea, which he decanted into a Thermos flask to accompany him to his beloved writing shed. Alice was unsurprised and untroubled by this non-reaction, saying that 'Mr Alan' was never very talkative in the mornings, whereas at other times of the day, he was always friendly and polite, sometimes interesting and occasionally funny.

Quite what the two of them chatted about I have no idea, and Alice never said. He certainly never talked about the book I was editing – his book – not even when I requested formal meetings about it, rather than trying to discuss it over a breakfast table at which I was something of an interloper. I would leave corrections, suggestions and even galley proofs at the house, all of which were received, if they were noticed at all, with indifference and pointed silence. Yet the slightest mention of the book he was now working on got him immediately excited and more than happy to discuss aspects of the plot and the dramatic high point where someone poisons Inspector Seeley and how he was researching all things deadly and horticultural. Much as I was delighted as a B & B editor that my author was being productive and that the phrase 'writer's block' was unknown to him (unlike some over-prolific authors where it should be), I found it increasingly frustrating not to have his feedback on my revisions to *Buried Above Ground*. I was well aware that if anything went badly wrong with that book, which had been commissioned by Hibbert's guardian angel and my boss Edward Jesser, then my career as a proper editor might be short-lived and could jeopardize my reasons for visiting Alice.

One evening, over a mediocre dinner in an Indian restaurant

220   Mike Ripley

called, confusingly, Five Spices to the Raj, I discussed my concern
with Alice. She rarely showed any interest in Hibbert's writing,
other than making the distinction between 'Mr Alan' when he
was in the house and 'Mr Duncan' when he was working in his
shed. To my knowledge, she never read any of his books, nor
expressed any interest in doing so, but she showed a tender
concern over my predicament. Her solution to it was eminently
simple.

'Ignore him,' she said, snapping a poppadum in half, 'like he
ignores you.'

'He doesn't ignore me,' I argued. 'In fact, you could say he
has welcomed me into his house. He certainly seems happy
enough with our . . . special arrangement . . . going on under
his roof. He always says good morning if I sleep over.'

'I try not to let you sleep too much,' she said with a wicked
grin which made me blush. 'But when he talks to you, you are
with me and he is Mr Alan. When you come to the house to talk
about his books, he has to be Mr Duncan, and Mr Duncan does
not like talking to people about his books.'

'I know he's not very sociable, but not talking to his editor
about a book he has submitted for publication is just crazy.'

'Maybe he is crazy. He doesn't talk to anyone about the books
he has written and he never reads them – or so he says.' She
jabbed the back of my hand with a jagged edge of her poppadum,
showering the tablecloth with crumbs. 'So why not ignore him?
If he makes no objections to your corrections, then he must accept
them, no?'

I let that sink in, marvelling at how Alice, who had never
shown any interest in the mechanics of publishing, was starting
to think like a publisher.

'You mean just steam ahead with any changes I think fit and
to hell with the author's sacred prose?'

'That's your job, isn't it?'

'Sort of, I suppose.'

'Or you could lock yourself in that shed with the famous
Duncan Torrens and shout at him until he talked to you.'

I shuddered at the thought of standing over Hibbert/Torrens
in that grubby shed as he hammered at that ancient typewriter,
standing over the unfilled grave he was so proud of.

'I like your first idea,' I said, and Alice gave me one of her sexiest smiles.

'I knew you would.'

FORTY-TWO

My edited version of *Buried Above Ground* – and I say 'my' because my edits outweighed Torrens' original script – went into production without any further consultation with the author. It was published on schedule, did well enough in pre-orders from libraries, and Edward Jesser even complimented me on a job well done and told me he had sent a note of congratulations to Alan Hibbert.

Alice, my spy in the Hibbert house, confirmed that he had read the letter with a big smile and far more enthusiasm than when he received his box of six author copies. At first sight he winced, perhaps at the changed title, perhaps at the cover, which he was seeing for the first time, then he shrugged and presented Alice with the first copy 'hot off the press' – an expression I had to explain to her, although she thought 'fresh from the oven' was better as I had helped cook it.

We had both giggled at that, and Alice had asked me to 'autograph' the book, claiming she would not read it unless I did (though I suspected she had no intention of reading it), and because I found it difficult to refuse her anything, I signed the title page of *Buried Above Ground* with the message: *To Russia with love. All my own work. Love, Roly xxx.*

It was not the first stupid thing I had done, and would not be the last, but at that moment, it seemed as if everything was going my way.

Alan Hibbert appeared happy enough with the way the book had turned out or at least had not complained to his former pupil Edward Jesser, which had been a serious concern of mine, and was busy in his shed on the next, which, as Duncan Torrens, he was happy to talk about when I stayed over in Dunkley, and was disturbingly enthusiastic about all the things in his garden which were poisonous.

Things changed shortly after he handed me his completed manuscript of the book which I was to retitle (without consultation)

The Herb Border, with not the slightest indication that he wished to discuss it. Flushed with my first success, I had no qualms about editing or rewriting the text and set about it with enthusiasm rather than trepidation, assuming that Hibbert would immediately become Torrens and start work on the next book.

It was not to be because Alan Hibbert had a stroke, albeit a minor one – what the doctor called a TIA. The question was had Duncan Torrens suffered as well?

With commendable quick thinking, Alice called for an ambulance and gave my name and office number as Hibbert's next of kin, though fortunately I was not called upon in that capacity. Hibbert spent two nights in hospital before being discharged with a bucketful of tablets to control his blood pressure and cholesterol, a reference to a physiotherapist, a diet sheet and a booklet on the benefits of physical exercise, all of which he studiously ignored.

Apart from an obvious weakness to his left leg when he walked and his left hand shaking when he carried anything, he seemed physically undamaged, but mentally it was another matter entirely. It was almost as if a brake had been applied to his brain, and the slowness of his thought process clearly distressed him and demonstrated itself in a shortness of temper and a tendency to snap at anyone who came near him. Fortunately, he had few social interactions, and poor Alice had to take the brunt of his violent mood swings.

She stuck it for four weeks before demanding that I get her out of the Dunkley house.

'Sick I can do. Crazy I will not stand,' she had said forcefully when she had me at her mercy. 'You must take me away from here.'

It was at that point that I met with Edward Jesser and told him about Hibbert's stroke.

'Will it affect his writing?' was his first question. 'Have you told anyone else?' was his second.

I reported what the doctors and nurses, who had assumed that Alice and I were Hibbert's carers, had said: that physical recovery was perfectly possible if he took his prescribed medicines and regular exercise, but his mental recovery was impossible to estimate. Certainly, he would be, or appear to be, slower in terms of thinking speed, and his memory may well have suffered.

224   Mike Ripley

'He still makes his daily trip to his writing shed, so he must be working on the next Inspector Seeley,' I told Edward without any justification at all, 'and I've not said a word to anyone here at B and B.'

That last was true and did not need qualifying further as absolutely no one outside of Boothby & Briggs would be remotely interested in Alan Hibbert or his health.

'That's good. Let's keep it that way. Alan has no relatives or, thank God, an agent to ask after him, and I don't think we need worry about nosey neighbours. Alan will have scared them off long ago. He'll come through this; he's a tough old boot.'

'There is one problem,' I said tentatively. 'He's not getting any younger, and he's living alone out there . . .'

'But he's not alone, is he? You sly dog, you!' And Edward Jesser did something I had never seen him do before or since – he winked at me. 'He's got Alice, our dynamic little Russian gymnast, hasn't he?'

Gymnast? Where did that come from? Had Hibbert been taking notes based on the noises coming from Alice's room – or, even worse, marking our performances – and reporting back to Edward?

'Not for long, I'm afraid,' I said, steeling myself. 'She wants to leave.'

'What have you done to her?'

'Me? Nothing. It's Alan. Alice thinks she lacks the professional capabilities to deal with him since the stroke.'

I thought a 'lack of professional capabilities' was a nice way of obfuscating Alice's decision that there was 'no fooking way I care for crazy man'.

'But I thought she had medical qualifications.'

'Did you check?'

Edward cleared his throat, or perhaps it was a growl.

'Then you'd better start looking for a replacement for her. Find an agency nurse, something like that. Alan can afford it.' He caught the surprise on my face. 'Oh, not on the royalties we pay him, but he has inherited money in the bank, and the house is mortgage free, so he might as well spend it on something useful. Find someone suitable and set it up, then I'll ring Alan and tell him he has to behave. I think he quite likes Alice and

Buried Above Ground

is quite amused by your . . . liaison . . . with her. How has he taken the news that she's jumping ship?'

'Quite well, I think, once Alice told him we were getting married.'

Just before she told me.

FORTY-THREE

'When did you last see your wife? For the tape, please.'

'About a year or so after the wedding.'

Inspector Walker showed neither surprise nor sympathy.

'Things just did not work out for us, and we agreed to a divorce. That would have been around the mid-nineties, so it must be nearly thirty years ago.'

'And you never kept in touch?'

'Why would we? The marriage only lasted months.'

Just long enough for Alice to persuade me to buy a house we could not afford, get her driving lessons and then buy her a car, all of it passing in something of a mad blur.

'That's not bad going for a marriage these days.'

'Actually the divorce rate was higher back then in the nineties than it is now.'

The inspector now did look surprised.

'I looked it up in the library,' I added.

'Where you work?'

'Yes, I went into the library service after being made redundant by the publishing firm I worked for.'

I hoped it didn't sound too over the top to say 'library service', as if I had answered some noble patriotic call to arms, even though it sometimes felt exactly like that.

'That would be Boothby and Briggs?'

'Technically Pabulator, the conglomerate which took over B and B.'

'And when was that exactly?'

'Twenty-first October 1999. That was when I got the boot; the takeover would have been the day before.'

'You sound bitter.'

'I was; still am, I suppose.'

She had no idea, and I wasn't going to tell her that I was thinking about how much Alice had drained me financially and

Buried Above Ground 227

how I was still suffering from that all these years later, rather than being made redundant.

'How did Alan Hibbert take it?'

'Much better than I did, but he had the advantage of being dead.' She gave me her exhausted schoolteacher expression until I behaved. 'He died earlier that year, before the takeover and the last novel he had written was rejected by the new regime in short order.'

'Did that upset you?'

'It was out of my hands; I was out of a job.'

She flipped a couple of pages in her notebook.

'Getting back to Alice Bulova . . .'

'Al*isa* Bulova, though she was Alice Wilkes for a while.'

'She was Russian.' It wasn't a question, so I just nodded but then she pointed at the tape recorder.

'Yes, she was. I think she came to London on some sort of student exchange and decided to stay. We hit it off because I'd done the same thing the other way and visited Russia as a student.'

'So you speak Russian?'

'A little, or I did to try and impress Alice. I've had no need of it since she left me.'

'She left you?'

With a mortgage I couldn't afford, and I'd had to sell my car to cover the payments on hers.

'Very much so. I think she always saw me as a way of escaping from Hibbert. After he had his first stroke. Probably a wise move, as he had others.'

'Did Alan Hibbert get on with her?'

'Yes, he did, surprisingly well given that he was a miserable old git who enjoyed living as a recluse. I think he was genuinely sorry to see her go.'

She flashed me the up-from-under-the-eyelashes look only women can do. 'Did he go to your wedding?'

'No. He was invited, but Hibbert didn't travel. It was a quiet, registry-office job, not the big-budget Hollywood production numbers they have today.'

'And you moved to Watford. Why Watford?'

I shrugged and held out my arms, palms upward.

She nodded emphatically at the tape recorder.

228 Mike Ripley

'I could commute into London easily.' And so, it turned out, could Alice. 'Plus, we were sure Alice would find another job pretty quickly.'

'And did she?'

'Not really. She tried a few things like dog walking and barmaid shifts at the local pub, but nothing substantial. Money became very tight and a bit of an issue between us. Then she started going out for the day and not coming back until the next.'

'Was she seeing Alan Hibbert?'

'No, he would have said something.'

'So you were still in touch with him.'

'I had to be, didn't I? I was still his editor, and I had a fax machine installed in his house so he could communicate with us at B and B without having to come to the office or use the phone. He had only ever rung to speak to Edward Jesser, who was no longer handling his books, and he hated dealing with secretaries or receptionists.'

'How often did you see him?'

'Hardly at all after Alice moved out. Any changes to his books or new contracts were done by fax. I think he quite liked using the fax machine; that way, he didn't have to deal with people.'

'So who looked after him?'

'I think Edward Jesser set him up with a series of house-keepers.' I tried to look as if I was scouring my memory. 'They were probably all Mrs Doubtfire types, not bright young sparks like Alice, and I've no idea how he got on with them, but I do remember he insisted they had their own transport and did not come from Dunkley. As time went on and he had more strokes, he needed regular visits from a nurse, and then there were the local social services. I think there were plans to have him moved to a hospice near the end, but nothing came of it.'

'Between the time Alisa Bulova left Dunkley to marry you and Hibbert's death, did she ever go back to see him?'

'No. There was no reason why she would.'

'Can you be sure of that?'

'No, but it seems unlikely she would, though she could have, I suppose. She had her own car, and I was in London three or four days a week, but she never said anything about going back

Buried Above Ground

to Dunkley, and I'm sure Alan Hibbert would have mentioned it. He had a soft spot for her.'

'As shown by him leaving her cash in his will.'

'That surprised me at the time.'

'Because you weren't mentioned in his will?'

'Oh no, I wasn't expecting anything. A writer leaving money to his editor? That would have been a shock.'

'But you knew about the bequest to Alice?'

'Of course. Alan's solicitor got in touch trying to find Alice to hand it over, but by that time we were divorced and I had no idea where she was.'

'You never kept in touch with her?'

'We were divorced; she'd walked out on me,' I said slowly and deliberately.

'And you never reported her missing?'

'Why would I? She wasn't missing – she'd left. I guessed that she'd gone back to wherever she'd lived previously in London before she started working for Hibbert.'

'What did she do in London, before going to Dunkley?'

'I have no idea. She never talked about her past life. Edward Jesser and Robina Robinson hired her from some agency in Soho. Perhaps Robina might know if they still exist.'

They didn't; I had checked.

'She never mentioned friends or family? Surely you were curious?'

I took a deep breath. 'When someone as ordinary and un-exciting as me makes a connection with a girl as pretty and vibrant as Alice, the last thing you think of doing is a background check.'

'So you were flattered by her attentions?'

'Damn right I was. It was a novel experience' – in more ways than one – 'for someone who had been described by a previous girlfriend as having been born at the age of forty-five.'

(Girlfriend in question: Robina Robinson.)

'You must have been upset when she left you.'

'I was distraught.'

Not to mention in severe financial difficulties.

'But you didn't look for her.'

'She said not to. That was actually the last thing she said as

230   Mike Ripley

she walked out the door: don't come looking for me; you won't find me. When she said things like that, you believed her.'

'Basically, you knew nothing about her.'

'I knew she was Russian, had family there and was probably marrying me in order to get a British passport, though she never did as far as I know.'

'There is no record of one being issued to her' – Inspector Toni Walker had been doing her homework – 'but I presume she still had a valid Russian passport.'

I did my best to look surprised. 'You think she went back to Russia?'

'We discovered her car had been found abandoned in one of the car parks at Heathrow, where it had been for over a month. Sadly, it was destroyed by the army as a precaution.'

'I'm sorry?'

'There had been mortar attacks on Heathrow by the IRA back then. The security people were taking no chances unfortunately.'

'Unfortunately?'

'It was a possible source of a sample of Alice's DNA.'

'Even after all this time?'

Now it was her turn to shrug. 'They got DNA off Richard III, didn't they? And he's been buried in a car park for nearly five hundred years. Amazing what the boffins can do these days.'

I did a double take as if I'd had a small electric shock. 'If you are looking for DNA, does that mean you haven't identified the body?'

'Not officially.' She licked her lips and cleared her throat before divulging gruesome details – probably part of her training. 'There were no clothing or identifiable goods with the body, and decomposition rules out a visual identification. All we know is it's a female, height around five foot two, aged between twenty and twenty-five. We need a comparison sample of Alice's DNA to match up with that taken from the corpse.'

'So it might not be Alice. Come to think of it, why did you assume it was her in the first place? Moreover, why have you let me assume that?'

She could not prevent her eyes from flitting towards the tape recorder. A sure sign of nerves, even though this was supposed

Buried Above Ground   231

to be an informal background research session for which I had volunteered. (Not that I really had much choice.)

'The likelihood of outsiders, either victim or murderer, randomly finding a vacant, concealed grave inside a garden shed just when conveniently needed is remote.' She took a breath. 'So it seems plausible that either the victim or the murderer knew about it beforehand and therefore had inside knowledge of Alan Hibbert's house in Dunkley.'

'Only the killer would have known about Hibbert's mock sarcophagus.'

'Why do you say that?'

If this had been a formal interview, it would have been when I started saying 'no comment' like they do on television in those long interrogation scenes which have become so popular.

'Because no victim would have presented her killer with an open grave just crying out to be filled.'

'Unless she knew the killer.'

I held up a hand to acknowledge the point. 'I know, I know. Most murders are committed by someone who is known to the victim – something many a crime writer forgets when it's convenient. Isn't it true that the perfect murder would be when a victim answers the doorbell to a complete stranger who shoots them from outside the house and then disappears to dispose of the gun? There is, of course, no CCTV coverage or doorbell camera footage.'

'You've thought about this.'

'I've had to; it's my job – or it was – as a crime-fiction editor. But such a scenario, where there is no motive, would hardly make a good book, would it?'

'I wouldn't know about that, but it would certainly give us, the police, the problem of no physical evidence, and we do rely on DNA an awful lot these days.'

'You'd be surprised, or perhaps not, how many crime writers still have anonymous corpses identified by their' – I made inverted commas in the air with my fingers, something I usually abhor – 'dental records, yet they never explain how the police knew which dentist to go to in order to find them. In this case, you've got the victim's DNA but don't know if it's Alice's DNA, right?'

232 Mike Ripley

'Pretty much. It didn't register on the National Database, but that only dates from 1995.'

'But you haven't said why you think it might be *Alice's* DNA.'

Inspector Walker looked down at the tabletop, avoiding eye contact. 'Everything points to the victim having knowledge of Alan Hibbert's house and garden, and Alice's name cropped up through enquiries to Hibbert's solicitors about likely family relatives. The only thing flagged up as interesting was that bequest to Alice Bulova, who we discovered fit the parameters of age and sex and whom nobody seems to have seen for more than twenty-five years. The solicitor was most upset he had never been able to trace her. So we had a name – or at least a possible identity if we could match the DNA, which is where we need your help in obtaining a sample.'

'How the devil am I supposed to do that?'

'Do you have any of her clothes or possessions on which we might find a trace?'

'Not a thing, and the house we lived in – briefly – I sold back in the nineties, or rather the bank did after they repossessed it, and it has probably had more owners since. Alice didn't have many personal *things*; she always said she liked to travel light. I don't suppose there's any trace of her left in Hibbert's house, is there?'

'Since it became a halfway house for refugees,' the inspector said with resignation, 'hundreds of people, families, have passed through there. It was as if by leaving the house in his will to a noble cause, Hibbert was deliberately muddying the waters for us.'

'It does rather,' I said quietly, 'but you don't suspect Hibbert, do you, whether it's Alice in that grave or not?'

'That's a conundrum for us. If it is Alice, why did he leave money in his will to her? And he registered his will with his solicitor two years before he died, which was two or three years after we think the body in the shed was killed. On the other hand, Hibbert had prepared that grave . . .'

'You seriously think he could have killed whoever the girl was, buried her and then sat in his shed bashing out his books?'

'Alternatively, can you imagine some random serial killer looking to dispose of a body just stumbling on a convenient grave hidden inside a garden shed and saying thank you very much? I mean the whole point of his book was that the body was hidden in plain sight, but the key word is *hidden*. And who else knew about the grave under the floorboards?'

'Well, I did,' I admitted thoughtfully, 'and so did Edward Jesser and probably Robina Robinson plus, of course, anyone who had read *Buried Above Ground.*'

'Like Jacon Archer.'

'You're not suggesting poor Jacon killed Alice, are you? That's insane. Jacon wasn't born when Alice worked for Alan Hibbert, or if he was, he would only have been a toddler. He'd most likely never heard of her.'

'But he suspected something.' She closed her notebook and leaned back in her chair, palms flat on the tabletop. 'That's why he was killed.'

FORTY-FOUR

Jacon Archer was the one I felt guilty about lying to.

Yes, he was a nerd and the last person you want to be trapped with at a bus stop when it was raining, as one female British crime writer once described the fictional detective created by a much more successful rival.

The problem was he was a reader and so obsessed with detective stories with carefully laid 'clues' that he was convinced he could not only spot them but follow them. His downfall was that he read too much and too intelligently. Had he not said that those later Duncan Torrens books had shown a marked increase in the quality of the writing? And he had enjoyed the last unpublished Inspector Seeley book, *The Missing Fabergé,* which had been so ignominiously consigned to a skip. At least he had good taste.

He was as observant as a good fictional detective should be and filed away odd bits of information in case they came in handy (they usually did in crime novels). He had picked up on the fact that I had been married, but he could not have known it was to Alice. He could not have known about Alice at all, but he had read *Buried Above Ground* and would have guessed – because that's what most fictional detectives do – that Hibbert's writing shed could be the catafalque or the sarcophagus or whatever that was intended, in the book, for a Cynthia who became a Kirstie – certainly not an Alice.

I wondered, though it was now far too late to speculate, whether he would have picked up on the clues in those last six or seven Inspector Seeley novels? Well, not so much clues as *hints.* Those consecutive titles taken from the *Meditations* of Marcus Aurelius – *Most Wretched of Deaths, Small Is the Span* and *One Who Is Afraid of Death* – might have raised an eyebrow or two on the faces of regular readers of the books of Duncan Torrens, an author not known for references to the classical world. Though again, the references might have gone over the heads of most Inspector Seeley fans.

Buried Above Ground

The following two titles – *Unlawful and Premeditated* and *Seamless Death* – could have been clues, but then allusions to death were almost compulsory in the titles of detective stories, even the cosiest of mysteries at what one might call the Jane Austen end of the crime-fiction spectrum. And the next, *The House Guest Who Never Left*, was surely a bit of a giveaway if, that is, you knew that Alan Hibbert had had a series of live-in home helps, one of whom had (suspiciously) not been seen for some time.

The Attainder was, admittedly, more obscure, being a coded reference to Hibbert changing his will two years – a not at all suspicious or small span of time – before his death, and no one except his solicitor could have known about that. So I don't suppose that could count as a 'fair play' clue, and Jacon Archer would probably have called foul over that one.

As one of the few people in the world to have read the unpublished *The Missing Fabergé*, Jacon and his fellow Gadabout website warriors would surely have noticed that Duncan Torrens had suddenly displayed an interest in Russian history, something he had never done before over the course of more than three dozen books.

If he had done more digging, or perhaps more reading, Jacon would surely have started to have suspicions and been able to put two and two together. The one thing which might have stumped him was the motive behind the crimes – not so much the murder of a young female (sadly a common-enough occurrence) or even the hiding of a body, but the subsequent transgressions.

In Jacon's world of crime (fiction), sins were mostly venal. Murder was committed because someone had been done out of an inheritance – or to make sure someone got an inheritance. The female victim who refused to divorce her wandering husband invariably controlled the money. The young, flighty couple wanted to get married but had no money and couldn't do so until a rich uncle/stepmother/elder brother had been bumped off. Back in that 'Golden Age', it seemed no one ever thought of working for a living – they had to acquire money by murder. To be fair, there was a lot of unemployment in the thirties, so good jobs for the feckless sons and, less often, daughters of the upper-middle classes were likely to be in short supply.

But poor Jacon had never got the chance to discover what really happened with those later Duncan Torrens books – or to tackle the clues, or hints, they contained to what had happened out at Dunkley. There again, he might have.

Thinking about it, I had not really lied to him, just not told him all the truth, and, oddly, it was a truth which both surprised and undid him at the end.

He had asked if I could give him a lift out to Dunkley, and I had told him I did not own a car, which was perfectly true – it had been sold years ago in my period of penury following Alice's debt-strewn departure – but I still had a clean driving licence and the ability to hire a vehicle from a small firm in High Barnet which specialized in anonymous small vans and not asking too many questions.

Jacon's big mistake was telling me in advance that he was going to visit Alan Hibbert's house in Dunkley, giving me plenty of time to be in the area and observe him from a distance. Of course, I knew where he would go, which gave me an advantage, and these days a small white van cruising the main street of even the most remote rural village would not be suspicious; simply another delivery of something ordered online.

Like most urban cyclists, Jacon automatically assumed that the lighter traffic in the countryside did not count as any sort of hazard, and freewheeling down the hill out of Dunkley, the wind in his face, he had no idea what was behind him.

It was a notoriously dangerous corner, and the trees into which he and his bicycle smashed were solid and unyielding. Almost fatal.

FORTY-FIVE

My last interview with Inspector Toni Walker took place in the library, which sounds like a phrase from a traditional detective story, but the reality was mundane rather than dramatic. She had paid a surprise visit to the local library to catch me at work and presumably off guard. As it was a quiet time – most time in the library is quiet these days – I arranged chairs for us in between the two free-standing shelf units displaying, naturally, our collection of crime novels and thrillers.

The shelving gave us a modicum of privacy from the few – those happy few – customers who usually drifted in and out during the afternoons, mostly young mothers killing time before collecting children on the school run. As we cheerfully ignored the unwritten law about observing complete silence, Val White, my erstwhile superior in the management team, had raised no objections whatsoever when Inspector Toni turned up unannounced but in full uniform and asked if she 'could have an informal word' with me.

Sensing the prospect of juicy gossip and no doubt in awe of the police uniform, Val White could hardly contain her glee at the situation, even offering to make the inspector a cup of tea, all the time never taking her eyes off me, as if expecting me to crumble under the humiliation or make a dash for the fire exit.

It must have confused Val White that I did not look more worried. I was surprised by the visit but not anxious. Inspector Walker had asked for another 'informal' word, and although she looked impressive in her clean and pressed uniform, black stockings and smart but sensible shoes, she was somehow far less threatening than when she had been on plain clothes detective duties. Added to which, she was alone and without a tape recorder or colleague to back up her version of what transpired between us. To me that meant that I didn't yet need a solicitor.

'I hope you don't mind me troubling you at work, Mr Wilkes,'

238 Mike Ripley

she said for openers, but her expression said she couldn't care less about my feelings on the matter.

'Not at all. It makes a nice break from the normal hurly-burly.'

She had the good grace not to do a double take in case she had missed a horde of enthusiastic book-groupers lurking behind the mind, body and wellness shelves, sadly one of our most popular sections. We were, however, unlikely to be overheard by any innocent bystanders apart from Val White, who made a point of loitering within earshot, slowly and carefully shelving and reorganizing books, occasionally examining individual volumes in case they had been vandalized or returned with inappropriate bookmarks in place.

'This was where you met Jacon Archer?' she asked, looking around as if it was a tourist spot or a regular meeting place for lovers.

'Yes, he came here to find me.' There was no point in being evasive, not with Val White in my eyeline.

'Well, he came to the right place, given his interest in crime.' She made a point of surveying the crime and thriller section in which we nestled.

'Oh, I don't think we have much in stock which would have appealed to young Jacon. He was solidly a Golden Age reader, and we don't carry a big selection, at least nothing he wouldn't have read. For most GA readers, the more obscure the title and the longer out of print it's been, the better.'

'From what I've seen on his website,' she said, nodding, 'he was something of an obsessive, and I'm really trying to under-stand him. Everything on his computer, his phone, his social media, everything in his bedroom at his mother's house, it's all geared to this Golden Age stuff.' She leaned forward in her chair, well aware of Val White's flapping ears. 'This is very much off the record, by the way.'

'Of course,' I said, thinking: *Who am I going to tell?*

'Is it normal? I mean, I know there are people who dress up as Sherlock Holmes and go to murder-mystery weekends.'

'Worse than that,' I said, 'I've come across married couples who pretend to be Tommy and Tuppence Beresford when they go to the supermarket.'

'Who?'

'Never mind, just accept it's part of their fantasy world and usually harmless.'

'Until they start playing detective for real?'

'Is that what you think Jacon was doing?'

'Don't you? You knew him – and his tastes in reading.'

'I'd hardly say I knew him, but I admit we shared *some* of the same interests when it came to crime fiction, and I do think he might fancy himself as an amateur detective.'

'Do you think he would have been any good at it?'

'What an odd question!' I must have spoken too loudly, as Val White's head turned sharply towards us like a surprised owl. 'How would I know?'

'You read the same sort of books.' She raised the palms of both hands as if presenting me with Exhibit A: the shelves of murder and mayhem stacked around us.

'It's all fiction, for entertainment purposes only. These aren't training manuals or do-it-yourself books. Not even the ones calling themselves police procedurals actually cover real procedure, which I suspect is actually dull and boring. Sorry, I meant painstaking and detailed, which never makes for a good page-turner. I can't think of one which would teach you how to be a real police detective, nor how to get away with murder.'

'How would you?'

'How would I what?'

'Get away with murder.' One corner of her mouth twitched in a hastily suppressed smile. 'Hypothetically, of course, as a reader of detective stories.'

'If I read the sort of books Jacon Archer liked,' I started, resisting the urge to go into full lecture mode, 'I would start by establishing an unbreakable alibi involving railway timetables, though you can't rely on them these days. Preferably you should have no obvious motive for the murder and no financial gain from it. Ideally, you wouldn't even know your victim.'

'So you get someone else to do your murder for you?'

'Or you swap murders with someone else who has a victim in mind. But that's been done,' I added. 'More than once in fact – or, I should say, fiction. The one thing a successful murderer needs, which is never covered in fiction, is luck. Even the most

240   Mike Ripley

stupid murderer can get away with it if they're lucky. You must know that, from your experience.'

'Actually I don't.'

'Excuse me?'

Now she did allow herself a smile – a sickly, almost simpering one. 'How many murders do the detectives solve in these books of yours?'

'Well, I wouldn't call them mine . . . but the standard formula is two murders solved per book, plus one averted. In the nick of time, of course. And of course with a new book every year, that soon mounts up.'

'Do you know how many murder cases a British police officer handles in an entire career?'

'Not a clue,' I said, which was a daft thing to say.

'I think the average works out at 1.7 – and no jokes about the 0.7 being an unidentified body part.'

'So you've already exceeded your quota, early in your career.'

'I beg your pardon?'

'I'm assuming you are early in your police career,' I said carefully, not wishing to annoy her, 'because it's not just the police officers who are getting younger; at my age, everyone is, and don't you have two murders to investigate in Dunkley?'

'Technically, two *deaths*, so I've now been told.' From her expression, I would not have liked to have been the person who told her.

She smoothed the material of her uniform skirt over her thighs before she continued. The uniform – I should have guessed.

'I don't understand,' I prompted.

She looked uncomfortable and squirmed slightly on her chair. 'I may have jumped to some conclusions far too early,' she started, lowering her voice, 'and to be honest, it was my first murder scene – at least I thought it was. I assumed that Jacon Archer had been bumped off the road by another vehicle, he'd smashed into a tree and then whoever had run him off the road had finished him off with a blow to the head and then thrown his bicycle in the river. With the reports we now have from forensics and the pathologist, it seems that Jacon impacting' – I winced at the word even if she did not – 'with a very solid oak tree was quite enough to kill him without any follow-up, and his

Buried Above Ground 241

bicycle could easily have rolled into the river under its own momentum.'

I almost felt sorry for her, but confession time was over, and she was moving on to the official statement she had clearly rehearsed.

'Due to lack of forensic evidence to the contrary, no CCTV, no vehicle registration recognition and not even tyre tracks, the death of Jacon Archer is being treated at best as an accident on a dangerous piece of road, at worst as a hit-and-run which is unlikely to be resolved unless someone owns up or a witness comes forward. The case has been passed over to Road Traffic.'

She paused to do some more unnecessary smoothing.

'As to the body we found in Alan Hibbert's writing shed, that was clearly a violent death, but given the time elapsed and the lack of a positive identification, that has been designated as a cold case and will no doubt end up in a dusty broom cupboard at the National Crime Agency.'

So Inspector Toni's hopes of glory as a detective had been snatched away from her and she was back in uniform, pounding a beat, but still she had pounded her way to me; in uniform but, I guessed, off duty.

'Does that mean you're off the case?' I asked as innocently as I could, wary of coming across as in any way smug.

To my surprise, she smiled.

'One of my superiors told me I should stop reading so many detective stories! Can you credit that? Everyone connected with those deaths in Dunkley had something to do with crime writing, you included.'

I waved a hand at the surrounding shelves. 'Only as a curator these days, not a provider, and my retirement from that isn't so far off.' I risked a sympathetic grin. 'Then we'll both be off the case. I take it you *are* off the case.'

'Being back in uniform gave it away, did it? I have to pass the files over, but I wanted to fill in as many gaps as possible before I do, and I thought you could help get my thoughts in order.'

'How?'

'By answering some questions about your ex-wife, Alice.' She blanched and squirmed on her chair, genuinely uncomfortable.

242 Mike Ripley

'I have no official reason to ask them, and you have no need to answer.'

So I could now answer 'no comment' with impunity, I thought, but decided to play it cool and helpful.

'Are you sure it's Alice that's buried in Hibbert's shed?'

'No – that's the problem. Identification has proved impossible. All we can say is that she is a person of interest because she was the one known resident of the house who disappeared roughly around the time death occurred. We have a DNA sample but nothing to match it with. You are sure you kept nothing of hers; her clothing perhaps?'

'Not a thing, I'm afraid,' I said apologetically. 'When she walked out on me, she took everything she had with her. I don't even have a photograph of her.'

'I was going to ask about that. Not even a selfie with her?'

'You forget, we're talking about the dark ages before mobile phones had cameras. Come to think of it, we didn't even have mobile phones.'

In all my dealings with Inspector Toni, I think that was the thing I told her that she found most difficult to believe, but it didn't throw her off track.

'Where did you last see Alice?'

'Just across the road here, in a pub called The Foresters one Friday evening. We signed our divorce papers over warm beer and a disappointing steak pie.'

'And you never saw her again?'

'No, I did not.'

She ran the tip of her tongue over her lips and narrowed her eyes. 'Why did you never report your wife missing, Mr Wilkes?'

'To me, she wasn't missing.' I shrugged. 'She was gone, out of my life, out of a too-hasty marriage. I hadn't thrown her out on the street.' I would have loved to see anyone try and do that to Alice. 'She said she was going to stay with old friends in London. I didn't ask for details. She had her car, and I had agreed to give her half the value of the house we had to sell – at a loss, I might add – which was quite a struggle for me, but Alice certainly wasn't destitute.'

'And then she came into some money when Alan Hibbert died in 1999, but his solicitor was unable to find her. He did,

Buried Above Ground 243

however, find a bank account in her maiden name. Did you know about that?'

'Of course I did. Alice had opened an account as soon as she arrived in this country and insisted on keeping it. All she had to do was show her passport and give an address. It's probably more difficult these days, but she was hardly a Russian oligarch doing money-laundering on the side.'

'She certainly wasn't doing that.' Inspector Toni placed her hands in her lap and interlinked her fingers. I sensed she was moving into prim schoolmistress mode. 'There was no movement in her account after 1994, after a large deposit from you.'

'The proceeds of the house sale; her share.'

'And then, in 1999, Alan Hibbert left her more money in his will, but by then the bank had declared the account dormant. *If* the body in Hibbert's shed is Alisa Bulova, and she was killed sometime in 1994, that would explain the lack of outgoings from the account.'

'There's a joke in there somewhere about the best way to stop a woman shopping,' I said without thinking.

'A very tasteless one, which, sadly, I've heard several times from fellow officers – male officers. But my point is if Hibbert killed her, why remember her in his will? You witnessed that will, Mr Wilkes – didn't it strike you as odd?'

'I can't say it did. When he drew up that will, Alice had been gone for at least a couple of years, out of my life and, as far as I knew, out of Alan's, but he had always got on with Alice, so a bequest wasn't that surprising, and he didn't have anyone else to leave anything to. Him leaving his house to the local authority as a refuge for asylum seekers, that was the big-money item and the one that would cause a stir locally, which would have pleased him.'

'And you were sure Hibbert was, as the phrase goes, of sound mind when he drew that up?'

'He was old and he was ill and a bit unsteady on his pins, but he was all there up here.' I tapped the side of my head with a forefinger.

'Still writing his books?'

'For sure and with more in the pipeline. He used to say he could never finish a book until he had had a good idea for the

244 Mike Ripley

next, which he couldn't wait to get started on. He was a one-man Inspector Seeley production line, but many crime writers are like that; they just can't stop themselves.'

'That's weird.'

'Not really, not in crime writing, though few get better the longer they go on.'

'Hibbert did though, didn't he?'

Now that did throw me for a moment. 'What makes you say that?'

'Not my opinion,' she said quickly. 'I'm no literary critic, but that was Jacon Archer's opinion, at least on the ones he'd read. He made copious notes of everything he read on his computer at home.'

Of course he did.

'But that's not what I meant,' she continued when I said nothing, 'when I said weird. What I meant was if Hibbert killed the girl, whether it was Alice or not, and buried her in that shed, it was pretty strange to go on sitting in there writing more detective stories with a body under his feet.'

'More than a tad ghoulish if true and even more so to remember Alice – if it was, is, Alice – in his will years later. That doesn't make much sense.'

'Unless he was very cleverly covering his tracks,' said the inspector.

FORTY-SIX

Of course it wasn't true. Alan Hibbert never sat typing away in his shed with a dead body under the floorboards as per the plot of *Buried Above Ground*.

Alan Hibbert never actually wrote a book after the much-edited *Buried Above Ground*. To be fair, he had the initial plot idea for what became *The Herb Border*, but he didn't write the published version of the book, nor any of the subsequent Inspector Seeley novels.

I did.

I never told Edward Jesser, or anyone at Boothby & Briggs, how severe Alan Hibbert's series of mini-strokes had been. They had not been physically incapacitating, and his doctor was reluctant to send him to hospital if he could be cared for at home. Yet the after-effects soon became apparent. The loss of his sense of balance made him walk with a drunken stagger, and there wasn't a door frame in the house he did not collide with or a step he did not stumble down.

Alice soon realized her new job was not going to be as easy as she must have first thought. From being a housekeeper for an extremely private, reclusive writer, she soon became part constant companion and part nurse to an ageing invalid whose memory was deteriorating rapidly.

Alice took this remarkably well, and I like to think it was because we had already established an amorous relationship which gave her every incentive to stay in Dunkley. I visited as often as I could, and Hibbert, as I've said, did not seem to mind or even be surprised to see me at the breakfast table at the weekends. There was no way I could regularly visit an author as low down the midlist pecking order as Duncan Torrens during office hours without arousing suspicion, but given his special relationship with Edward Jesser, I was expected to know that our author was well and, most importantly, working on his next book.

I was lucky not just to have Alice as an ally but in the fact

246 Mike Ripley

that Hibbert was a virtual hermit who had always refused to do public appearances or talk to journalists. In the event, no one in the office thought it odd that Hibbert should have a fax machine installed so that he could discuss/accept/reject editorial suggestions from his editor (me) from the comfort of his own home. Edward Jesser actually approved of the idea, commending me for being so 'efficient', though I think he secretly dreaded the thought that Hibbert might, one day, turn up at the office unannounced.

Should anyone ask – and no one ever did – how the next Duncan Torrens was coming along, I had a fistful of received faxes (written by me and sent by Alice on an agreed timetable) to refer to. Any new Torrens manuscript would arrive in the traditional way; in the post, messily typed on sheets of foolscap paper, which probably would have been impossible to send by fax.

Fortunately, I was able to acquire an ancient Underwood identical to the one in Hibbert's writing shed at an auction of surplus local government office equipment. Finding ribbons for the machine proved more difficult, but I was lucky to find half a dozen unused ones in a junk shop in Camden, though they cost me more than the monstrous machine they fitted. Foolscap paper was less of a problem as Hibbert had bought in bulk and had a huge stock, which Alice was able to easily pilfer.

By the time I had completed *The Herb Border* and delivered the manuscript (to myself), Alan Hibbert was, to all intents and purposes, completely out of the picture. Alice was keeping him comfortably inactive with plenty of cigarettes and a bottle of whisky always close to hand. He had not stopped visiting his writing shed, and never worried about how his latest book turned out, although, Alice said, he looked 'pleased as Punch' when she was able to put a finished copy into his hands.

Even Robina Robinson said, in one of our departmental meetings, that it was 'a good one' which would keep the fans happy, and Edward Jesser remarked that, 'The old boy is, like fine wine, actually getting better with age.' He then, and I should have seen it coming, said, 'I wonder what he's got for us for next year?'

Fortunately, I had had an idea, which was just as well because Duncan Torrens hadn't had one for several months.

Wearing my editor's hat, I had noticed that Inspector Seeley's sidekick who fulfilled the 'Dr Watson' function, Sergeant Gerry Grimes, had always been a slightly anonymous character and also seemed to be androgynous. It was always just 'Grimes' or 'Sergeant' and only occasionally 'Gerry'; never 'he said' or 'he' did this, that or the other. Just about the only personal information Torrens had divulged was that the sergeant was partial to a half pint of lager now and then.

It was curious that Torrens had persisted over so many books with a need to keep Grimes' sex a secret, and that his previous editor, Edward Jesser, had not queried it. I could not come up with a good reason for Torrens to have done that deliberately and thought that 'outing' Gerry as Geraldine would spice up the books, but I ran the idea past Edward Jesser first, claiming that it had come (by fax) from Hibbert himself.

Edward had roared with laughter and, delighted, said that it added 'a bit of zip and zing' to the Inspector Seeley saga.

'I once asked him about Grimes, you know,' Edward confided to me, 'saying that I never knew whether they ran for the ladies' or the gents' when they were caught short. Alan just growled at me and said Sergeant Grimes wasn't important; Gideon Seeley was the hero. But I suspect the old boy just forgot to allocate a sex to the character right at the start and was too embarrassed to admit he'd made a mistake. It'll be a nice surprise for regular readers; really perk them up! Good move on Alan's part. There's life in the old dog yet.'

There was indeed, but not much. I don't think he ever registered the sex change I imposed on one of his most established supporting cast members, so rapidly was he deteriorating mentally. He certainly wasn't up to writing anything or even reading proofs of what he was supposed to have written, though I had a file of faxes at the office to say he had.

Confined to the house, Hibbert seemed to accept a life of total passivity, allowing Alice, with whom he got on famously even when he forgot her name, to sit him down with a bottle of Scotch and a pack of cigarettes in front of all the joys of daytime television. At the time, we put it down to the effects of the mini-strokes he had suffered, though now I would say the dementia had well and truly set in.

248   Mike Ripley

I really thought poor Alan's days were numbered and that my new career as a ghost writer, which I was thoroughly enjoying, would be short-lived. It was probably Alan's condition which inspired, rather gloomily, the title I chose: *Most Wretched of Deaths*, carefully adding a copy of Marcus Aurelius's *Meditations* to his bookshelves to confound the curious.

Most Wretched was a great success by Boothby & Briggs' standards, even getting a review of almost a quarter of a column inch in a national newspaper, and Edward Jesser sent down a memo for me to fax to Hibbert saying, basically, more of the same please.

So the boss was happy, the writer was happy and even Robina Robinson noted, through gritted teeth at a sales meeting, that sales of the latest Duncan Torrens had shown a pleasant spike. Duncan Torrens was oblivious to all this, and the only person unhappy with the situation was Alice.

I had always known that our relationship served as something of a release valve for Alice's emotions.

At first, she seemed happy, positively delighted, to be out of London and isolated in the countryside in Dunkley. Perhaps there was something in London she needed to get away from, and I know I should have pressed her on this, but I was too caught up in our developing physical relationship. Love at first sight is probably possible, though statistically unlikely, but lust at first sight is another matter, and it was soon clear to me that Alice was blessed with an enormous capacity for lust and an enthusiasm for experimentation.

I admit I was an unlikely choice of sex mate for Alice (she had once actually used that term, announcing, quite seriously, 'I do not want a soul mate; I want a sex mate'). I may have been a dozen years older, and there was no doubt she was the senior partner, but I could understand, if I stopped to think about it, why I appealed to her. Out in the countryside, free from whatever had inhibited her in London, she seemed to be able to let herself go but lacked anyone to go *with*. She must have realized early on that life in Dunkley with Alan Hibbert might be safe and relatively comfortable, but it would be frustrating, in more ways than one, if she was deprived of energetic male company. And that was where I scored: quite simply, I was the only unattached

Buried Above Ground

male under sixty with whom she had regular social contact, plus I had a car and an expense account – or at least she thought I did and, to my folly, I did not deny it until it was too late.

Alice may have been extremely physical, not to say animalistic, but she was not stupid. She very quickly realized that I was doing more than just editing the Inspector Seeley books and was happy to become involved in the deception (though I did not see it as deception at the time) by sending faxes purporting to come from Hibbert, although it was unlikely he ever realized he had a fax machine.

I should have taken more notice of that first warning sign, when she asked me how the new book was going and immediately turned it into a joke by adding, 'You have a very strict editor, you know.' By the time she got to asking the more important question – 'Who gets the money for your books?' – we were married.

It was what the casual observer might have described as a whirlwind romance, except for the fact that there were no casual observers. We had no guests at the wedding apart from Edward Jesser and his wife because neither of us had any close friends. I had work colleagues, of course, but the ones I invited all had other commitments that afternoon, although there was an office whip-round for us, and we did get a card and a John Lewis voucher out of it.

We had arranged for an agency nurse to babysit Alan Hibbert on the day, a Hibbert who had no idea what we were doing or that Alice was preparing to leave his employ, though we were genuinely worried about that as they really did seem to get on well together.

If it wasn't exactly a whirlwind affair, everything seemed to happen in a tornado generated by a hyper-active Alice. I do not remember making any significant decisions about getting married, the wedding or buying the house in Watford and, on reflection, do not remember being asked to make any. Alice was totally in control of the situation, even interviewing suitable carers to replace her in Hibbert's house, stressing to candidates that Mr Hibbert was often confused but harmless. He might occasionally retreat to his writing shed but was not to be disturbed there. No attempt should be made to curb his consumption of alcohol or tobacco, and his local doctor was always on call. All matters arising, particularly incoming mail and faxes, would be dealt with by his trusted editor Mr Wilkes, who would call regularly.

But not as regularly as he should have, as Mr Wilkes had more on his plate than he had bargained for.

I was struggling with another Inspector Seeley novel, which would have been the second I had written 'from scratch' with no input from Duncan Torrens and a new central character, Geraldine Grimes, to incorporate, hopefully seamlessly. I began to appreciate the trite, overused comment by reviewers about 'the difficult second novel'. Plus, I had my normal workload of editing at B & B and was using every spare moment to negotiate a mortgage on a house in Watford which had taken Alice's fancy.

Financially, it was just about manageable, by exaggerating my career prospects to my bank manager, pretending that Alice was still employed by Alan Hibbert and by putting every penny of my savings towards the deposit, but it left little margin for error. The situation became even more precarious when Alice announced that if she was to find a job, she needed a car, which surprised me as until then I had no idea that she could drive or that she had a British driving licence.

That, really, was where the trouble began. A casual acquaintance would have labelled me an innocent – and with some justification. A close male friend would have scoffed in disgust and applied a much cruder epithet to reflect the way I was submissive to my new wife – a term so crude it would never have been allowed in a Boothby & Briggs novel. But I had few casual acquaintances and no close male friends and so traded in my trusty but ageing Volvo (inherited from my mother) and bought Alice her freedom in the shape of a slightly used (one careful lady owner) Renault Clio, while I became a bus-and-train commuter.

Would things have been different if Alice had not had that car? Probably not. I soon discovered that when I was at work, Alice would be out in the car somewhere doing I did not know what and seeing I did not know who, although from the mileage on the odometer, the amount of petrol I had to replace and the odd car parking receipt found in the footwell, it was clear that she was driving into Central London on a fairly regular basis.

Buried Above Ground

When I questioned her, which I did only rarely and usually when an unexpected credit-card bill had arrived, she would say only that she had been to see old friends whom she had missed whilst she had been isolated out at Dunkley – something I could not possibly deprive her of, could I? I should have pressed her further about friends I had not met, had not come to our wedding and of whom she had never spoken before, or at the very least asked her how the job-hunting was going. And I really should have asked earlier where the thick wad of twenty-pound notes held in a roll with a rubber band which I found in her make-up bag had come from.

When I did press her to tell me where she was getting great wodges of cash (I had found several by this point) and why it was not being used to help with the mounting domestic bills, we were in her car and driving along a country road. Things became heated quickly – and then violent as I grabbed Alice's handbag from the back seat and began to go through its contents.

We struggled over the bag, both of us constrained by our seat belts and Alice attempting to control the car as it sped along a twisty country lane. Bizarrely, I could only think of how many Russian obscenities I remembered from my student days.

Being, I now realize, a better driver than I ever was, Alice manoeuvred the car, steering one-handed, off the road and on to a grassy verge. As she stamped on the brake, we were both jerked forwards and then back, and somehow my right elbow smashed into Alice's nose, stunning her long enough for me to get out of my seat belt, out of the car and round to the driver's side, open the door and pull her out as soon as she released her own seat belt.

I held her by the shoulders against the car, horrified at the sight of blood pouring from her nose and fumbling for a hand-kerchief, hoping it was clean. She grabbed it from me and held it up to staunch the flow, breathing deeply. Neither of us spoke, both of us in shock.

Alice recovered first. She bunched up the now red-spotted handkerchief and threw it to the ground.

'I want a divorce,' she said.

Then she swung her right fist and landed what I am told is an upper cut on the point of my jaw.

In my head, I came back with an instantly sardonic 'And so do I', but in fact the next thing I knew, I was lying in damp grass, my mouth full of blood from a bitten tongue, and I was crying. Divorce proceedings started the next morning, and Alice and I spoke probably less than a hundred words to each other over the next two years, the majority of those words revolving around money.

Naive and innocent I might have been, but once my eyes had cleared from behind a sheen of pure lust, I realized that I had married a vampire who was determined to drain me. So what did I do? I let her.

It seemed the only thing to do to ensure a quick exit from the relationship and avoid confrontation. There was no need to tell anyone at work of our problems – no one was remotely interested in my private life – and there were no relatives offering toe-curling condolences, plus we had not been long enough in our house in Watford to have nosey neighbours.

As far as I knew, Alice had no family in the country, and I was blissfully ignorant of the London friends she visited in the car I had bought her. I presumed, once she walked out, that she was living with them, but I did not want to know.

It was a period of constant stress for me. I had to maintain my productivity at work, sell the house (at a considerable loss) in Watford along with the contents (apart from my book collection), find digs for myself, and plan and write another Inspector Seeley novel. Had Alice ever been able to read it, she might have recognized herself in the murdered female victim in *Small Is the Span*. In the end, I was grateful that very few people actually read it.

Eventually, I had to come clean and tell the personnel people at Boothby & Briggs that I was no longer married and had changed my address. The news was met with a sniff and a curled lip from Robina Robinson and a big sympathetic sigh from Edward Jesser, who then spoiled things by saying, 'Pity; Alan was very fond of her.'

It may sound incredible, but I did not miss Alice, not even her sexual enthusiasms. I had made a mistake and had to pay for it, which, in cash terms, I did dearly. Mentally, I tried to think of anything but my impending penury and concentrated on editing the latest Duncan Torrens and writing the next one.

Buried Above Ground 253

I had been mostly truthful with Inspector Toni when I had said the last time I saw Alice was one early Friday evening in The Foresters pub near the public library I would, a few years later, end up working in. The management team running it has, of course, changed many times in the years since – and its pricelist even more often – so there was little hope, at this distance, of finding anyone to confirm or dispute that.

Alice had demanded the meeting, I innocently supposed to mark a final farewell; I should have known better.

'How much do you make for writing Mr Hibbert's books?' was her opening gambit.

'Nothing,' I said.

'You think I'm a fool? Does your company know you are paying yourself twice? Do you think they might be interested?'

I was not shocked by her direct approach, and given her behaviour during the divorce, I might have expected it. For once, though, I had no reason to lie to her and explained that all royalties from Duncan Torrens' books went to Alan Hibbert and I hadn't touched a penny.

She did not believe me, but thinking quickly, I said I could prove it by showing her Hibbert's royalty statements and bank statements, several of which I knew remained unopened in his writing shed out at Dunkley.

'Then we must go there and you can show me.'

I remember those almost as her parting words, spoken with undisguised greed, demanding proof that I was not hiding assets she clearly thought she was entitled to.

I said that it would be a good time to go right then as Hibbert's present carer was not a live-in nurse and would have gone home, having left him his dinner, and I carried a spare set of keys to the house and shed. Luckily for me, she agreed immediately, and, even luckier for me, it would be dark by the time we got there.

After a frostily silent journey, I told Alice to park on the road just beyond Hibbert's house so as not to disturb him. It would be easy enough to sneak around the side of the house and into the garden.

What a pity Alice had never read *Small Is the Span*; she would

254   Mike Ripley

not have been so comfortable allowing me to walk behind her, but then to her I was anything but a threat.

I undid the buckle on the narrow leather belt on my trousers, slid it free of the belt loops and twisted the ends around both hands to secure my grip. Even though I had imagined and acted out the move many times before describing it in *Small Is the Span*, I was surprised how easy it was to loop the belt over Alice's head and I suppose the technical term is garrotte her.

After quietly entering the house and being reassured by the thunder of snoring coming from Alan's bedroom, I armed myself with a small torch and a black bin liner before returning to the garden, and got to work. It took me most of the night to ease up the floorboards of the shed to reveal the ready-made grave, deposit a naked Alice in the void and then, using a bucket and garden spade, transfer enough soil from the compost heap to cover the body. The floorboards went back easily enough, and I doubted very much that anyone – if anyone came in there at all – would notice that their footsteps no longer rang hollow.

To that point, someone like Jacon Archer might have deduced that the means and motive for the crime had already been blueprinted in the works of Duncan Torrens, but what happened after was not plotted, merely improvisation fuelled by dumb luck.

It was not yet fully dawn when I started up Alice's car, and I was sure I had not been seen by anyone. Perhaps the Clio had, but I could not remember hearing any cars passing during the night, and in any case, there was nothing I could do about that.

I drove towards Watford and then across North London to get to Heathrow, avoiding the M25 and its cameras. I stopped frequently every time I spotted a public litter bin in order to deposit an item of Alice's clothing, spreading them evenly over about forty-five miles of suburban roads and God knows how many local council recycling operations. Her handbag, which I emptied of cash and her driving licence and passport (to be burned later), went into a roadside skip in Stanmore under several layers of plasterboard and the ripped-out guts of a bathroom.

At Heathrow, I left the car in the long-stay car park, took the shuttle bus to the terminal and caught a blissfully empty

Buried Above Ground

Tube into Central London. It had been an idea I had been considering for a plot point in a future Inspector Seeley book, and in fact I did use it in *The House Guest Who Never Left*, though in that version the murderer did not fall asleep on the Piccadilly Line and go three stations past his stop. And unlike my fictional character, I did not concern myself with any forensic fallout. There were no bloodstains to worry about, and my fingerprints and DNA in Alice's car could easily be explained as I had ridden in, and driven, it many times when we were a couple.

It was a lucky bonus that the car was, eventually, found to be suspicious and destroyed by the Bomb Squad, and, in a way, I had another bonus in the words Alice used to prompt me in to action when she asked me how much I earned from the Duncan Torrens books I was writing.

Until then, as I had truthfully told her, I had made nothing, but with Alice out of the way, I decided it was time for the worker to be paid for his labour. I picked a building society in the nearest town to Dunkley and opened an account in the name of Alan George Hibbert, using his real address, verified by the electoral register and a recent electricity bill easily removed on one of my visits, with a cash deposit of £100. It was easy for me to pass a suitably worded fax message, with a convincingly forged signature, to the accounts department at Boothby & Briggs, informing them of Hibbert's 'new' banking details. Thus I was able to authorize (to myself) the advances for another five Inspector Seeley books as well as collect biannual royalties on his sales. I was never going to get rich, but being able to draw on that building society account went some way to relieving the financial pressure Alice had put me under.

But I was not greedy, though I could have been. In one of his lucid moments, Hibbert insisted that I look at the will he had drawn up. It was one of those do-it-yourself kits which had not been lodged with a solicitor, and he wanted me to witness his signature – though by that time I was probably more proficient at that than he was. I was genuinely shocked to discover that he proposed to leave his house and garden to me and the last thing I wanted was to inherit a crime scene. It took me an hour to convince him that turning the house into a refugee centre would be a far better use of his house and might help other economic migrants like Alice, whom he had remembered with a specific bequest. Alan had always felt strongly about the treatment of immigrants, holding remarkably liberal views on the subject even though on other topics, and in his fiction, he came across as a true-blue Tory.

I typed up a new draft will (in my bedsit, not in the garden shed) and faxed it to Alan's solicitor in St Albans with a note asking him to add his solicitor's official, and expensive, imprimatur and requesting a meeting for signature in Dunkley as Alan was now too frail to travel. I was happy to witness the event and not be, legally, a beneficiary, thereby removing one of the main motives for murder in the type of detective story beloved by Jacon Archer.

Alan Hibbert died, and when the posthumous novel *The Missing Fabergé* was rejected by B & B, so did Duncan Torrens. In retrospect, it was an unusual Seeley novel, more of a thriller than a whodunit, going back into Russian history as it did. To be honest, I had run out of ideas for Seeley, Grimes and the gang and resorted to my student interest in all things Russian, which may have included, subconsciously, Alice. With the death of Edward Jesser, the takeover by Pabulator – who immediately got rid of the office fax machine – and the coup in the editorial department by Robina Robinson, that became irrelevant. My income from Duncan Torrens' books dried up completely, and I had to find work stacking shelves in local libraries.

And basically, for more than twenty-five years, nothing happened until Jacon Archer appeared on the scene and began asking questions.

Since his death, and the discovery of the body of an unidentified female out at Dunkley, I have been expecting the arrival of a police officer bearing handcuffs and the regulation warning about saying things I might rely on later in court.

Ideally, because I think she deserves it, it would have been Inspector Toni Walker, but it has been six months now since I have seen or heard from her. Perhaps I never will again.

I know I have been lucky, but then as one of my favourite anti-heroes in crime fiction always maintained: it's better to be lucky than good.

With retirement and a miserable pension looming, I might have to reinvent myself again as a crime writer.

If only it wasn't so hard to think up a credible plot.

APPENDIX

References you may have missed.

Part One

(page 5) The novel *Caviar Cat*, which was Roly's first attempt at a reader's report, was actually written by Katharine Morton, a student on the crime writing course the author taught for Cambridge University in 2008. It was very good and a great regret that we could not interest a publisher in it. (But that's publishers for you!)

(page 33) The famous crime writer with a character who disliked the term 'crime writing' was Michael Innes (Professor J.I.M. Stewart) in *Appleby's Answer* (1973).

(page 37) As one famous crime writer of the Golden Age said (I paraphrase): anyone who wrote that much either had an overactive thyroid or a problem with the Inland Revenue. It was Dorothy L. Sayers, of course.

(page 40) Technical shooting scripts from two episodes of *Callan* were indeed found in a skip outside the Teddington Lock television studios, where they had been filmed in 1969 but the recordings since lost. The scripts surfaced on eBay in 2012 where they were purchased by a fan and were subsequently recreated in *Callan Uncovered 2* (2015).

(page 41) '. . . there already was a British detective character called Maxwell Archer?' Maxwell, not Lew, Archer was created by Hugh Clevely (1898–1964) who also wrote as Tod Claymore.

(page 53) The author with contradictory physical descriptions on his early Penguin paperback editions was Len Deighton.

(page 57) 'If twenty doesn't make you a writer, what number does?' Reginald Hill, cited in his obituary in *The Guardian* in 2012.

260   Mike Ripley

Part Two

(page 71) The initial title for Adam Diment's *The Dolly Dolly Spy* (1967) was *The Runes of Death*, and Alistair MacLean suggested *Polynya* as a title for what became *Ice Station Zebra* in 1963.

(page 84) '. . . a Turkish bath, no weapon is found and all the usual suspects are stark naked' refers to the famous short story *The Tea Leaf* by Edgar Jepson and Robert Eustace (1929).

(page 86) *Why Shoot the Butler?* Written by Georgette Heyer (1902–1974).

(page 111) '. . . dictate to a secretary or typist . . .' Several bestselling authors dictated their books, most notably Edgar Wallace and Peter Cheney. The 'supremely confident' thriller writer who treated himself to a gold-plated typewriter was Ian Fleming.

(page 112) '. . . maybe he picked Duncan Torrens because it sounded Scottish.' John Broxholme (1930–2001) used this reasoning when he adopted the pen name Duncan Kyle.

(page 114) '. . . he sees dead people, like the ghosts of murder victims, and they help him solve the case.' This happens in the Commissario Ricciardi mysteries by Italian crime writer Maurizio de Giovanni.

Part Three

(page 126) '. . . Americans, who arrived big time in the nineties.' Both Patricia Cornwell and John Grisham made their debuts in the UK in 1991.

(page 128) The crime writer who got an unjustified reputation for always putting animals in danger was Peter Guttridge.

(page 131) 'Can you think of any other crime writer who had a character without a defined gender?' Sarah Caudwell, who created the magnificent Professor Hilary Tamar in *Thus Was Adonis Murdered* in 1981.

(page 154) '. . . boiled to death in a copper vat in a country brewery.' This occurred in *There's Trouble Brewing* in 1937 by Nicholas Blake (1904–1972), the pen name of Cecil Day-Lewis, poet laureate and father of Daniel.

Buried Above Ground

(page 156) For just how tricky a business, note Dr Bickleigh's predicament in *Malice Aforethought* by Francis Iles in 1931.

Part Four

(page 174) The spoof campaign against Gorbachev was called THUG – Thriller writers Hoping to Unseat Gorbachev – and was proposed by Gavin Lyall (1932–2003).

(page 187) 'There have been cases when a popular actor has been instrumental in getting a crime novel turned into successful television, but it is really rather rare.' Notable examples in the UK were Ian McShane's role in getting Jonathan Gash's *Lovejoy* books on to the BBC and David Jason selecting Rodney Wingfield's *Inspector Frost* novels for ITV.

(page 187) '. . . finally appearing two years after the death of the author . . .' refers to Alan Hunter (1922–2005) and his 'George Gently' novels.

Part Five

(page 234) '. . . as one female British crime writer once described the fictional detective created by a much more successful rival'. This was Sarah Caudwell (again) who described P.D. James' fictional policeman Adam Dalgliesh as a good detective and a passable poet, but you wouldn't want to . . .

(page 240) 'And of course with a new book every year, that soon mounts up.' After his retirement from writing fiction, the creator of Inspector Morse, Colin Dexter (1930–2017) was told that his thirteen novels had contained seventy-three violent deaths in the Oxford area.

(page 256) 'It's better to be lucky than good' – as often said by Fitzroy Maclean Angel in *Just Another Angel* (1988).